Capricorn Games

Robert Silverberg was born in New York, studied at Columbia University, and now lives near San Francisco. He is the author of countless short stories, many novels, and a substantial amount of non-fiction on archaeological and historical themes. He has been President of the Science Fiction Writers of America, was guest of honour at the World Science Fiction Convention in Heidelberg in 1970, and at the British Science Fiction Convention in Manchester in 1976. He has won two Hugo Awards and three Nebulas. He enjoys gardening, with a particular interest in fuchsias and cacti, travelling, contemporary literature and music, and mediaeval geography.

His most recent books include *A Time of Changes*, *Unfamiliar Territory*, *Born With the Dead*, *The Stochastic Man*, *Downward to the Earth*, *New Dimensions 7*, and *Across a Billion Years*.

Previously published by
Robert Silverberg in Pan Books

Downward to the Earth

Robert Silverberg

Capricorn Games

Pan Books London and Sydney

The stories in this collection were originally published in the following books:

'Capricorn Games' in *The Far Side of Time*, edited by Roger Elwood. (Dodd, Mead and Company, 1974)

'The Science Fiction Hall of Fame' in *Infinity Five*, edited by Roger Elwood. (Lancer Books, Inc., 1973)

'Ms. Found in an Abandoned Time Machine' in *Ten Tomorrows*, edited by Roger Elwood. (Fawcett Publications, Inc., 1973)

'Breckenridge and the Continuum' in *Showcase*, edited by Roger Elwood. (Harper & Row Publishers, Inc., 1973)

'Ship-Sister, Star-Sister' in *Frontier: Tomorrow's Alternatives*, edited by Roger Elwood. (Macmillan Publishing Co., Inc., 1973)

'A Sea of Faces' in *Universe #4*, edited by Terry Carr. (Random House, Inc., 1974)

'The Dybbuk of Mazel Tov IV' in *Wandering Stars*, edited by Jack Dann. (Harper & Row Publishers, Inc., 1974)

'Getting Across' in *Future City*, edited by Roger Elwood. (Simon & Schuster, 1973)

First published 1978 by Victor Gollancz Ltd
This edition published 1979 by Pan Books Ltd,
Cavaye Place, London SW10 9PG
© Robert Silverberg 1973, 1974, 1975, 1976
ISBN 0 330 25631 9
Printed and bound in Great Britain by
Richard Clay (The Chaucer Press) Ltd., Bungay, Suffolk

Contents

Capricorn games

Nikki stepped into the conical field of the ultrasonic cleanser, wriggling so that the unheard droning out of the machine's stubby snout could more effectively shear her skin of dead epidermal tissue, globules of dried sweat, dabs of yesterday's scents, and other debris; after three minutes she emerged clean, bouncy, ready for the party. She programmed her party outfit: green buskins, lemon-yellow tunic of gauzy film, pale-orange cape soft as a clam's mantle, and nothing underneath but Nikki – smooth, glistening, satiny Nikki. Her body was tuned and fit. The party was in her honour, though she was the only one who knew that. Today was her birthday, the seventh of January, 1999, twenty-four years old, no sign yet of bodily decay. Old Steiner had gathered an extraordinary assortment of guests: he promised to display a reader of minds, a billionaire, an authentic Byzantine duke, an Arab rabbi, a man who had married his own daughter, and other marvels. All of these, of course, subordinate to the true guest of honour, the evening's prize, the real birthday boy, the lion of the season, the celebrated Nicholson, who had lived a thousand years and who said he could help others to do the same. Nikki ... Nicholson. Happy assonance, portending close harmony. You will show me, dear Nicholson, how I can live forever and never grow old. A cosy, soothing idea.

The sky beyond the sleek curve of her window was black, snow-dappled; she imagined she could hear the rusty howl of the wind and feel the sway of the frost-gripped building, ninety stories high. This was the worst winter she had ever known. Snow fell almost every day, a planetary snow, a global shiver, not even sparing the tropics. Ice hard as iron bands bound the streets of New York. Walls were slippery, the air had a cutting edge. Tonight Jupiter gleamed fiercely in the blackness like a diamond in a raven's forehead. Thank God she didn't have to go outside. She could wait out the winter within this tower. The mail came by pneumatic tube. The penthouse restaurant fed her. She had friends on a dozen floors. The building was a world, warm, snug. Let it snow. Let the sour gales come. Nikki checked herself in the all-around mirror: very nice, very nice. Sweet filmy yellow folds. Hint of thigh, hint of breasts. More than a hint when there's a light source behind her. She glowed. Fluffed her short glossy black hair. Dab of scent. Everyone loved her. Beauty is a magnet: repels some, attracts many, leaves no one unmoved. It was nine o'clock.

'Upstairs,' she said to the elevator. 'Steiner's place.'

'Eighty-eighth floor,' the elevator said.

'I know that. You're so sweet.'

Music in the hallway: Mozart, crystalline and sinuous. The door to Steiner's apartment was a half-barrel of chromed steel, like the entrance to a bank vault. Nikki smiled into the scanner. The barrel revolved. Steiner held his hands like cups, centimetres from her chest, by way of greeting. 'Beautiful,' he murmured.

'So glad you asked me to come.'

'Practically everybody's here already. It's a wonderful party, love.'

She kissed his shaggy cheek. In October they had met in the elevator. He was past sixty and looked less than forty. When she touched his body she perceived it as an object encased in milky ice, like a mammoth fresh out of the Siberian permafrost. They had been lovers for two weeks. Autumn had given way to winter and Nikki had passed out of his life, but he had kept his word about the parties: here she was, invited.

'Alexius Ducas,' said a short, wide man with a dense black beard, parted in the middle. He bowed. A good flourish. Steiner evaporated and she was in the keeping of the Byzantine duke. He manoeuvred her at once across the thick white carpet to a place where clusters of spotlights, sprouting like angry fungi from the wall, revealed the contours of her body. Others turned to look. Duke Alexius favoured her with a heavy stare. But she felt no excitement. Byzantium had been over for a long time. He brought her a goblet of chilled green wine and said, 'Are you ever in the Aegean Sea? My family has its ancestral castle on an island eighteen kilometres east of—'

'Excuse me, but which is the man named Nicholson?'

'Nicholson is merely the name he currently uses. He claims to have had a shop in Constantinople during the reign of my ancestor the Basileus Manuel Comnenus.' A patronizing click, tongue on teeth. 'Only a shopkeeper.' The Byzantine eyes sparkled ferociously. 'How beautiful you are!'

'Which one is he?'

'There. By the couch.'

Nikki saw only a wall of backs. She tilted to the left and peered. No use. She would get to him later. Alexius Ducas continued to offer her his body with his eyes. She whispered languidly, 'Tell me all about Byzantium.'

He got as far as Constantine the Great before he bored her. She finished her wine, and coyly extending the glass, persuaded a smooth young man passing by to refill it for her. The Byzantine looked sad. 'The empire then was divided,' he said, 'among—'

'This is my birthday,' she announced.

'Yours also? My congratulations. Are you as old as—'

'Not nearly. Not by half. I won't even be five hundred for some time,' she said, and turned to take her glass. The smooth young man did not wait to be captured. The party engulfed him like an avalanche. Sixty, eighty guests, all in motion. The draperies were pulled back, revealing the full fury of the snowstorm. No one was watching it. Steiner's apartment was like a movie set: great porcelain garden stools, Ming or even Sung; walls painted with flat sheets of bronze and scarlet; pre-Columbian artefacts in spotlit niches; sculptures like aluminium spider webs; Dürer etchings; the loot of the ages. Squat shaven-headed servants, Mayas or Khmers or perhaps Olmecs, circulated impassively offering trays of delicacies: caviar, sea urchins, bits of roasted meat, tiny sausages, burritos in startling chili sauce. Hands darted unceasingly from trays to lips. This was a gathering of life-eaters, world-swallowers. Duke Alexius was stroking her arm. 'I will leave at midnight,' he said gently. 'It would be a delight if you left with me.'

'I have other plans,' she told him.

'Even so.' He bowed courteously, outwardly undisappointed. 'Possibly another time. My card?' It appeared as if by magic in his hand: a sliver of tawny cardboard, elaborately engraved. She put it in her purse and the room swallowed him. Instantly a big, wild-eyed man took his place before her. 'You've never heard of me,' he began.

'Is that a boast or an apology?'

'I'm quite ordinary. I work for Steiner. He thought it would be amusing to invite me to one of his parties.'

'What do you do?'

'Invoices and debarkations. Isn't this an amazing place?'

'What's your sign?' Nikki asked him.

'Libra.'

'I'm Capricorn. Tonight's my birthday as well as *his*. If you're really Libra, you're wasting your time with me. Do you have a name?'

'Martin Bliss.'

'Nikki.'

'There isn't any Mrs Bliss, hah-hah.'

Nikki licked her lips. 'I'm hungry. Would you get me some canapés?'

She was gone as soon as he moved towards the food. Circumnavigating the long room – past the string quintet, past the bartender's throne, past the window – until she had a good view of the man called Nicholson. He didn't disappoint her. He was slender, supple, not tall, strong in the shoulders. A man of presence and authority. She wanted to put her lips to him and suck immortality out. His head was a flat triangle, brutal cheekbones, thin lips, dark mat of curly hair, no beard, no moustache. His eyes were keen, electric, intolerably wise. He must have seen everything twice at the very least. Nikki had read his book. Everyone had. He had been a king, a lama, a slave trader, a slave. Always taking pains to conceal his implausible longevity, now offering his terrible secret freely to the members of the Book-of-the-Month-Club. Why had he chosen to surface and reveal himself? Because this is the necessary moment of revelation, he had said. When he must

12

stand forth as what he is, so that he might impart his gift to others, lest he lose it. Lest he lose it. At the stroke of the new century he must share his prize of life. A dozen people surrounded him, catching his glow. He glanced through a palisade of shoulders and locked his eyes on hers; Nikki felt impaled, exalted, chosen. Warmth spread through her loins like a river of molten tungsten, like a stream of hot honey. She started to go to him. A corpse got in her way. Death's head, parchment skin, nightmare eyes. A scaly hand brushed her bare biceps. A frightful eroded voice croaked, 'How old do you think I am?'

'Oh, God!'

'How old?'

'Two thousand?'

'I'm fifty-eight. I won't live to see fifty-nine. Here, smoke one of these.'

With trembling hands he offered her a tiny ivory tube. There was a Gothic monogram near one end – FXB – and a translucent green capsule at the other. She pressed the capsule and a flickering blue flame sprouted. She inhaled. 'What is it?' she asked.

'My own mixture. Soma Number Five. You like it?'

'I'm smeared,' she said. 'Absolutely smeared. Oh, God!' The walls were flowing. The snow had turned to tin foil. An instant hit. The corpse had a golden halo. Dollar signs rose into view like stigmata on his furrowed forehead. She heard the crash of the surf, the roar of the waves. The deck was heaving. The masts were cracking. Woman overboard, she cried, and heard her inaudible voice disappearing down a tunnel of echoes, boingg boingg boingg. She clutched at his frail wrists. 'You bastard, what did you *do* to me?'

'I'm Francis Xavier Byrne.'

Oh. The billionaire. Byrne Industries, the great conglomerate. Steiner had promised her a billionaire tonight.

'Are you going to die soon?' she asked.

'No later than Easter. Money can't help me now. I'm a walking metastasis.' He opened his ruffled shirt. Something bright and metallic, like chain mail, covered his chest. 'Life-support system,' he confided. 'It operates me. Take it off for half an hour and I'd be finished. Are you a Capricorn?'

'How did you know?'

'I may be dying, but I'm not stupid. You have the Capricorn gleam in your eyes. What am I?'

She hesitated. His eyes were gleaming too. Self-made man, fantastic business sense, energy, arrogance. Capricorn, of course. No, too easy. 'Leo,' she said.

'No. Try again.' He pressed another monogrammed tube into her hand and strode away. She hadn't yet come down from the last one, although the most flamboyant effects had ebbed. Party guests swirled and flowed around her. She could no longer see Nicholson. The snow seemed to be turning to hail, little hard particles spattering the vast windows and leaving white abraded tracks: or were her perceptions merely sharper? The roar of conversation seemed to rise and fall as if someone were adjusting a volume control. The lights fluctuated in a counterpointed rhythm. She felt dizzy. A tray of golden cocktails went past her and she hissed, 'Where's the bathroom?'

Down the hall. Five strangers clustered outside it, talking in scaly whispers. She floated through them, grabbed the sink's cold edge, thrust her face to the oval concave mirror. A death's head. Parchment skin, nightmare eyes. No! No! She blinked and her own features reappeared. Shivering, she made an effort to pull herself together. The medicine cabinet held a tempting collection of drugs, Steiner's all-purpose remedies. Without looking at labels Nikki seized a handful of vials and gobbled pills at random. A flat red one, a tapering green one, a succulent yellow gelatine capsule. Maybe headache remedies, maybe hallucinogens. Who knows, who cares? We Capricorns are not always as cautious as you think.

Someone knocked at the bathroom door. She answered and found the bland, hopeful face of Martin Bliss hovering near the ceiling. Eyes protruding faintly, cheeks florid. 'They said you were sick. Can I do anything for you?' So kind, so sweet. She touched his arm, grazed his cheek with her lips. Beyond him in the hall stood a broad-bodied man with close-cropped blond hair, glacial blue eyes, a plump perfect face. His smile was intense and brilliant. 'That's easy,' he said. 'Capricorn.'

'Can you guess my—' She stopped, stunned. 'Sign?' she finished, voice very small. 'How did you do that? Oh.'

'Yes. I'm that one.'

She felt more than naked, stripped down to the ganglia, to the synapses. 'What's the trick?'

'No trick. I listen. I hear.'

'You hear people thinking?'

'More or less. Do you think it's a party game?' He was beautiful but terrifying, like a Samurai sword in motion. She wanted him but she didn't dare. He's got my number, she thought. I would never have any secrets from him. He said sadly, 'I don't mind that. I know I frighten a lot of people. Some don't care.'

'What's your name?'

'Tom,' he said. 'Hello, Nikki.'

'I feel very sorry for you.'

'Not really. You can kid yourself if you need to. But you can't kid me. Anyway, you don't sleep with men you feel sorry for.'

'I don't sleep with you.'

'You will,' he said.

'I thought you were just a mind-reader. They didn't tell me you did prophecies too.'

He leaned close and smiled. The smile demolished her. She had to fight to keep from falling. 'I've got your number, all right,' he said in a low harsh voice. 'I'll call you next Tuesday.' As he walked away he said, 'You're wrong. I'm a Virgo. Believe it or not.'

Nikki returned, numb, to the living room. '. . . the figure of the mandala,' Nicholson was saying. His voice was dark, focused, a pure basso cantante. 'The essential thing that every mandala has is a centre: the place where everything is born, the eye of God's mind, the heart of darkness and of light, the core of the storm. All right: you must move towards the centre, find the vortex at the boundary of Yang and Yin, place yourself right at the mandala's midpoint. *Centre yourself*. Do you follow the metaphor? Centre yourself at *now*, the eternal *now*. To move off centre is to move forward towards death, backwards towards birth, always the fatal polar swings; but if you're capable of positioning yourself constantly at the focus of the mandala, right on centre, you have access to the fountain of renewal, you become an organism capable of constant self-healing, constant self-replenishment, constant expansion into regions beyond self. Do you follow? The power of—'

Steiner, at her elbow, said tenderly, 'How beautiful you are in the first moments of erotic fixation.'

'It's a marvellous party.'

'Are you meeting interesting people?'

'Is there any other kind?' she asked.

Nicholson abruptly detached himself from the circle of his audience and strode across the room, alone, in a quick decisive knight's move towards the bar. Nikki, hurrying to intercept him, collided with a shaven-headed tray-bearing servant. The tray slid smoothly from the man's thick fingertips and launched itself into the air like a spinning shield; a rainfall of skewered meat in an oily green curry sauce spattered the white carpet. The servant was utterly motionless. He stood frozen like some sort of Mexican stone idol, thick-necked, flat-nosed, for a long painful moment; then he turned his head slowly to the left and regretfully contemplated his rigid outspread hand, shorn of its tray; finally he swung his head towards Nikki, and his normally expressionless granite face took on for a quick flickering instant a look of total hatred, a coruscating emanation of contempt and disgust that faded immediately. He laughed: hu-hu-hu, a neighing snicker. His superiority was overwhelming. Nikki floundered in quicksands of humiliation. Hastily she escaped, a zig and a zag, around the tumbled goodies and across to the bar. Nicholson, still by himself. Her face went crimson. She felt short of breath. Hunting for words, tongue all thumbs. Finally, in a catapulting blurt: 'Happy birthday!'

'Thank you,' he said solemnly.

'Are you enjoying your birthday?'

'Very much.'

'I'm amazed that they don't bore you. I mean, having had so many of them.'

'I don't bore easily.' He was awesomely calm, drawing on some bottomless reservoir of patience. He gave her a look that was at the same time warm and impersonal. 'I find everything interesting,' he said.

'That's curious. I said more or less the same thing to Steiner just a few minutes ago. You know, it's my birthday too.'

'Really?'

'The seventh of January, 1975, for me.'

'Hello 1975. I'm—' He laughed. 'It sounds absolutely absurd, doesn't it?'

'The seventh of January, 982.'

'You've been doing your homework.'

'I've read your book,' she said. 'Can I make a silly remark? My God, you don't look like you're a thousand and seventeen years old.'

'How should I look?'

'More like him,' she said, indicating Francis Xavier Byrne. Nicholson chuckled. She wondered if he liked her. Maybe. Maybe. Nikki risked some eye contact. He was hardly a centimetre taller than she was, which made it a terrifyingly intimate experience. He regarded her steadily, centredly; she imagined a throbbing mandala surrounding him, luminous turquoise spokes emanating from his heart, radiant red and green spider-web rings connecting them. Reaching from her loins, she threw a loop of desire around him. Her eyes were explicit. His were veiled. She felt him calmly retreating. Take me inside, she pleaded, take me to one of the back rooms. Pour life into me. She said, 'How will you choose the people you're going to instruct in the secret?'

'Intuitively.'

'Refusing anybody who asks directly, of course.'

'Refusing anybody who asks.'

'Did *you* ask?'

'You said you read my book.'

'Oh. Yes. I remember: you didn't know what was happening, you didn't understand anything until it was over.'

'I was a simple lad,' he said. 'That was a long time ago.' His eyes were alive again. He's drawn to me. He sees that I'm his kind, that I deserve him. Capricorn, Capricorn, Capricorn, you and me, he-goat and she-goat. Play my game, Cap. 'How are you named?' he asked.

'Nikki.'

'A beautiful name. A beautiful woman.'

The emptiness of the compliments devastated her. She realized she had arrived with mysterious suddenness at a necessary point of tactical withdrawal; retreat was obligatory, lest she push too hard and destroy the tenuous contact so tensely established. She thanked him with a glance and gracefully slipped away, pivoting towards Martin Bliss, slipping her arm through his. Bliss quivered at the gesture, glowed, leaped into a higher energy state. She resonated to his vibrations, going up and up. She was at the heart of the party, the centre of the mandala: standing flat-footed, legs slightly apart, making her body a polar axis, with lines of force zooming up out of the earth, up through the basement levels of this building, up the eighty-eight stories of it, up through her sex, her heart, her head. This is how it must feel, she thought, when undyingness is conferred on you. A moment of spontaneous grace, the kindling of an inner light. She looked love at poor sappy Bliss. You dear heart, you dumb walking pun. The string quintet made molten sounds. 'What is that?' she asked. 'Brahms?' Bliss offered to find out. Alone, she was vulnerable to Francis Xavier Byrne, who brought her down with a single cadaverous glance.

'Have you guessed it yet?' he asked. 'The sign.'

She stared through his ragged cancerous body, blazing with decomposition. 'Scorpio,' she told him hoarsely.

'Right! Right!' He pulled a pendant from his breast and draped its golden chain over her head. 'For you,' he rasped, and fled. She fondled it. A smooth green stone. Jade? Emerald? Lightly engraved on its domed face was the looped cross, the crux ansata. Beautiful. The gift of life, from the dying man. She waved fondly to him across a forest of heads and winked. Bliss returned.

'They're playing something by Schönberg,' he reported. *Verklärte Nacht.*

'How lovely.' She flipped the pendant and let it fall back against her breasts. 'Do you like it?'

'I'm sure you didn't have it a moment ago.'

'It sprouted,' she told him. She felt high, but not as high as she had been just after leaving Nicholson. That sense of herself as focal point had departed. The party seemed chaotic. Couples were forming, dissolving, re-forming; shadowy figures were stealing away in twos and threes towards the bedrooms; the servants were more obsessively thrusting their trays of drinks and snacks at the remaining guests; the hail had reverted to snow, and feathery masses silently struck the windows, sticking there, revealing their glistening mandalic structures for painfully brief moments before they deliquesced. Nikki struggled to regain her centred position. She indulged in a cheering fantasy: Nicholson coming to her, formally touching her cheek, telling her, 'You will be one of the elect.' In less than twelve months the time would come for him to gather with his seven still unnamed disciples to see in the new century, and he would take their hands into his hands, he would pump the vitality of the undying into their bodies, sharing with them the secret that had been shared with him a thousand years ago. Who? Who? Who? Me. Me. Me. But where had Nicholson gone? His aura, his glow, that cone of imaginary light that had appeared to surround him – nowhere.

A man with a lacquered orange wig began furiously to quarrel, almost under Nikki's nose, with a much younger woman wearing festoons of bioluminescent pearls. Man and wife, evidently. They were both sharp-featured, with glossy, protuberant eyes, rigid faces, cheek muscles working intensely. Live together long enough, come to look alike. Their dispute had a stale, ritualistic flavour, as though they had staged it all too many times before: they were explaining to each other the events that had caused the quarrel, interpreting them, recapitulating them, shading them, justifying, attacking, defending – you said this because and that led me to respond that way because ... no, on the contrary I said this because you said that – all of it in a quiet screechy tone, sickening, agonizing, pure death.

'He's her biological father,' a man next to Nikki said. 'She was one of the first of the in vitro babies, and he was the donor, and five years ago he tracked her down and married her. A loophole in the law.' Five years? They sounded as if they had been married for fifty. Walls of pain and boredom encased them. Only their eyes were alive. Nikki found it impossible to imagine those two in bed, bodies entwined in the act of love. Act of love, she thought, and laughed. Where was Nicholson? Duke Alexius, flushed and sweat-beaded, bowed to her. 'I will leave soon,' he announced, and she received the announcement gravely but without reacting, as though he had merely commented on the fluctuations of the storm, or had spoken in Greek. He bowed again and went away. Nicholson? Nicholson? She grew calm again, finding her centre. He will come to me when he is ready. There was contact between us, and it was real and good.

Bliss, beside her, gestured and said, 'A rabbi of Syrian birth, formerly Muslim, highly regarded among Jewish theologians.'

She nodded but didn't look.

'An astronaut just back from Mars. I've never seen anyone's skin tanned quite that colour.'

The astronaut held no interest for her. She worked at kicking herself back into high. The party was approaching a climactic moment, she felt, a time when commitments were being made and decisions taken. The clink of ice in glasses, the foggy vapours of psychedelic inhalants, the press of warm flesh all about her – she was wired into everything, she was alive and receptive, she was entering into the twitching hour, the hour of galvanic jerks. She grew wild and reckless. Impulsively she kissed Bliss, straining on tiptoes, jabbing her tongue deep into his startled mouth. Then she broke free. Someone was playing with the lights: they grew redder, then gained force and zoomed to blue-white ferocity. Far across the room a crowd was surging and billowing around the fallen figure of Francis Xavier Byrne, slumped loose-jointedly against the base of the bar. His eyes were open but glassy. Nicholson crouched over him, reaching into his shirt, making delicate adjustments of the controls of the chain mail beneath. 'It's all right,' Steiner was saying. 'Give him some air. It's all right!' Confusion. Hubbub. A torrent of tangled input.

'—they say there's been a permanent change in the weather patterns. Colder winters from now on, because of accumulations of dust in the atmosphere that screen the sun's rays. Until we freeze altogether by around the year 2200—'

'—but the carbon dioxide is supposed to start a greenhouse effect that's causing *warmer* weather, I thought, and—'

'—the proposal to generate electrical power from—'

'—the San Andreas fault—'

'—financed by debentures convertible into—'

'—capsules of botulism toxin—'

'—to be distributed at a ratio of one per thousand families, throughout Greenland and the Kamchatka Metropolitan Area—'

'—in the sixteenth century, when you could actually hope to found your own empire in some unknown part of the—'

'—unresolved conflicts of Capricorn personality—'

'—intense concentration and meditation upon the completed mandala so that the contents of the work are transferred to and identified with the mind and body of the beholder. I mean, technically what occurs is the reabsorption of cosmic forces. In the process of construction these forces—'

'—butterflies, which are no longer to be found anywhere in—'

'—were projected out from the chaos of the unconscious; in the process of absorption, the powers are drawn back in again—'

'—reflecting transformations of the DNA in the light-collecting organ, which—'

'—the snow—'

'—a thousand years, can you imagine that? And—'

'—her body—'

'—formerly a toad—'

'—just back from Mars, and there's that *look* in his eye—'

'Hold me,' Nikki said. 'Just hold me. I'm very dizzy.'

'Would you like a drink?'

'Just hold me.' She pressed against cool sweet-smelling

fabric. His chest, unyielding beneath it. Steiner. Very male. He steadied her, but only for a moment. Other responsibilities summoned him. When he released her, she swayed. He beckoned to someone else, blond, soft-faced. The mind-reader, Tom. Passing her along the chain from man to man.

'You feel better now,' the telepath told her.

'Are you positive of that?'

'Very.'

'Can you read any mind in the room?' she asked.

He nodded.

'Even *his*?'

Again a nod. 'He's the clearest of all. He's been using it so long, all the channels are worn deep.'

'Then he really is a thousand years old?'

'You didn't believe it?'

Nikki shrugged. 'Sometimes I don't know what I believe.'

'He's *old*.'

'You'd be the one to know.'

'He's a phenomenon. He's absolutely extraordinary.' A pause, quick, stabbing. 'Would you like to see into his mind?'

'How can I?'

'I'll pitch you right in, if you'd like me to.' The glacial eyes flashed sudden mischievous warmth. 'Yes?'

'I'm not sure I want to.'

'You're very sure. You're curious as hell. Don't kid me. Don't play games, Nikki. You want to see into him.'

'Maybe.' Grudgingly.

'You do. Believe me, you do. Here. Relax, let your shoulders slump a little, loosen up, make yourself receptive, and I'll establish the link.'

'Wait,' she said.

But it was too late. The mind-reader serenely parted her consciousness like Moses doing the Red Sea, and rammed something into her forehead, something thick but insubstantial, a truncheon of fog. She quivered and recoiled. She felt violated. It was like her first time in bed, in that moment when all the fooling around at last was over, the kissing and the nibbling and the stroking, and suddenly there was this object deep inside her body. She had never forgotten that sense of being impaled. But of course it had been not only an intrusion but also a source of ecstasy. As was this. The object within her was the consciousness of Nicholson. In wonder she explored its surface, rigid and weathered, pitted with the myriad ablations of re-entry. Ran her trembling hands over its bronzy roughness. Remained outside it. Tom the mind-reader gave her a nudge. Go on, go on. Deeper. Don't hold back. She folded herself around Nicholson and drifted into him like ectoplasm seeping into sand. Suddenly she lost her bearings. The discrete and impermeable boundary marking the end of her self and the beginning of his became indistinct. It was impossible to distinguish between her experiences and his, nor could she separate the pulsations of her nervous system from the impulses travelling along his. Phantom memories assailed and engulfed her. She was transformed into a node of pure perception, a steady cool isolated eye, surveying and recording. Images flashed. She was toiling upwards along a dazzling snowy crest, with jagged Himalayan fangs hanging above her in the white sky and a warm-muzzled yak snuffling wearily at her side. A platoon of swarthy-skinned little men accompanied her, slanty eyes, heavy coats, thick boots. The stink of rancid butter, the cutting edge of an impossible wind: and there, gleaming in the sudden sunlight, a pile of fire-bright yellow plaster with a thousand winking windows, a building, a lamasery strung along a mountain ridge. The nasal sound of distant horns and trumpets. The hoarse chanting of lotus-legged monks. What were they chanting? Om? Om? Om? *Om*, and flies buzzed around her nose, and she lay hunkered in a flimsy canoe, coursing silently down a midnight river in the heart of Africa, drowning in humidity. Brawny naked men with purple-black skins crouching close. Sweaty fronds dangling from flamboyantly excessive shrubbery; the snouts of crocodiles rising out of the dark water like toothy flowers; great nauseating orchids blossoming high in the smooth-shanked trees. And on shore, five white men in Elizabethan costume, wide-brimmed hats, drooping sweaty collars, lace, fancy buckles, curling red beards. Errol Flynn as Sir Francis Drake, blunderbuss dangling in crook of arm. The white men laughing, beckoning, shouting to the men in the canoe. Am I slave or slavemaster? No answer. Only a blurring and a new vision: autumn leaves blowing across the open doorways of straw-thatched huts, shivering oxen crouched in bare stubble-strewn fields, grim long-moustachioed men with close-cropped hair riding diagonal courses towards the horizon. Crusaders, are they? Or warriors of Hungary on their way to meet the dread Mongols? Defenders of the imperilled Anglo-Saxon realm against the Norman invaders? They could be any of these. But always that steady cool eye, always that unmoving consciousness at the centre of every scene. *Him*, eternal, all-enduring. And then: the train rolling westward, belching white smoke, the plains unrolling infinityward, the big brown fierce-eyed bison standing in shaggy clumps along the right of way, the man with turbulent shoulder-length hair laughing, slapping a twenty-dollar gold piece on the table, picking up his rifle – .50-calibre breech-loading Springfield – he aims casually through the door of the moving train, he squeezes off a shot, another, another. Three shaggy brown corpses beside the tracks, and the train rolls onward, honking raucously. Her arm and shoulder tingled with the impact of those shots. Then: a foetid waterfront, bales of cloves and peppers and cinnamon, small brown-skinned men in turbans and loincloths arguing under a terrible sun. Tiny irregular silver coins glittering in the palm of her hand. The jabber of some Malabar dialect counterpointed with fluid mocking Portuguese. Do we sail now with Vasco da Gama? Perhaps. And then a grey Teutonic street, windswept, mediaeval, bleak Lutheran faces scowling from leaded windows. And then the Gobi steppe, with horsemen and campfires and dark tents. And then New York City, unmistakably New York City, with square automobiles scurrying between the stubby skyscrappers like glossy beetles, a scene out of some silent movie. And then. And then. Everywhere, everything, all times, all places, a discontinuous flow of events but always that clarity of vision, that rock-steady perception, that solid mind at the centre, that unshakeable identity, that unchanging self—

—with whom I am inextricably enmeshed—

There was no 'I', there was no 'he', there was only the one ever-perceiving point of view. But abruptly she felt a change of focus, a distancing effect, a separation of self and self, so that she was looking at him as he lived his many lives, seeing him from the outside, seeing him plainly changing identities as others might change clothing, growing beards and moustaches, shaving them, cropping his hair, letting his hair grow, adopting new fashions, learning languages, forging documents. She saw him in all his thousand years of guises and subterfuges, saw him real and unified and centred beneath his obligatory camouflages—

—and saw him seeing her—

Instantly contact broke. She staggered. Arms caught her. She pulled away from the smiling plump-faced blond man, muttering, 'What have you done? You didn't tell me you'd show *me* to *him*.'

'How else can there be a linkage?' the telepath asked.

'You didn't tell me. You should have told me.' Everything was lost. She couldn't bear to be in the same room as Nicholson now. Tom reached for her, but she stumbled past him, stepping on people. They winked up at her. Someone stroked her leg. She forced her way through improbable laocoons, three women and two servants, five men and a tablecloth. A glass door, a gleaming silvery handle: she pushed. Out onto the terrace. The purity of the gale might cleanse her. Behind her, faint gasps, a few shrill screams, annoyed expostulations: 'Close that thing!' She slammed it. Alone in the night, eighty-eight storeys above street level, she offered herself to the storm. Her filmy tunic shielded her not at all. Snowflakes burned against her breasts. Her nipples hardened and rose like fiery beacons, jutting against the soft fabric. The snow stung her throat, her shoulders, her arms. Far below, the wind churned newly fallen crystals into spiral galaxies. The street was invisible. Thermal confusions brought updraughts that seized the edge of her tunic and whipped it outward from her body. Fierce, cold particles of hail were driven into her bare pale thighs. She stood with her back to the party. Did anyone in there notice her? Would someone think she was contemplating suicide, and come rushing gallantly out to save her? Capricorns didn't commit suicide. They might threaten it, yes, they might even tell themselves quite earnestly that they were really going to do it, but it was only a game, only a game. No one came to her. She didn't turn. Gripping the railing, she fought to calm herself.

No use. Not even the bitter air could help. Frost in her eyelashes, snow on her lips. The pendant Byrne had given her blazed between her breasts. The air was white with a throbbing green underglow. It seared her eyes. She was off-centre and floundering. She felt herself still reverberating through the centuries, going back and forth across the orbit of Nicholson's interminable life. What year is this? Is it 1386, 1912, 1532, 1779, 1043, 1977, 1235, 1129, 1836? So many centuries. So many lives. And yet always the one true self, changeless, unchangeable.

Gradually the resonances died away. Nicholson's unending epochs no longer filled her mind with terrible noise. She began to shiver, not from fear but merely from cold, and tugged at her moist tunic, trying to shield her nakedness. Melting snow left hot clammy tracks across her breasts and belly. A halo of steam surrounded her. Her heart pounded.

She wondered if what she had experienced had been genuine contact with Nicholson's soul, or rather only some trick of Tom's, a simulation of contact. Was it possible, after all, even for Tom to create a linkage between two nontelepathic minds such as hers and Nicholson's? Maybe Tom had fabricated it all himself, using images borrowed from Nicholson's book.

In that case there might still be hope for her.

A delusion, she knew. A fantasy born of the desperate optimism of the hopeless. But nevertheless—

She found the handle, let herself back into the party. A gust accompanied her, sweeping snow inward. People stared. She was like death arriving at the feast. Doglike, she shook off the searing snowflakes. Her clothes were wet and stuck to her skin; she might as well have been naked. 'You poor shivering thing,' a woman said. She pulled Nikki into a tight embrace. It was the sharp-faced woman, the bulgy-eyed bottle-born one, bride of her own father. Her hands travelled swiftly over Nikki's body, caressing her breasts, touching her cheek, her forearm, her haunch. 'Come inside with me,' she crooned. 'I'll make you warm.' Her lips grazed Nikki's. A playful tongue sought hers. For a moment, needing the warmth, Nikki gave herself to the embrace. Then she pulled away. 'No,' she said. 'Some other time. Please.' Wriggling free, she started across the room. An endless journey. Like crossing the Sahara by pogo stick. Voices, faces, laughter. A dryness in her throat. Then she was in front of Nicholson.

Well. Now or never.

'I have to talk to you,' she said.

'Of course.' His eyes were merciless. No wrath in them, not even disdain, only an incredible patience more terrifying than anger or scorn. She would not let herself bend before that cool level gaze.

She said, 'A few minutes ago, did you have an odd experience, a sense that someone was – well, looking into your mind? I know it sounds foolish, but—'

'Yes. It happened.' So calm. How did he stay that close to his centre? That unwavering eye, that uniquely self-contained self, perceiving all – the lamasery, the slave depot, the railroad train, everything, all time gone by all time to come – how did he manage to be so tranquil? She knew she never could learn such calmness. She knew he knew it. He has my number, all right. She found that she was looking at his cheekbones, at his forehead, at his lips. Not into his eyes.

'You have the wrong image of me,' she told him.

'It isn't an image,' he said. 'What I have is you.'

'No.'

'Face yourself, Nikki. If you can figure out where to look.' He laughed. Gently, but she was demolished.

An odd thing, then. She forced herself to stare into his eyes and felt a snapping of awareness from one mode into some other, and he turned into an old man. That mask of changeless early maturity dissolved and she saw the frightening yellowed eyes, the maze of furrows and gullies, the toothless gums, the drooling lips, the hollow throat, the self beneath the face. A thousand years, a thousand years! And every moment of those thousand years was visible. 'You're old,' she whispered. 'You disgust me. I wouldn't want to be like you, not for anything!' She backed away, shaking. 'An old, old, old man. All a masquerade!'

He smiled. 'Isn't that pathetic?'

'Me or you? *Me or you?*'

He didn't answer. She was bewildered. When she was five paces away from him there came another snapping of awareness, a second changing of phase, and suddenly he was himself again, taut-skinned, erect, appearing to be perhaps thirty-five years old. A globe of silence hung betwen them. The force of his rejection was withering. She summoned her last strength for a parting glare. *I didn't want you either, friend, not any single part of you.* He saluted cordially. Dismissal.

Martin Bliss, grinning vacantly, stood near the bar. 'Let's go,' she said savagely. 'Take me home!'

'But—'

'It's just a few floors below.' She thrust her arm through his. He blinked, shrugged, fell into step.

'I'll call you Tuesday, Nikki,' Tom said as they swept past him.

Downstairs, on her home turf, she felt better. In the bedroom they quickly dropped their clothes. His body was pink, hairy, serviceable. She turned the bed on and it began to murmur and throb. 'How old do you think I am?' she asked.

'Twenty-six?' Bliss said vaguely.

'Bastard!' She pulled him down on top of her. Her hands raked his skin. Her thighs parted. Go on. Like an animal, she thought. Like an animal! She was getting older moment by moment, she was dying in his arms.

'You're much better than I expected,' she said eventually.

He looked down, baffled, amazed. 'You could have chosen anyone at that party. Anyone.'

'Almost anyone,' she said.

When he was asleep she slipped out of bed. Snow was still falling. She heard the thunk of bullets and the whine of wounded bison. She heard the clangour of swords on shields.

She heard lamas chanting: Om, Om, Om. No sleep for her this night, none. The clock was ticking like a bomb. The century was flowing remorselessly towards its finish. She checked her face for wrinkles in the bathroom mirror. Smooth, smooth, all smooth under the blue fluorescent glow. Her eyes looked bloody. Her nipples were still hard. She took a little alabaster jar from one of the bathroom cabinets and three slender red capsules fell out of it, into her palm. Happy birthday, dear Nikki, happy birthday to you. She swallowed all three. Went back to bed. Waited, listening to the slap of snow on glass, for the visions to come and carry her away.

The science fiction hall of fame

The look in his remote grey eyes was haunted, terrified, beaten, as he came running in from the Projectorium. His shoulders were slumped; I had never before seen him betray the slightest surrender to despair, but now I was chilled by the completeness of his capitulation. With a shaking hand he thrust at me a slender yellow data slip, marked in red with the arcane symbols of cosmic computation. 'No use,' he muttered. 'There's absolutely no use trying to fight any longer!'

'You mean—'

'Tonight,' he said huskily, 'the universe irrevocably enters the penumbra of the null point!'

The day Armstrong and Aldrin stepped out onto the surface of the moon – it was Sunday, July 20, 1969, remember? – I stayed home, planning to watch the whole thing on television. But it happened that I met an interesting woman at Leon and Helene's party the night before, and she came home with me. Her name is gone from my mind, if I ever knew it, but I remember how she looked: long soft golden hair, heart-shaped face with prominent ruddy cheeks, gentle grey-blue eyes, plump breasts, slender legs. I remember, too, how she wandered around my apartment, studying the crowded shelves of old paperbacks and magazines. 'You're really into sci-fi, aren't you?' she said at last. And laughed and said, 'I guess this must be your big weekend, then! Wow, the moon!' But it was all a big joke to her, that men should be cavorting around up there when there was still so much work left to do on earth. We had a shower and I made lunch and we settled down in front of the set to wait for the men to come out of their module, and – very easily, without a sense of transition – we found ourselves starting to screw, and it went on and on, one of those impossible impersonal mechanical screws in which body grinds against body for centuries, no feeling, no excitement, and as I rocked rhythmically on top of her, unable either to come or to quit, I heard Walter Cronkite telling the world that the module hatch was opening. I wanted to break free of her so I could watch, but she clawed at my back. With a distinct effort I pulled myself up on my elbows, pivoted the upper part of my body so I had a view of the screen, and waited for the ecstasy to hit me. Just as the first wavery image of an upside-down spaceman came into view on that ladder, she moaned and bucked her hips wildly and went into a frenzied climax. I felt nothing. Nothing. Eventually she left, and I showered and had a snack and watched the replay of the moonwalk on the eleven o'clock news. And still I felt nothing.

'What is the answer?' said Gertrude Stein, about to die. Alice B. Toklas remained silent. 'In that case,' Miss Stein went on, 'what is the question?'

Extract from *History of the Imperium*, Koeckert and Hallis, third edition (revised):

The galactic empire was organized 190 standard universal centuries ago by the joint, simultaneous, and unanimous resolution of the governing bodies of eleven hundred worlds. By the present day the hegemony of the empire has spread to thirteen galactic sectors and embraces many thousands of planets, all of which entered the empire willingly and gladly. To remain outside the empire is to confess civic insanity, for the Imperium is unquestionably regarded throughout the cosmos as the most wholly sane construct ever created by the sentient mind. The decision-making processes of the Imperium are invariably determined by recourse to the Hermosillo Equations, which provide unambiguous and incontrovertibly rational guidance in any question of public policy. Thus the many worlds of the empire form a single coherent unit, as perfectly interrelated socially, politically, and economically as its component worlds are interrelated by the workings of the universal laws of gravitation.

Perhaps I spend too much time on other planets and in remote galaxies. It's an embarrassing addiction, this science fiction. (Horrible jingle! It jangles in my brain like an idiot's singsong chant.) Look at my bookshelves: hundreds of well-worn paperbacks, arranged alphabetically by authors, Aschenbach-Barger-Capwell-De Soto-Friedrich, all the greats of the genre out to Waldman and Zenger. The collection of magazines, every issue of everything back to the summer of 1953, a complete run of *Nova*, most issues of *Deep Space*, a thick file of *Tomorrow*. I suppose some of those magazines are quite rare now, though I've never looked closely into the feverish world of the s-f collector. I simply accumulate the publications I buy at the newsstand, never throwing any of them away. How could I part with them? Slices of my past, those magazines, those books. I can give dates to changes in my spirit, alterations in my consciousness, merely by picking up old magazines and reflecting on the associations they evoke. This issue showing the ropy-armed purple monster: it went on sale the month I discovered sex. This issue, cover painting of exploding spaceships: I read it my first month in college, by way of relief from Aquinas and Plato. Mileposts, landmarks, waterlines. An embarrassing addiction. My friends are good-humoured about it. They think science fiction is a literature for children – God knows, they may be right – and they indulge my fancy for it in an affectionate way, giving me some fat anthology for Christmas, leaving a stack of current magazines on my desk while I'm out to lunch. But they wonder about me. Sometimes I wonder too. At the age of thirty-four should I still be able to react with such boyish enthusiasm to, say, Capwell's Solar League novels or Waldman's 'Mindleech' series? What is there about the present that drives me so obsessively towards the future? The grey and vacant present, the tantalizing, inaccessible future.

His eyes were glittering with irrepressible excitement as he handed her the gleaming yellow dome that was the thought-transference helmet. 'Put it on,' he said tenderly.

'I'm afraid, Riik.'

'Don't be. What's there to fear?'

'Myself. The real me. I'll be wide open, Riik. I fear what you may see in me, what it may do to you, to *us*.'

'Is it so ugly inside you?' he asked.

'Sometimes I think so.'

'Sometimes everybody thinks that about himself, Juun. It's the old neurotic self-hatred welling up, the garbage that we can't escape until we're totally sane. You'll find that kind of stuff in me, too, once we have the helmets on. Ignore it. It isn't real. It isn't going to be a determining factor in our lives.'

'Do you love me, Riik?'

'The helmet will answer that better than I can.'

'All right. All right.' She smiled nervously. Then with exaggerated care she lifted the helmet, put it in place, adjusted it, smoothed a vagrant golden curl back under the helmet's rim. He nodded and donned his own.

'Ready?' he asked.

'Ready.'

'Now!'

He threw the switch. Their minds surged towards one another.

Then—

Oneness!

My mind is cluttered with other men's fantasies: robots, androids, starships, giant computers, predatory energy globes, false messiahs, real messiahs, visitors from distant worlds, time machines, gravity repellers. Punch my buttons and I offer you parables from the works of Hartzell or Marcus, appropriate philosophical gems borrowed from the collected editorial utterances of David Coughlin, or concepts dredged from my meditations on De Soto. I am a walking mass of secondhand imagination. I am the flesh-and-blood personification of the Science Fiction Hall of Fame.

'At last,' cried Professor Kholgoltz triumphantly. 'The machine is finished! The last solenoid is installed! Feed power, Hagley. Feed power! Now we will have the Answer we have sought for so many years!'

He gestured to his assistant, who gradually brought the great computer throbbingly to life. A subtle, barely perceptible glow of energy pervaded the air : the neutrino flux that the master equations had predicted. In the amphitheatre adjoining the laboratory, ten thousand people sat tensely frozen. All about the world, millions more, linked by satellite relay, waited with similar intensity. The professor nodded. Another gesture, and Hagley, with a grand flourish, fed the question tape – programmed under the supervision of a corps of multispan-trained philosophers – into the gaping maw of the input slot.

'The meaning of life,' murmured Kholgoltz. 'The solution to the ultimate riddle. In just another moment it will be in our hands.'

An ominous rumbling sound came from the depths of the mighty thinking machine. And then—

My recurring nightmare : A beam of dense emerald light penetrates my bedroom and lifts me with an irresistible force from my bed. I float through the window and hover high above the city. A zone of blackness engulfs me and I find myself transported to an endless onyx-walled tunnel-like hallway. I am alone. I wait, and nothing happens, and after an interminable length of time I begin to walk forward, keeping close to the left side of the hall. I am aware now that towering cone-shaped beings with saucer-sized orange eyes and rubbery bodies are gliding past me on the right, paying no attention to me. I walk for days. Finally the hallway splits : nine identical tunnels confront me. Randomly I choose the leftmost one. It is just like the last, except that the beings moving towards me now are animated purple starfish, rough-skinned, many-tentacled, a globe of pale white fire glowing at their cores. Days again. I feel no hunger, no fatigue; I just go marching on. The tunnel forks once more. Seventeen options this time. I choose the rightmost branch. No change in the texture of the tunnel – smooth as always, glossy, bright with an inexplicable inner radiance – but now the beings flowing past me are spherical, translucent, paramecioid things filled with churning misty organs. On to the next forking place. And on. And on.

Fork after fork, choice after choice, nothing the same, nothing ever different. I keep walking. On. On. On. I walk forever. I never leave the tunnel.

What's the purpose of life, anyway? Who if anybody put us here, and why? Is the whole cosmos merely a gigantic accident? Or was there a conscious and determined Prime Cause? What about free will? Do we have any, or are we only acting out the dictates of some unimaginable, unalterable programme that was stencilled into the fabric of reality a billion billion years ago?

Big resonant questions. The kind an adolescent asks when he first begins to wrestle with the nature of the universe. What am I doing brooding over such stuff at my age? Who am I fooling?

This is the place. I have reached the centre of the universe, where all vortices meet, where everything is tranquil, the zone of stormlessness. I drift becalmed, moving in a shallow orbit. This is ultimate peace. This is the edge of union with the All. In my tranquillity I experience a vision of the brawling, tempestuous universe that surrounds me. In every quadrant there are wars, quarrels, conspiracies, murders, air crashes, frictional losses, dimming suns, transfers of energy, colliding planets, a multitude of entropic interchanges. But here everything is perfectly still. Here is where I wish to be.

Yes! If only I could remain forever!

How, though? There's no way. Already I feel the tug of inexorable forces, and I have only just arrived. There is no everlasting peace. We constantly rocket past that miraculous centre towards one zone of turbulence or another, driven always towards the periphery, driven, driven, helpless. I am drawn away from the place of peace. I spin wildly. The centrifuge of ego keeps me churning. Let me go back! Let me go! Let me lose myself in that place at the heart of the tumbling galaxies!

*

Never to die. That's part of the attraction. To live in a thousand civilizations yet to come, to see the future millennia unfold, to participate vicariously in the ultimate evolution of mankind – how to achieve all that, except through these books and magazines? That's what they give me: life eternal and a cosmic perspective. At any rate they give it to me from one page to the next.

The signal sped across the black bowl of night, picked up again and again by ultrawave repeater stations that kicked it to higher energy states. A thousand trembling laser nodes were converted to vapour in order to hasten the message to the galactic communications centre on Manipool VI, where the emperor awaited news of the revolt. Through the data dome at last the story tumbled. Worlds aflame! Millions dead! The talismans of the Imperium trampled upon!

'We have no choice,' said the emperor calmly. 'Destroy the entire Rigel system at once.'

The problem that arises when you try to regard science fiction as adult literature is that it's doubly removed from our 'real' concerns. Ordinary mainstream fiction, your Faulkner and Dostoevsky and Hemingway, is by definition made-up stuff – the first remove. But at least it derives directly from experience, from contemplation of the empirical world of tangible daily phenomena. And so, while we are able to accept *The Possessed*, say, as an abstract thing, a verbal object, a construct of nouns and verbs and adjectives and adverbs, and while we can take it purely as a story, an aggregation of incidents and conversations and expository passages describing invented individuals and events, we can also *make use of it* as a guide to a certain aspect of Russian nineteenth-century sensibility and as a key to pre-revolutionary radical thought. That is, it is of the nature of an historical artefact, a legacy of its own era, with real and identifiable extra-literary values. Because it simulates actual people moving within a plausible and comprehensible real-world human situation, we can draw information from Dostoevsky's book that could conceivably aid us in understanding our own lives. What about science fiction, though, dealing with unreal situations set in places that do not exist and in eras that have not yet occurred? Can we take the adventures of Captain Zap in the eightieth century as a blueprint for self-discovery? Can we accept the collision of stellar federations in the Andromeda Nebula as an interpretation of the relationship of the United States and the Soviet Union circa 1950? I suppose we can, provided we can accept a science fiction story on a rarefied metaphorical level, as a set of symbolic structures generated in some way by the author's real-world experience. But it's much easier to hang in there with Captain Zap on his own level, for the sheer gaudy fun of it. And that's kiddie stuff.

Therefore we have two possible evaluations of science fiction:

—That it is simple-minded escape literature, lacking relevance to daily life and useful only as self-contained diversion.

—That its value is subtle and elusive, accessible only to those capable and willing to penetrate the experiential substructure concealed by those broad metaphors of galactic empires and supernormal powers.

I oscillate between the two attitudes. Sometimes I embrace both simultaneously. That's a trick I learned from science fiction, incidentally: 'multispan logic', it was called in Zenger's famous novel *The Mind Plateau*. It took his hero twenty years of ascetic study in the cloisters of the Brothers of Aldebaran to master the trick. I've accomplished it in twenty years of reading *Nova* and *Deep Space* and *Solar Quarterly*. Yes: multispan logic. Yes. The art of embracing contradictory theses. Maybe 'dynamic schizophrenia' would be a more expressive term, I don't know.

Is this the centre? Am I there? I doubt it. Will I know it when I reach it, or will I deny it as I frequently do, will I say, *What else is there, where else should I look?*

The alien was a repellent thing, all lines and angles, its tendrils quivering menacingly, its slit-wide eyes revealing a sombre bloodshot curiosity. Mortenson was unable to focus clearly on the creature; it kept slipping off at the edges into some other plane of being, an odd rippling effect that he found morbidly disquieting. It was no more than fifty metres from him now, and advancing steadily. When it gets to within ten metres, he thought, I'm going to blast it no matter what.

Five steps more; then an eerie metamorphosis. In place of this thing of harsh angular threat there stood a beaming, happy Golkon! The plump little creature waved its chubby tentacles and cooed a gleeful greeting!

'I am love,' the Golkon declared. 'I am the bringer of happiness! I welcome you to this world, dear friend!'

What do I fear? I fear the future. I fear the infinite possibilities that lie ahead. They fascinate and terrify me. I never thought I would admit that, even to myself. But what other interpretation can I place on my dream? That multitude of tunnels, that infinity of strange beings, all drifting towards me as I walk on and on? The embodiment of my basic fear. Hence my compulsive reading of science fiction: I crave road signs, I want a map of the territory that I must enter. That we all must enter. Yet the maps themselves are frightening. Perhaps I should look backwards instead. It would be less terrifying to read historical novels. Yet I feed on these fantasies that obsess and frighten me. I derive energy from them. If I renounced them, what would nourish me?

The blood-collectors were out tonight, roving in thirsty packs across the blasted land. From the stone-walled safety of his cell he could hear them baying, could hear also the terrible cries of the victims, the old women, the straggling children. Four, five nights a week now, the fanged monsters broke loose and went marauding, and each night there were fewer humans left to hold back the tide. That was bad enough, but there was worse: his own craving. How much longer could he keep himself locked up in here? How long before he too was out there, prowling, questing for blood?

*

When I went to the newsstand at lunchtime to pick up the latest issue of *Tomorrow,* I found the first number of a new magazine: *Worlds of Wonder*. That startled me. It must be nine or ten years since anybody risked bringing out a new s-f title. We have our handful of long-established standbys, most of them founded in the thirties and even the twenties, which seem to be going to go on forever; but the failure of nearly all the younger magazines in the fifties was so emphatic that I suppose I came to assume there never again would be any new titles. Yet here is *Worlds of Wonder,* out today. There's nothing extraordinary about it. Except for the name it might very well be *Deep Space* or *Solar*. The format is the usual one, the size of *The Reader's Digest*. The cover painting, unsurprisingly, is by Greenstone. The stories are by Aschenbach, Marcus, and some lesser names. The editor is Roy Schaefer, whom I remember as a competent but unspectacular writer in the fifties and sixties. I suppose I should be pleased that I'll have six more issues a year to keep me amused. In fact I feel vaguely threatened, as though the tunnel of my dreams has sprouted an unexpected new fork.

The time machine hangs before me in the laboratory, a glittering golden ovoid suspended in ebony struts. Richards and Halleck smile nervously as I approach it. This, after all, is the climax of our years of research, and so much emotion rides on the success of the voyage I am about to take that every moment now seems freighted with heavy symbolic import. Our experiments with rats and rabbits seemed successful; but how can we know what it is to travel in time until a human being has made the journey?

All right. I enter the machine. Crisply we crackle instructions to one another across the intercom. Setting? Fifth of May, 2500 AD – a jump of nearly three and a half centuries. Power level? Energy feed? Go. Go. Dislocation circuit activated? Yes. All systems go. Bon voyage!

The control panel goes crazy. Dials spin. Lights flash. Everything's zapping at once. I plunge forward in time, going, going, going!

When everything is calm again I commence the emergence routines. The time capsule must be opened just so, unhurriedly. My hands tremble in anticipation of the strange new world that awaits me. A thousand hypotheses tumble through my brain. At last the hatch opens. 'Hello,' says Richards, 'Hi there,' Halleck says. We are still in the laboratory.

'I don't understand,' I say. 'My meters show definite temporal transfer.'

'There was,' says Richards. 'You went forward to 2500 AD, as planned. But you're still here.'

'Where?'

'*Here*.'

Halleck laughs. 'You know what happened, Mike? You *did* travel in time. You jumped forward three hundred and whatever years. But you brought the whole present along with you. You pulled our own time into the future. It's like tugging a doughnut through its own hole. You seé? Our work is kaput, Mike. We've got our answer. The present is always with us, no matter how far out we go.'

Once about five years ago I took some acid, a little purple pill that a friend of mine mailed me from New Mexico. I had read a good deal about the psychedelics and I wasn't at all afraid: eager, in fact, hungry for the experience. I was going to float up into the cosmos and embrace it all. I was going to become a part of the nebulas and the supernovas, and they were going to become part of me; or rather, I would at last come to recognize that we had been part of each other all along. In other words, I imagined that LSD would be like an input of five hundred s-f novels all at once: a mind-blowing charge of imagery, emotion, strangeness, and transport to incredible unknowable places. The drug took about an hour to hit me. I saw the walls begin to flow and billow, and cascades of light streamed from the ceiling. Time became jumbled, and I thought three hours had gone by, but it was only about twenty minutes. Holly was with me. 'What are you feeling?' she asked. 'Is it mystical?' She asked a lot of questions like that. 'I don't know,'

I said. 'It's very pretty, but I just don't know.' The drug wore off in about seven hours, but my nervous system was keyed up and lights kept exploding behind my eyes when I tried to got to sleep. So I sat up all night and read Marcus's *Starflame* novels, both of them, before dawn.

There is no galactic empire. There never will be any galactic empire. All is chaos. Everything is random. Galactic empires are puerile power-fantasies. Do I truly believe this? If not, why do I say it? Do I enjoy bringing myself down?

'Look over there!' the mutant whispered. Carter looked. An entire corner of the room had disappeared – melted away, as though it had been erased. Carter could see the street outside, the traffic, the building across the way. 'Over there!' the mutant said. 'Look!' The chair was gone. 'Look!' The ceiling vanished. 'Look! Look! Look!' Carter's head whirled. Everything was going, vanishing at the command of the inexorable golden-eyed mutant. 'Do you see the stars?' the mutant asked. He snapped his fingers. 'No!' Carter cried. 'Don't!' Too late. The stars also were gone.

Sometimes I slip into what I consider the science fiction experience in everyday life. I mean, I can be sitting at my desk typing a report, or standing in the subway train waiting for the long grinding sweaty ride to end, when I feel a buzz, a rush, an upward movement of the soul similar to what I felt the time I took acid, and suddenly I see myself in an entirely new perspective – as a visitor from some other time, some other place, isolated in a world of alien beings known as earth. Everything seems unfamiliar and baffling. I get that sense of doubleness, of *déjà vu*, as though I have read about this subway in some science fiction novel, as though I have seen this office described in a fantasy story, far away, long ago. The real world thus becomes something science fictional to me for twenty or thirty seconds at a stretch. The textures slide; the fabric strains. Sometimes, when that has happened to me, I think it's more exciting than having a fantasy world become 'real' as I read. And sometimes I think I'm coming apart.

While we were sleeping there had been tragedy aboard our mighty starship. Our captain, our leader, our guide for two full generations, had been murdered in his bed! 'Let me see it again!' I insisted, and Timothy held out the hologram. Yes! No doubt of it! I could see the blood stains in his thick white hair, I could see the frozen mask of anguish on his strong-featured face. Dead! The captain was dead! 'What now?' I asked. 'What will happen?'

'The civil war has already started on E Deck,' Timothy said.

Perhaps what I really fear is not so much a dizzying multiplicity of futures but rather the absence of futures. When I end, will the universe end? Nothingness, emptiness, the void that awaits us all, the tunnel that leads not to everywhere but to nowhere – is that the only destination? If it is, is there any reason to feel fear? Why should I fear it? Nothingness is peace. Our nada who art in nada, nada be thy name, thy kingdom nada, thy will be nada, in nada as it is in nada. Hail nothing full of nothing, nothing is with thee. That's Hemingway. He felt the nada pressing in on all sides. Hemingway never wrote a word of science fiction. Eventually he delivered himself cheerfully to the great nada with a shotgun blast.

My friend Leon reminds me in some ways of Henry Dark-dawn in De Soto's classic *Cosmos* trilogy. (If I said he reminded me of Stephen Dedalus or Raskolnikov or Julien Sorel, you would naturally need no further descriptions to know what I mean, but Henry Darkdawn is probably outside your range of literary experience. The De Soto trilogy deals with the formation, expansion, and decay of a quasi-religious movement spanning several galaxies in the years 30,000 to 35,000 AD, and Darkdawn is a charismatic prophet, human but immortal or at any rate extraordinarily long-lived, who combines within himself the functions of Moses, Jesus and St Paul: seer, intermediary with higher powers, organizer, leader, and ultimately martyr.) What makes the series so beautiful is the way De Soto gets inside Darkdawn's character, so that he's not merely a distant bas-relief – The Prophet – but a warm, breathing human being. That is, you see him warts and all – a sophisticated concept for science fiction, which tends to run heavily to marble statues in place of living protagonists.

Leon, of course, is unlikely ever to found a galaxy-spanning cult, but he has much of the intensity that I associate with Darkdawn. Oddly, he's quite tall – six feet two, I'd say – and has conventional good looks; people of his type don't generally run to high inner voltage, I've observed. But despite his natural physical advantages something must have compressed and redirected Leon's soul when he was young, because he's a brooder, a dreamer, a fire-breather, always coming up with visionary plans for reorganizing our office, stuff like that. He's the one who usually leaves s-f magazines on my desk as gifts, but he's also the one who pokes the most fun at me for reading what he considers to be trash. You see his contradictory nature right there. He's shy and aggressive, tough and vulnerable, confident and uncertain, the whole crazy human mix, everything right up front.

Last Tuesday I had dinner at his house. I often go there. His wife Helene is a superb cook. She and I had an affair five years ago that lasted about six months. Leon knew about it after the third meeting, but he never has said a word to me. Judging by Helene's desperate ardour, she and Leon must not have a very good sexual relationship; when she was in bed with me she seemed to want everything at once, every position, every kind of sensation, as though she had been deprived much too long. Possibly Leon was pleased that I was taking some of the sexual pressure off him, and has silently regretted that I no longer sleep with his wife. (I ended the affair because she was drawing too much energy from me and because I was having difficulties meeting Leon's frank, open gaze.)

Last Tuesday just before dinner Helene went into the kitchen to check the oven. Leon excused himself and headed for the bathroom. Alone, I stood a moment by the bookshelf, checking in my automatic way to see if they had any s-f, and then

I followed Helene into the kitchen to refill my glass from the martini pitcher in the refrigerator. Suddenly she was up against me, clinging tight, her lips seeking mine. She muttered my name; she dug her fingertips into my back. 'Hey,' I said softly. 'Wait a second! We agreed that we weren't going to start that stuff again!'

'I want you!'

'Don't, Helene.' Gently I prised her free of me. 'Don't complicate things. Please.'

I wriggled loose. She backed away from me, head down, and sullenly went to the stove. As I turned I saw Leon in the doorway. He must have witnessed the entire scene. His dark eyes were glossy with half-suppressed tears; his lips were quivering. Without saying anything he took the pitcher from me, filled his martini glass and drank the cocktail at a gulp. Then he went into the living room, and ten minutes later we were talking office politics as though nothing had happened. Yes, Leon, you're Henry Darkdawn to the last inch. Out of such stuff as you, Leon, are prophets created. Out of such stuff as you are cosmic martyrs made.

No one could tell the difference any longer. The sleek, slippery android had totally engulfed its maker's personality.

I stood at the edge of the cliff, staring in horror at the red, swollen thing that had been the life-giving sun of Earth.

The horde of robots—

The alien spaceship, plunging in a wild spiral—

Laughing, she opened her fist. The Q-bomb lay in the centre of her palm. 'Ten seconds,' she said.

How warm it is tonight! A dank glove of humidity enfolds me. Sleep will not come. I feel a terrible pressure all around me. Yes! The beam of green light! At last, at last, at last! Cradling me, lifting me, floating me through the open window. High over the dark city. On and on, through the void, out of space and time. To the tunnel. Setting me down. Here. Here. Yes, exactly as I imagined it would be: the onyx walls, the sourceless dull gleam, the curving vault far overhead, the silent alien figures drifting towards me. Here. The tunnel, at last. I take the first step forward. Another. Another. I am launched on my journey.

Ms. found in
an abandoned time machine

If life is to be worth living at all, we have to have at least the
illusion that we are capable of making sweeping changes in the
world we live in. I say *at least the illusion*. Real ability to effect
change would obviously be preferable, but not all of us can
get to that level, and even the illusion of power offers hope,
and hope sustains life. The point is not to be a puppet, not to
be a passive plaything of karma. I think you'll agree that
sweeping changes in society have to be made. Who will make
them, if not you and me? If we tell ourselves that we're
helpless, that meaningful reform is impossible, that the status
quo is here for keeps, then we might as well not bother going
on living, don't you think? I mean, if the bus is breaking down
and the driver is freaking out on junk and all the doors are
jammed, it's cooler to take the cyanide than to wait around for
the inevitable messy smashup. But naturally we don't want to
let ourselves believe that we're helpless. We want to think that
we can grab the wheel and get the bus back on course and
steer it safely to the repair shop. Right? Right. That's what
we want to think. Even if it's only an illusion. Because sometimes – who knows? – you can firm up an illusion and make it
real.

The cast of characters. Thomas C——, our chief protagonist,
age twenty. As we first encounter him he lies asleep with
strands of his own long brown hair casually wrapped across his
mouth. Tie-dyed jeans and an ECOLOGY NOW! sweat shirt are
crumpled at the foot of the bed. He was raised in Elephant
Mound, Wisconsin, and this is his third year at the university.
He appears to be sleeping peacefully but through his dreaming
mind flit disturbing phantoms: Lee Harvey Oswald, George
Lincoln Rockwell, Neil Armstrong, Arthur Bremer, Sirhan
Sirhan, Hubert Humphrey, Mao Tse-tung, Lieutenant William

Calley, John Lennon. Each in turn announces himself, does a light-footed little dance expressive of his character, vanishes and reappears elsewhere in Thomas's cerebral cortex. On the wall of Thomas's room are various contemporary totems: a giant photograph of Spiro Agnew playing golf, a gaudy VOTE FOR MCGOVERN sticker, and banners that variously proclaim FREE ANGELA, SUPPORT YOUR LOCAL PIG FORCE, POWER TO THE PEOPLE, and CHE LIVES! Thomas has an extremely contemporary sensibility, circa 1970–72. By 1997 he will feel terribly nostalgic for the causes and artefacts of his youth, as his grandfather now is for raccoon coats, bathtub gin, and flagpole sitters. He will say things like 'Try it, you'll like it' or 'Sock it to me' and no one under forty will laugh.

Asleep next to him is Katherine F——, blonde, nineteen years old. Ordinarily she wears steel-rimmed glasses, green hip-hugger bells, a silken purple poncho, and a macramé shawl, but she wears none of these things now. Katherine is not dreaming but her next REM cycle is due shortly. She comes from Moose Valley, Minnesota, and lost her virginity at the age of fourteen while watching a Mastroianni-Loren flick at the North Star Drive-In. During her seduction she never took her eyes from the screen for a period longer than thirty seconds. Nowadays she's much more heavily into the responsiveness thing, but back then she was trying hard to be cool. Four hours ago she and Thomas performed an act of mutual oral-genital stimulation that is illegal in seventeen states and the Republic of Vietnam (South), although there is hope of changing that before long.

On the floor by the side of the bed is Thomas's dog Fidel, part beagle, part terrier. He is asleep too. Attached to Fidel's collar is a Day-Glow streamer that reads THREE WOOFS FOR PET LIB.

Without God, said one of the Karamazov boys, everything is possible. I suppose that's true enough, if you conceive of God as the force that holds things together, that keeps water from flowing uphill and the sun from rising in the west. But what a limited concept of God that is! *Au contraire*, Fyodor: *with*

God everything is possible. And I would like to be God for a little while.

Q. *What did you do?*

A. *I yelled at Sergeant Bacon and told him to go and start searching hooches and get your people moving right on – not the hooches but the bunkers – and I started over to Mitchell's location. I came back out. Meadlo was still standing there with a group of Vietnamese, and I yelled at Meadlo and asked him – I told him if he couldn't move all those people, to get rid of them.*

Q. *Did you fire into that group of people?*

A. *No, sir, I did not.*

Q. *After that incident, what did you do?*

A. *Well, I told my men to get on across the ditch and to get into position after I had fired into the ditch.*

Q. *Now, did you have a chance to look and observe what was in the ditch?*

A. *Yes, sir.*

Q. *And what did you see?*

A. *Dead people, sir.*

Q. *Did you see any appearance of anybody being alive in there?*

A. *No, sir.*

This is Thomas talking. Listen to me. Just listen. Suppose you had a machine that would enable you to fix everything that's wrong in the world. Let's say that it draws on all the resources of modern technology, not to mention the powers of a rich, well-stocked imagination and a highly developed ethical sense. The machine can do anything. It makes you invisible; it gives you a way of slipping backwards and forwards in time; it provides telepathic access to the minds of others; it lets you reach into those minds and c-h-a-n-g-e them. And so forth. Call this machine whatever you want. Call it Everybody's Fantasy Actualizer. Call it a Time Machine Mark Nine. Call it a God Box. Call it a magic wand, if you like. Okay. I give you a magic wand. And you give me a magic wand too, because reader and writer have to be allies, co-conspirators. You and me, with our magic wands. What will you do with yours? What will I do with mine? Let's go.

The Revenge of the Indians. On the plains ten miles west of Grand Otter Falls, Nebraska, the tribes assemble. By pickup truck, camper, Chevrolet, bicycle, and microbus they arrive from every corner of the nation, the delegations of angry redskins. Here are the Onondagas, the Oglallas, the Hunkpapas, the Jicarillas, the Punxsatawneys, the Kickapoos, the Gros Ventres, the Nez Percés, the Lenni Lenapes, the Wepawaugs, the Pamunkeys, the Penobscots, and all that crowd. They are clad in the regalia that the white man expects them to wear: feather bonnets, buckskin leggings, painted faces, tomahawks. See the great bonfire burn! See the leaping sweatshiny braves dance the scalping dance! Listen to their weird barbaric cries! What terror these savages must inspire in the plump suburbanites who watch them on Channel Four!

Now the council meeting begins. The pipe passes. Grunts of approval are heard. The mighty Navaho chieftain, Hosteen Dollars, is the main orator. He speaks for the strongest of the tribes, for the puissant Navahos own motels, gift shops, oil wells, banks, coal mines, and supermarkets. They hold the lucrative national distributorships for the superb pottery of their Hopi and Pueblo neighbours. Quietly they have accumulated vast wealth and power, which they have surreptitiously devoted to the welfare of their less fortunate kinsmen of other tribes. Now the arsenal is fully stocked: the tanks, the flamethrowers, the automatic rifles, the halftracks, the crop-dusters primed with napalm. Only the Big Bang is missing. But that lack, Hosteen Dollars declares, has now been remedied through miraculous intervention. 'This is our moment!' he cries. 'Hiawatha! Hiawatha!' Solemnly I descend from the skies, drifting in a slow downward spiral, landing lithely on my feet. I am naked but for a fringed breechclout. My coppery skin gleams glossily. Cradled in my arms is a hydrogen bomb, armed and ready. 'The Big Bang!' I cry. 'Here, brothers! Here!' By nightfall Washington is a heap of radioactive ash. At dawn the Acting President capitulates. Hosteen Dollars goes on national television to explain the new system of reservations, and the roundup of palefaces commences.

Marin County District Attorney Bruce Bales, who disqualified himself as Angela Davis's prosecutor, said yesterday he was 'shocked beyond belief' at her acquittal.

In a bitter reaction, Bales said, 'I think the jury fell for the very emotional pitch offered by the defence. She didn't even take the stand to deny her guilt. Despite what has happened, I still maintain she was as responsible for the death of Judge Haley and the crippling of my assistant, Gary Thomas, as Jonathan Jackson. Undoubtedly more so, because of her age, experience, and intelligence.'

Governor Ronald Reagan, a spokesman at the capital said, was not available for comment on the verdict.

The day we trashed the Pentagon was simply beautiful, a landmark in the history of the Movement. It took years of planning and a tremendous cooperative effort, but the results were worth the heroic struggle and then some.

This is how we did it:

With the help of our IBM 2020 multiphasic we plotted a ring of access points around the whole District of Columbia. Three sites were in Maryland – Hyattsville, Suitland, and Wheaton – and two were on the Virginia side, at McLean and Merrifield. At each access point we dropped a vertical shaft six hundred feet deep, using our Hughes fluid-intake rotary reamer coupled with a GM twin-core extractor unit. Every night we transported the excavation tailings by truck to Kentucky and Tennessee, dumping them as fill in strip-mining scars. When we reached the six-hundred-foot level we began laying down a thirty-six-inch pipeline route straight to the Pentagon from each of our five loci, employing an LTV molecular compactor to convert the soil castings into semi-liquid form. This slurry we pumped into five huge adjacent underground retaining pockets that we carved with our Gardner-Denver hemispherical subsurface backhoe. When the pipelines were laid we started to pump the stored slurry towards the Pentagon at a constant rate calculated for us by our little XDS computer and monitored at five-hundred-metre intervals along the route by our Control Data 106a sensor system. The pumps, of course, were heavy-duty Briggs and Stratton 580s.

Over a period of eight months we succeeded in replacing the subsoil beneath the Pentagon's foundation with an immense pool of slurry, taking care, however, to avoid causing any seismological disturbances that the Pentagon's own equipment might detect. For this part of the operation we employed Bausch and Lomb spectrophotometers and Perkin-Elmer scanners, rigged in series with a Honeywell 990 vibration-damping integrator. Our timing was perfect. On the evening of July 3 we pierced the critical destruct threshold. The Pentagon was now floating on a lake of mud nearly a kilometre in diameter. A triple bank of Dow autonomic stabilizers maintained the building at its normal elevation; we used Ampex homeostasis equipment to regulate flotation pressures. At noon on the Fourth of July Katherine and I held a press conference on the steps of the Library of Congress, attended chiefly by representatives of the underground media although there were a few nonfreak reporters there too. I demanded an immediate end to all Amerikan overseas military adventures and gave the President one hour to reply. There was no response from the White House, of course, and at five minutes to one I activated the sluices by whistling three bars of 'The Star-Spangled Banner' into a pay telephone outside FBI headquarters. By doing so I initiated a slurry-removal process and by five after one the Pentagon was sinking. It went down slowly enough so that there was no loss of life: the evacuation was complete within two hours and the uppermost floor of the building didn't go under the mud until five in the afternoon.

Two lions that killed a youth at the Portland Zoo Saturday night were dead today, victims of a night-time rifleman.

Roger Dean Adams, nineteen years old, of Portland, was the youth who was killed. The zoo was closed Saturday night when he and two companions entered the zoo by climbing a fence.

The companions said that the Adams youth first lowered himself over the side of the grizzly bear pit, clinging by his hands to the edge of the wall, then pulling himself up. He tried it again at the lions' pit after first sitting on the edge.

Kenneth Franklin Bowers of Portland, one of young Adams's companions, said the youth lowered himself over the edge and as he hung by his fingers he kicked at the lions. One slapped at him, hit his foot, and the youth fell to the floor of the pit, sixteen feet below the rim of the wall. The lions then mauled him and it appeared that he bled to death after an artery in his neck was slashed.

One of the lions, Caesar, a sixteen-year-old male, was killed last night by two bullets from a foreign-made rifle. Sis, an eleven-year-old female, was shot in the spine. She died this morning.

The police said they had few clues to the shootings.

Jack Marks, the zoo director, said the zoo would prosecute anyone charged with the shootings. 'You'd have to be sick to shoot an animal that has done nothing wrong by its own standards,' Mr Marks said. 'No right-thinking person would go into the zoo in the middle of the night and shoot an animal in captivity.'

Do you want me to tell you who I really am? You may think I am a college student of the second half of the twentieth century but in fact I am a visitor from the far future, born in a year which by your system of reckoning would be called AD 2806. I can try to describe my native era to you, but there is little likelihood you would comprehend what I say. For instance, does it mean anything to you when I tell you that I have two womb-mothers, one ovarian and one uterine, and that my spermfather in the somatic line was, strictly speaking, part dolphin and part ocelot? Or that I celebrated my fifth neuron-gate raising by taking part in an expedition to Proxy Nine, where I learned the eleven soul-diving drills and the seven contrary mantras? The trouble is that from your point of view we have moved beyond the technological into the incomprehensible. You could explain television to a man of the eleventh century in such a way that he would grasp the essential concept if not the actual operative principles ('We have this box on which we are able to make pictures of far-away places appear, and we do this by taming the same power that makes lightning leap across the sky'), but how can I find even the basic words to help you visualize our simplest toys?

At any rate it was eye-festival time and for my project I chose to live in the year 1972. This required a good deal of preparation. Certain physical alterations were necessary – synthesizing body hair, for example – but the really difficult part was creating the cultural camouflage. I had to pick up speech patterns, historical background, a whole sense of *context*. (I also had to create a convincing autobiography. The time-field effect provides travellers like myself with an instant retroactive existence in the past, an established background of schooling and parentage and whatnot stretching over any desired period prior to point of arrival, but only if the appropriate programming is done.) I drew on the services of our leading historians and archaeologists, who supplied me with everything I needed, including an intensive training in late-twentieth-century youth culture. How glib I became! I can talk all your dialects: macrobiotics, ecology, hallucinogens, lib-sub-aleph, rock, astrology, yoga. Are you a *sanpaku* Capricorn? Are you plagued by sexism, bum trips, wobbly karma, malign planetary conjunctions? Ask me for advice. I know this stuff. I'm into everything that's current. I'm with the Revolution all the way.

Do you want to know something else? I think I may not be the only time traveller who's here right now. I'm starting to form a theory that this entire generation may have come here from the future.

BELFAST, Northern Ireland, May 28 – Six people were killed early today in a big bomb explosion in Short Strand, a Roman Catholic section of Belfast.

Three of the dead, all men, were identified later as members

of the Irish Republican Army. Security forces said they
believed the bomb blew up accidentally while it was being
taken to another part of the city.

One of the dead was identified as a well-known IRA explo-
sives expert who had been high on the British Army's wanted
list for some time. The three other victims, two men and a
woman, could not be identified immediately.

Seventeen persons, including several children, were injured
by the explosion, and twenty houses in the narrow street were
so badly damaged that they will have to be demolished.

One day I woke up and could not breathe. All that day and
through the days after, in the green parks and in the rooms of
friends and even beside the sea, I could not breathe. The air
was used up. Each thing I saw that was ugly was ugly because
of man – man-made or man-touched. And so I left my friends
and lived alone.

EUGENE, Ore. (UPI) – A retired chef and his dog were buried
together recently as per the master's wish.

Horace Lee Edwards, seventy-one years old, had lived alone
with his dog for twenty-two years, since it was a pup. He
expressed the wish that when he died the dog be buried with
him.

Members of Mr Edwards's family put the dog to death
after Mr Edwards's illness. It was placed at its master's feet
in his coffin.

I accept chaos. I am not sure whether it accepts me.

A memo to the Actualizer.

Dear Machine:
We need more assassins. The system itself is fundamentally
violent and we have tried to transform it through love. That
didn't work. We gave them flowers and they gave us bullets.
All right. We've reached such a miserable point that the
only way we can fight their violence is with violence of our

own. *The time has come to rip off the rippers-off. Therefore, old machine, your assignment for today is to turn out a corps of capable assassins, a cadre of convincing-looking artificial human beings who will serve the needs of the Movement. Killer androids, that's what we want.*

These are the specs:

AGE – *between nineteen and twenty-five years old.*
HEIGHT – *from five feet five to five feet nine.*
WEIGHT – *on the low side, or else very heavy.*
RACE – *white, more or less.*
RELIGION – *former Christian, now agnostic or atheist. Ex-Fundamentalist will do nicely.*
PSYCHOLOGICAL PROFILE – *intense, weird, a loner, a loser. A bad sexual history: impotence, premature ejaculation, inability to find willing partners. A bad relationship with siblings (if any) and parents. Subject should be a hobbyist (stamp or coin collecting, trapshooting, cross-country running, etc.) but not an 'intellectual'. A touch of paranoia is desirable. Also free-floating ambitions impossible to fulfil.*
POLITICAL CONVICTIONS – *any. Preferably highly flexible. Willing to call himself a libertarian anarchist on Tuesday and a dedicated Marxist on Thursday if he thinks it'll get him somewhere to make the switch. Willing to shoot with equal enthusiasm at presidential candidates, incumbent senators, baseball players, rock stars, traffic cops, or any other components of the mysterious 'they' that hog the glory and keep him from attaining his true place in the universe.*

Okay. You can supply the trimmings yourself, machine. Any colour eyes so long as the eyes are a little bit on the glassy hyperthyroid side. Any colour hair, although it will help if the hair is prematurely thinning and our man blames his lack of success with women in part on that. Any marital history (single, divorced, widowed, married) provided whatever liaison may have existed was unsatisfactory. The

rest is up to you. Get with the job and use your creativity.
Start stamping them out in quantity:

Oswald Sirhan Bremer Ray Czolgosz Guiteau
Oswald Sirhan Bremer Ray Czolgosz Guiteau
Oswald Sirhan Bremer Ray Czolgosz Guiteau
Oswald Sirhan Bremer Ray Czolgosz Guiteau
Oswald Sirhan Bremer Ray Czolgosz Guiteau
Oswald Sirhan Bremer Ray Czolgosz Guiteau
Oswald Sirhan Bremer Ray Czolgosz Guiteau
Oswald Sirhan Bremer Ray Czolgosz Guiteau

Give us the men. We'll find uses for them. And when they've
done their filthy thing we'll throw them back into the karmic
hopper to be recycled, and God help us all.

Every day thousands of ships routinely stain the sea with oily
wastes. When an oil tanker has discharged its cargo, it must
add weight of some other kind to remain stable; this is usually
done by filling some of the ship's storage tanks with sea water.
Before it can take on a new load of oil, the tanker must flush
this watery ballast from its tanks; and as the water is pumped
out, it takes with it the oily scum that had remained in the
tanks when the last cargo was unloaded. Until 1964 each such
flushing of an average 40,000-ton tanker sent eighty-three tons
of oil into the sea. Improved flushing procedures have cut the
usual oil discharge to about three tons. But there are so many
tankers afloat – more than 4,000 of them – that they nevertheless release several million tons of oil a year in this fashion.
The 44,000 passenger, cargo, military, and pleasure ships now
in service add an equal amount of pollution by flushing oily
wastes from their bilges. All told, according to one scientific
estimate, man may be putting as much as ten million tons of
oil a year into the sea. When the explorer Thor Heyerdahl
made a 3,200-mile voyage from North Africa to the West
Indies in a boat of papyrus reeds in the summer of 1970, he
saw 'a continuous stretch of at least 1,400 miles of open
Atlantic polluted by floating lumps of solidified, asphalt-like
oil'. French oceanographer Jacques Yves Cousteau estimates

that 40 per cent of the world's sea life has disappeared in the present century. The beaches near Boston Harbor have an average oil accumulation of 21.8 pounds of oil per mile, a figure that climbs to 1,750 pounds per mile on one stretch on Cape Cod. The Scientific Centre of Monaco reports: 'On the Mediterranean seaboard practically all the beaches are soiled by the petroleum refineries, and the sea bottom, which serves as a food reserve for marine fauna, is rendered barren by the same factors.'

It's a coolish spring day and here I am in Washington, D.C. That's the Capitol down there, and there's the White House. I can't see the Washington Monument, because they haven't finished it yet, and of course there isn't any Lincoln Memorial, because Honest Abe is alive and well on Pennsylvania Avenue. Today is Friday, April 14, 1865. And here I am. Far out!

—We hold the power to effect change. Very well, what shall we change? The whole ugly racial thing?

—That's cool. But how do we go about it?

—Well, what about uprooting the entire institution of slavery by going back to the sixteenth century and blocking it at the outset?

—No, too many ramifications: we'd have to alter the dynamics of the entire imperialist-colonial thrust, and that's just too big a job even for a bunch of gods. Omnipotent we may be, but not indefatigable. If we blocked that impulse there, it would only crop up somewhere else along the time-line; no force that powerful can be stifled altogether.

—What we need is a pinpoint way of reversing the racial mess. Let us find a single event that lies at a crucial nexus in the history of black/white relations in the United States and unhappen it. Any suggestions?

—Sure, Thomas. The Lincoln assassination.

—Far out! Run it through the machine; see what the consequences would be.

So we do the simulations and twenty times out of twenty they come out with a recommend that we de-assassinate Lincoln. Groovy. Any baboon with a rifle can do an assassination, but only we can do a de-assassination. *Alors:* Lincoln goes on to complete his second term. The weak, ineffectual Andrew Johnson remains Vice-President, and the Radical Republican faction in Congress doesn't succeed in enacting its 'humble the proud traitors' screw-the-South policies. Under Lincoln's even-handed guidance the South will be rebuilt sanely and welcomed back into the Union; there won't be any vindictive Reconstruction era, and there won't be the equally vindictive Jim Crow reaction against the carpetbaggers that led to all the lynchings and restrictive laws, and maybe we can blot out a century of racial bitterness. Maybe.

That's Ford's Theatre over there. *Our American Cousin* is playing tonight. Right now John Wilkes Booth is holed up in some downtown hotel, I suppose, oiling his gun, rehearsing his speech. 'Sic semper tyrannis!' is what he'll shout, and he'll blow away poor old Abe.

—One ticket for tonight's performance, please.

Look at the elegant ladies and gentlemen descending from their carriages. They know the President will be at the theatre, and they're wearing their finest finery. And yes! That's the White House buggy! Is that imperious-looking lady Mary Todd Lincoln? It has to be. And there's the President, stepping right off the five-dollar bill. Greying beard, stooped shoulders, weary eyes, tired, wrinkled face. Poor old Abe. Am I doing you much of a favour by saving you tonight? Don't you want to lay your burden down? But history needs you, man. All dem li'l black boys and girls, dey needs you. The President waves. I wave back. Greetings from the twentieth century, Mr Lincoln! I'm here to rob you of your martyrdom!

Curtain going up. Abe smiles in his box. I can't follow the play. Words, just words. Time crawls, tick-tock, tick-tock, tick-tock. Ten o'clock at last. The moment's coming close. There, do you see him? There: the wild-eyed man with the big gun. Wow, that gun's the size of a cannon! And he's creeping up on the President. Why doesn't anybody notice? Is the play so goddamned interesting that nobody notices—

'Hey! Hey you, John Wilkes Booth! Look over here, man! Look at me!'

Everybody turns as I shout. Booth turns too, and I rise and extend my arm and fire, not even needing to aim, just turning the weapon into an extension of my pointing hand as the Zen exercises have shown me how to do. The sound of the shot expands, filling the theatre with a terrible reverberating boom, and Booth topples, blood fountaining from his chest. Now, finally, the President's bodyguards break from their freeze and come scrambling forward. I'm sorry, John. Nothing personal. History was in need of some changing, is all. Goodbye, 1865. Goodbye, President Abe. You've got an extension of your lease, thanks to me. The rest is up to you.

Our freedom ... our liberation ... can only come through a transformation of social structure and relationships ... no one group can be free while another is still held in bonds. We want to build a world where people can choose their futures, where they can love without dependency games, where they do not starve. We want to create a world where men and women can relate to each other and to children as sharing, loving equals. We must eliminate the twin oppressors ... hierarchical and exploitative capitalism and its myths that keep us so securely in bonds ... sexism, racism, and other evils created by those who rule to keep the rest of us apart.

—Do you, Alexander, take this man to be your lawful wedded mate?
  —I do.
  —Do you, George, take this man to be your lawful wedded mate?
  —I do.
  —Then, George and Alexander, by the power vested in me by the State of New York as ordained minister of the First Congregational Gay Communion of Upper Manhattan, I do hereby pronounce you man and man, wedded before God and in the eyes of mankind, and may you love happily ever after.

It's all done with the aid of a lot of science fiction gadgetry. I won't apologize for that part of it. Apologies just aren't necessary. If you need gadgetry to get yourself off, you use gadgetry; the superficials simply don't enter into any real consideration of how you get where you want to be from where you're at. The aim is to eradicate the well-known evils of our society, and if we have to get there by means of time machines, thought-amplification headbands, anti-uptightness rays, molecular interpenetrator beams, superheterodyning levitator rods, and all the rest of that gaudy comic-book paraphernalia, so be it. It's the results that count.

Like I mean, take the day I blew the President's mind. You think I could have done that without all this gadgetry? Listen, simply getting into the White House is a trip and a half. You can't get hold of a reliable map of the interior of the White House, the part that the tourists aren't allowed to see; the maps that exist are phonies, and actually they keep rearranging the rooms so that espionage agents and assassins won't be able to find their way around. What is a bedroom one month is an office the next and a switchboard room the month after that. Some rooms can be folded up and removed altogether. It's a whole wild cloak-and-dagger number. So we set up our ultrasonic intercavitation scanner in Lafayette Park and got ourselves a trustworthy holographic representation of the inside of the building. That data enabled me to get my bearings once I was in there. But I also needed to be able to find the President in a hurry. Our method was to slap a beep transponder on him, which we did by catching the White House's head salad chef, zonking him on narcoleptic strobes, and programming him to hide the gimmick inside a tomato. The President ate the tomato at dinnertime and from that moment on we could trace him easily. Also the pattern of interference waves coming from the transponder told us whether anyone was with him.

So okay. I waited until he was alone one night, off in the Mauve Room rummaging through his file of autographed photos of football stars, and I levitated to a point ninety feet directly above that room, used our neutrino-flux desensitizer to knock out the White House security shield, and plummeted down via interpenetrator beam. I landed right in front of him. Give him credit: he didn't start to yell. He backed away and started to go for some kind of alarm button, but I said, 'Cool it, Mr President, you aren't going to get hurt. I just want to talk. Can you spare five minutes for a little rap?' And I beamed him with the conceptutron to relax him and make him receptive. 'Okay, chief?'

'You may speak, son,' he replied. 'I'm always eager to hear the voice of the public, and I'm particularly concerned with being responsive to the needs and problems of our younger generation. Our gallant young people who—'

'Groovy, Dick. Okay: now dig this. The country's falling apart, right? The ecology is deteriorating, the cities are decaying, the blacks are up in arms, the right-wingers are stocking up on napalm, the kids are getting maimed in one crazy foreign war after another, the prisons are creating criminals instead of rehabilitating them, the Victorian sexual codes are turning millions of potentially beautiful human beings into sickniks, the drug laws don't make any sense, the women are still hung up on the mother-chauffeur-cook-chambermaid trip, the men are still into the booze-guns-broads trip, the population is still growing and filling up the clean open spaces, the economic structure is set up to be self-destructive since capital and labour are in cahoots to screw the consumer, and so on. I'm sure you know the problems, since you're the President and you read a lot of newspapers. Okay. How did we get into this bummer? By accident? No. Through bad karma? I don't really think so. Through inescapable deterministic forces? Uh-uh. We got into it through dumbness, greed, and inertia. We're so greedy we don't even realize that it's ourselves we're robbing. But it can be fixed, Dick, *it can all be fixed!* We just have to wake up! And you're the man who can do it. Don't you want to go down in history as the man who helped this great country get itself together? You and thirty influential congressmen and five members of the Supreme Court can do it. All you have to do is start reshaping the national consciousness through some executive directives backed up with congressional action. Get on the tube, man, and tell all your silent majoritarians to shape up. Proclaim the reign of love. No more war, hear? It's over tomorrow. No more economic growth:

we just settle for what we have and we start cleaning up the rivers and lakes and forests. No more babies to be used as status symbols and pacifiers for idle housewives: from now on people will do babies only for the sake of bringing groovy new human beings into the world, two or three to a couple. As of tomorrow we abolish all laws against stuff that people do without hurting other people. And so on. We proclaim a new Bill of Rights granting every individual the right to a full and productive life according to his own style. Will you do that?'

'Well—'

'Let me make one thing perfectly clear,' I said. 'You're *going* to do it. You're going to decree an end to all the garbage that's been going down in this country. You know how I know you're going to do it? Because I've got this shiny little metal tube in my hand and it emits vibrations that are real strong stuff, vibrations that are going to get your head together when I press the button. Ready or not, here I go. One, two, three ... *zap.*'

'Right on, baby,' the President said.

The rest is history.

Oh. Oh. Oh. Oh, God. If it could only be that easy. One, two, three, zap. But it doesn't work like that. I don't have any magic wand. What makes you think I did? How was I able to trick you into a suspension of disbelief? You, reader, sitting there on your rear end, what do you think I really am? A miracle man? Some kind of superbeing from Galaxy Ten? I'll tell you what I really am, me, Thomas C——. I'm a bunch of symbols on a piece of paper. I'm just something abstract trapped within a mere fiction. A 'hero' in a 'story'. Helpless, disembodied, unreal. UNREAL! Whereas you out there – you have eyes, lungs feet, arms, a brain, a mouth, all that good stuff. You can function. You can move. You can act. Work for the Revolution! Strive for change! You're operating in the real world; you can do it if anybody can! Struggle towards ... umph ... glub ... Hey, get your filthy hands off me – Power to the people! Down with the fascist pigs ... hey –help – HELP!

Breckenridge and the continuum

Then Breckenridge said, 'I suppose I could tell you the story of Oedipus King of Thieves tonight.'

The late-afternoon sky was awful: grey, mottled, fierce. It resonated with a strange electricity. Breckenridge had never grown used to that sky. Day after day, as they crossed the desert, it transfixed him with the pain of incomprehensible loss.

'Oedipus King of Thieves,' Scarp murmured. Arios nodded. Horn looked towards the sky. Militor frowned. 'Oedipus,' said Horn. 'King of Thieves,' Arios said.

Breckenridge and his four companions were camped in a ruined pavilion in the desert – a handsome place of granite pillars and black marble floors, constructed perhaps for some delicious paramour of some forgotten prince of the city-building folk. The pavilion lay only a short distance outside the walls of the great dead city that they would enter, at last, in the morning. Once, maybe, this place had been a summer resort, a place for sherbet and swimming, in that vanished time when this desert had bloomed and peacocks had strolled through fragrant gardens. A fantasy out of the Thousand and One Nights: long ago, long ago, thousands of years ago. How confusing it was for Breckenridge to remember that that mighty city, now withered by time, had been founded and had thrived and had perished all in an era far less ancient than his own. The bonds that bound the continuum had loosened. He flapped in the time-gales.

'Tell your story,' Militor said.

They were restless, eager; they nodded their heads, they shifted positions. Scarp added fuel to the campfire. The sun was dropping behind the bare low hills that marked the desert's western edge; the day's smothering heat was suddenly rushing skyward, and a thin wind whistled through the colonnade of grooved grey pillars that surrounded the pavilion. Grains of pinkish sand danced in a steady stream across the floor of polished stone on which Breckenridge and those who travelled with him squatted. The lofty western wall of the nearby city was already sleeved in shadow.

Breckenridge drew his flimsy cloak closer around himself. He stared in turn at each of the four hooded figures facing him. He pressed his fingers against the cold smooth stone to anchor himself. In a low droning voice he said, 'This Oedipus was monarch of the land of Thieves, and a bold and turbulent man. He conceived an illicit desire for Eurydice his mother. Forcing his passions upon her, he grew so violent that in their coupling she lost her life. Stricken with guilt and fearing that her kinsmen would exact reprisals, Oedipus escaped his kingdom through the air, having fashioned wings for himself under the guidance of the magician Prospero; but he flew too high and came within the ambit of the chariot of his father Apollo, god of the sun. Wrathful over this intrusion, Apollo engulfed Oedipus in heat, and the wax binding the feathers of his wings was melted. For a full day and a night Oedipus tumbled downward across the heavens, plummeting finally into the ocean, sinking through the sea's floor into the dark world below. There he dwells for all eternity, blind and lame; but each spring he reappears among men, and as he limps across the fields green grasses spring up in his tracks.'

There was silence. Darkness was overtaking the sky. The four rounded fragments of the shattered old moon emerged and commenced their elegant, baffling saraband, spinning slowly, soaking one another in shifting patterns of cool white light. In the north the glittering violet and green bands of the aurora flickered with terrible abruptness, like the streaky glow of some monstrous searchlight. Breckenridge felt himself penetrated by gaudy ions, roasting him to the core. He waited, trembling.

'Is that all?' Militor said eventually. 'Is that how it ends?'

'There's no more to the story,' Breckenridge replied. 'Are you disappointed?'

'The meaning is obscure. Why the incest? Why did he fly

too high? Why was his father angry? Why does Oedipus reappear every spring? None of it makes sense. Am I too shallow to comprehend the relationships? I don't believe that I am.'

'Oh, it's old stuff,' said Scarp. 'The tale of the eternal return. The dead king bringing the new year's fertility. Surely you recognize it, Militor.' The aurora flashed with redoubled frenzy, a coded beacon, crying out, SPACE AND TIME, SPACE AND TIME, SPACE AND TIME. 'You should have been able to follow the outline of the story,' Scarp said. 'We've heard it a thousand times in a thousand forms.'

—SPACE AND TIME—

'Indeed we have,' Militor said. 'But the components of any satisfying tale have to have some logical necessity of sequence, some essential connection.' —SPACE— 'What we've just heard is a mass of random floating fragments. I see the semblance of myth but not the inner truth.'

—TIME—

'A myth holds truth,' Scarp insisted, 'no matter how garbled its form, no matter how many irrelevant interpolations have entered it. The interpolations may even be one species of truth, and not the lowest species at that.'

The Dow Jones Industrial Average, Breckenridge thought, closed today at 1100432.86—

'At any rate, he told it poorly,' Arios observed. 'No drama, no intensity, merely a bald outline of events. I've heard better from you on other nights, Breckenridge. Scheherazade and the Forty Giants – now, that was a story! Don Quixote and the Fountain of Youth, yes! But this – this—'

Scarp shook his head. 'The strength of a myth lies in its content, not in the melody of its telling. I sense the inherent power of tonight's tale. I find it acceptable.'

'Thank you,' Breckenridge said quietly. He threw sour glares at Militor and Arios. It was hateful when they quibbled over the stories he told them. What gift did he have for these four strange beings, anyhow, except his stories? When they received that gift with poor grace they were denying him his sole claim to their fellowship.

A million years from nowhere—
SPACE – TIME—
Apollo – Jesus – Apollo—

The wind grew chillier. No one spoke. Beasts howled on the
desert. Breckenridge lay back, feeling an ache in his shoulders,
and wriggled against the cold stone floor.

Merry my wife, Cassandra my daughter, Noel my son—
SPACE – TIME—
SPACE—

His eyes hurt from the aurora's frosty glow. He felt himself
stretched across the cosmos, torn between then and now,
breaking, breaking, ripping into fragments like the moon—

The stars had come out. He contemplated the early constellations. They were unfamiliar; no matter how often Scarp or
Horn pointed out the patterns to him, he saw only random
sprinklings of light. In his other life he had been able to
identify at least the more conspicuous constellations, but they
did not seem to be here. How long does it take to effect a
complete redistribution of the heavens? A million years? Ten
million? Thank God Mars and Jupiter still were visible, the
orange dot and the brilliant white one, to tell him that this
place was his own world, his own solar system. Images danced
in his aching skull. He saw everything double, suddenly. There
was Pegasus, there was Orion, there was Sagittarius. An over-
lay, a mask of realities superimposed on realities.

'Listen to this music,' Horn said after a long while, produc-
ing a fragile device of wheels and spindles from beneath his
cloak. He caressed it and delicate sounds came forth: crystalline, comforting, the music of dreams, sliding into the range of
audibility with no perceptible instant of attack. Shortly Scarp
began a wordless song, and one by one the others joined him
– first Horn, then Militor, and lastly, in a dry, buzzing monotone, Arios.

'What are you singing?' Breckenridge asked.

'The hymn of Oedipus King of Thieves,' Scarp told him.

*

Had it been such a bad life? He had been healthy, prosperous, and beloved. His father was managing partner of Falkner, Breckenridge & Company, one of the most stable of the Wall Street houses, and Breckenridge, after coming up through the ranks in the family tradition, putting in his time as a customer's man and his time in the bond department and his time as a floor trader, was a partner too, only ten years out of Dartmouth. What was wrong with that? His draw in 1972 was $83,500 — not as much as he had hoped for out of a partnership, but not bad, not bad at all, and next year might be much better. He had a wife and two children, an apartment on East 73rd Street, a country cabin on Candlewood Lake, a fair-sized schooner that he kept in a Gulf Coast marina, and a handsome young mistress in an apartment of her own on the Upper West Side. What was wrong with that? When he burst through the fabric of the continuum and found himself in an unimaginably altered world at the end of time, he was astonished not that such a thing might happen but that it had happened to someone as settled and well established as himself.

While they slept a corona of golden light sprang into being along the top of the city wall; the glow awakened Breckenridge, and he sat up quickly, thinking that the city was on fire. But the light seemed cool and supple, and appeared to be propagated in easy rippling waves, more like the aurora than like the raw blaze of flames. It sprang from the very rim of the wall and leaped high, casting blurred, rounded shadows at cross-angles to the sharp crisp shadows that the fragmented moon created. There seemed also to be a deep segment of blackness in the side of the wall; looking closely, Breckenridge saw that the huge gate on the wall's western face was standing open. Without telling the others he left the camp and crossed the flat sandy wasteland, coming to the gate after a brisk march of about an hour. Nothing prevented him from entering. Just within the wall was a wide cobbled plaza, and beyond that stretched broad avenues lined with buildings of a strange sort, rounded and rubbery, porous of texture, all humps and parapets. Black unfenced wells at the centre of each major intersection plunged to infinite depths. Brecken-ridge had been told that the city was empty, that it had been uninhabited for centuries since the spoiling of the climate in this part of the world, so he was surprised to find it occupied; pale figures flitted silently about, moving like wraiths, as though there were empty space between their feet and the pavement. He approached one and another and a third, but when he tried to speak no words would leave his lips. He seized one of the city dwellers by the wrist, a slender black-haired girl in a soft grey robe, and held her tightly, hoping that contact would lead to contact. Her dark sombre eyes studied him without show of fear and she made no effort to break away. I am Noel Breckenridge, he said – Noel III – and I was born in the town of Greenwich, Connecticut in the year of Our Lord 1940, my wife's name is Merry and my daughter is Cassandra and my son is Noel Breckenridge IV, and I am not as coarse or stupid as you may think me to be. She made no reply and showed no change of expression. He asked, Can you understand anything I'm saying to you? Her face re-mained wholly blank. He asked, Can you even hear the sound of my voice? There was no response. He went on: What is your name? What is this city called? When was it abandoned? What year is this on any calendar that I can comprehend? What do you know about me that I need to know? She continued to regard him in an altogether neutral way. He pulled her against his body and gripped her thin shoulders with his fingertips and kissed her urgently, forcing his tongue be-tween her teeth. An instant later he found himself sprawled not far from the campsite with his face in the sand and sand in his mouth. Only a dream, he thought wearily, only a dream.

He was having lunch with Harry Munsey at the Merchants and Shippers Club: sleek chrome-and-redwood premises, sixty stories above William Street in the heart of the financial district. Subdued light fixtures glowed like pulsing red suns; waiters moved past the tables like silent moons. The club was over a century old, although the skyscraper in which it occupied a penthouse suite had been erected only in 1968 –

its fourth home, or maybe its fifth. Membership was limited to white male Christians, sober and responsible, who held important positions in the New York securities industry. There was nothing in the club's written constitution that explicitly limited its membership to white male Christians, but all the same there had never been any members who had not been white, male, and Christian. No one with a firm grasp of reality thought there ever would be.

Harry Munsey, like Noel Breckenridge, was white, male, and Christian. They had gone to Dartmouth together and they had entered Wall Street together, Breckenridge going into his family's firm and Munsey into his, and they had lunch together almost every day and saw each other almost every Saturday night, and each had slept with the other's wife, though each believed that the other knew nothing about that.

On the third martini Munsey said, 'What's bugging you today, Noel?'

A dozen years ago Munsey had been an all-Ivy halfback; he was a big, powerful man, bigger even than Breckenridge, who was not a small man. Munsey's face was pink and unlined and his eyes were alive and youthful, but he had lost all his hair before he turned thirty.

'Is something bugging me?'

'Something's bugging you, yes. Why else would you look so untight after you've had two and a half martinis?'

Breckenridge had found it difficult to grow used to the sight of the massive bright dome that was Munsey's skull.

He said, 'All right. So I'm bugged.'

'Want to talk about it?'

'No.'

'Okay,' Munsey said.

Breckenridge finished his drink. 'As a matter of fact, I'm oppressed by a sophomoric sense of the meaninglessness of life, if you have to know.'

'Really?'

'Really.'

'The meaninglessness of life?'

'Life is empty, dumb, and mechanical,' Breckenridge said.

'*Your* life?'

'Life.'

'I know a lot of people who'd like to live your life. They'd trade with you, even up, asset for asset, liability for liability, life for life.'

Breckenridge shook his head. 'They're fools, then.'

'It's that bad?'

'It all seems so pointless, Harry. Everything. We have a good time and con ourselves into thinking it means something. But what is there, actually? The pursuit of money? I have enough money. After a certain point it's just a game. French restaurants? Trips to Europe? Drinking? Sex? Swimming pools? Jesus! We're born, we grow up, we do a lot of stuff, we grow old, we die. Is that all? Jesus, Harry, is that *all*?'

Munsey looked embarrassed. 'Well there's family,' he suggested. 'Marriage, fatherhood, knowing that you're linking yourself into the great chain of life. Bringing forth a new generation. Transmitting your ideals, your standards, your traditions, everything that distinguishes us from the apes we used to be. Doesn't that count?'

Shrugging, Breckenridge said, 'All right. Having kids, you say. We bring them into the world, we wipe their noses, we teach them to be little men and women, we send them to the right schools and get them into the right clubs, and they grow up to be carbon copies of their parents: lawyers or brokers or clubwomen or whatever—'

The lights fluttering. The aurora: red, green, violet, red, green. The straining fabric – the moon, the broken moon – the aurora – the lights – the fire atop the walls—

'—or else they grow up and deliberately fashion themselves into the opposites of their parents, and somewhere along the way the parents die off, and the kids have kids, and the cycle starts around again. Around and around, generation after generation, Noel Breckenridge III, Noel Breckenridge IV, Noel Breckenridge XVI—'

Arios – Scarp – Militor – Horn—

The city – the gate—

'—making money, spending money, living high, building

nothing real, just occupying space on the planet for a little while, and what for? What for? What does it all mean?'

The granite pillars – the aurora – SPACE AND TIME—

'You're on a bummer today, Noel,' Munsey said.

'I know. Aren't you sorry you asked what was bugging me?'

'Not particularly. Everybody goes through a phase like this.'

'When he's seventeen, yes.'

'And later, too.'

'It's more than a phase,' Breckenridge said. 'It's a sickness. If I had any guts, Harry, I'd drop out. Drop right out and try to work out some meanings in the privacy of my own head.'

'Why don't you? You can afford it. Go on. Why not?'

'I don't know,' said Breckenridge.

Such strange constellations. Such a terrible sky.

Such a cold wind blowing out of tomorrow.

'I think it may be time for another martini,' Munsey said.

They had been crossing the desert for a long time now – forty days and forty nights, Breckenridge liked to tell himself, but probably it had been more than that – and they moved at an unsparing pace, marching from dawn to sunset with as few rest periods as possible. The air was thin. His lungs felt leathery. Because he was the biggest man in the group, he carried the heaviest pack. That didn't bother him.

What did bother him was how little he knew about this expedition, its purposes, its origin, even how he had come to be a part of it. But asking such questions seemed somehow naïve and awkward, and he never did. He went along, doing his share – making camp, cleaning up in the mornings – and tried to keep his companions amused with his stories. They demanded stories fom him every night. 'Tell us your myths,' they urged. 'Tell us the legends and fables you learned in your childhood.'

After weeks of sharing this trek with them he knew little more about the other four than he had at the outset. His favourite among them was Scarp, who was sympathetic and flexible. He liked the hostile, contemptuous Militor the least.

Horn – dreamy, poetic, unworldly, aloof – was beyond his reach; Arios, the most dry and objective and scientific of the group, did not seem worth trying to reach. So far as Breckenridge could determine they were human, although their skins were oddly glossy and of a peculiar olive hue, something on the far side of swarthy. They had strange noses, narrow, high-bridged, noses of a kind he had never seen before, extremely fragile, like the noses of purebred society women carried to the ultimate possibilities of their design.

The desert was beautiful. A gaudy desolation, all dunes and sandy ripples, streaked blue and red and gold and green with brilliant oxides.

Sometimes when the aurora was going full blast – SPACE! TIME! SPACE! TIME! – the desert seemed merely to be a mirror for the sky. But in the morning, when the electronic furies of the aurora had died away, the sand still reverberated with its own inner pulses of bright colour.

And the sun – pale, remorseless – Apollo's deathless fires—

I am Noel Breckenridge and I am nine years old and this is how I spent my summer vacation—

Oh Lord Jesus forgive me.

Scattered everywhere on the desert were outcroppings of ancient ruins – colonnades, halls of statuary, guardposts, summer pavilions, hunting lodges, the stumps of antique walls, and invariably the marchers made their camp beside one of these. They studied each ruin, measured its dimensions, recorded its salient details, poked at its sand-shrouded foundations. Around Scarp's neck hung a kind of mechanized map, a teardrop-shaped black instrument that could be made to emit—

PING!

—sounds which daily guided them towards the next ruin in the chain leading to the city. Scarp also carried a compact humming machine that generated sweet water from handfuls of sand. For solid food they subsisted on small yellow pellets, quite tasty.

PING!

At the beginning Breckenridge had felt constant fatigue, but under the grinding exertions of the march he had grown steadily in strength and endurance, and now he felt he could continue forever, never tiring, parading—

PING!

—endlessly back and forth across this desert which perhaps spanned the entire world. The dead city, though, was their destination, and finally it was in view. They were to remain there for an indefinite stay. He was not yet sure whether these four were archaeologists or pilgrims. Perhaps both, he thought. Or maybe neither. Or maybe neither.

'How do you think you can make your life more meaningful, then?' Munsey asked.

'I don't know. I don't have any idea what would work for me. But I do know who the people are whose lives *do* have meaning.'

'Who?'

'The creators, Harry. The shapers, the makers, the begetters. Beethoven, Rembrandt, Dr Salk, Einstein, Shakespeare, that bunch. It isn't enough just to live. It isn't even enough just to have a good mind, to think clear thoughts. You have to add something to the sum of humanity's accomplishments, something real, something valuable. You have to *give*. Mozart. Newton. Columbus. Those who are able to reach into the well of creation, into that hot boiling chaos of raw energy down there, and pull something out, shape it, make something unique and new out of it. Making money isn't enough. Making more Breckenridges or Munseys isn't enough, either. You know what I'm saying, Harry? The well of creation. The reservoir of life, which is God. Do you ever think you believe in God? Do you wake up in the middle of the night sometimes saying, Yes, yes, there *is* Something after all, I believe, I believe! I'm not talking about churchgoing now, you understand. Churchgoing's nothing but a conditioned reflex these days, a twitch, a tic. I'm talking about faith. Belief. The state of enlightenment. I'm not talking about God as an old man with long white whiskers either, Harry. I mean something abstract, a force, a power, a current, a reservoir of energy underlying everything and connecting everything. God is that reservoir. That reservoir is God. I think of that reservoir as being something like the sea of molten lava down beneath the earth's crust: it's there, it's full of heat and power, it's accessible for those who know the way. Plato was able to tap into the reservoir. Van Gogh. Joyce. Schubert. El Greco. A few lucky ones know how to reach it. Most of us can't. Most of us can't. For those who can't, God is dead. Worse: for them, He never lived at all. Oh, Christ, how awful it is to be trapped in an era where everybody goes around like some sort of zombie, cut off from the energies of the spirit, ashamed even to admit there are such energies. I hate it. I hate the whole stinking twentieth century, do you know that? Am I making any sense? Do I seem terribly drunk? Am I embarrassing you, Harry? Harry? Harry?'

In the morning they struck camp and set out on the final leg of their journey towards the city. The sand here had a disturbing crusty quality: white saline outcroppings gave Breckenridge the feeling that they were crossing a tundra rather than a desert. The sky was clear and pale, and in its bleached cloudlessness it took on something of the quality of a shield, of a mirror, seizing the morning heat that rose from the ground and hurling it inexorably back, so that the five marchers felt themselves trapped in an infinite baffle of unendurable dry smothering warmth.

As they moved cityward Militor and Arios chattered compulsively, falling after a while into a quarrel over certain obscure and controversial points of historical theory. Breckenridge had heard them have this argument at least a dozen times in the last two weeks, and no doubt they had been battling it out for years. The main area of contention was the origin of the city. Who were its builders? Militor believed they were colonists from some other planet, strangers to earth, representatives of some alien species of immeasurable grandeur and nobility, who had crossed space thousands of years ago to build this gigantic monument on Asia's flank. Nonsense, retorted Arios: the city was plainly the work of human beings, unusually gifted and energetic but human nonetheless. Why multiply hypotheses needlessly? Here is the city; humans have built many cities nearly as great as this one in their long history; this city is only quantitatively superior to the others, merely a bit more daringly conceived; to invoke extraterrestrial architects is to dabble gratuitously in fantasy. But Militor maintained his position. Humans, he said, were plainly incapable of such immense constructions. Neither in this present decadent epoch, when any sort of effort is too great, nor at any time in the past could human resources have been equal to such a task as the building of this city must have been. Breckenridge had his doubts about that, having seen what the twentieth century had accomplished. He tended to side with Arios. But indeed the city was extraordinary, Breckenridge admitted: an ultimate urban glory, a supernal Babylon, a consummate Persepolis, the soul's own hymn in brick and stone. The wall that girdled it was at least two hundred feet high – why pour so much energy into a wall? Were no better means of defence at hand, or was the wall mere exuberant decoration? – and, judging by the easy angle of its curve, it must be hundreds of miles in circumference. A city larger than New York, more sprawling even than Los Angeles, a giant antenna of turbulent consciousness set like a colossal gem into this vast plain, a throbbing antenna for all the radiance of the stars: yes, it was overwhelming, it was devastating to contemplate the planning and the building of it, it seemed almost to require the hypothesis of a superior alien race. And yet he refused to accept that hypothesis. Arios, he thought, I am with you.

The city was uninhabited, a hulk, a ruin. Why? What had happened here to turn this garden plain into a salt-crusted waste? The builders grew too proud, said Militor. They defied the gods, they overreached even their own powers, and stumbling, they fell headlong into decay. The life went out of the soil, the sky gave no rain, the spirit lost its energies; the city perished and was forgotten, and was whispered about by mythmakers, a city out of time, a city at the end of the world, a mighty mass of dead wonders, a habitation for jackals, a place where no one went. We are the first in centuries, said Scarp, to seek this city.

Halfway between dawn and noon they reached the wall and stood before the great gate. The gate alone was fifty feet high, a curving slab of burnished blue metal set smoothly into a recess in the tawny stucco of the wall. Breckenridge saw no way of opening it, no winch, no portcullis, no handles, no knobs. He feared that the impatient Militor would merely blow a hole in it. But, groping along the base of the gate, they found a small doorway, man-high and barely man-wide, near the left-hand edge. Ancient hinges yielded at a push. Scarp led the way inside.

The city was as Breckenridge remembered it from his dream: the cobbled plaza, the broad avenues, the humped and rubbery buildings. The fierce sunlight, deflected and refracted by the undulant roof lines, reverberated from every flat surface and rebounded in showers of brilliant energy. Breckenridge shaded his eyes. It was as though the sky were full of pulsars. His soul was frying on a cosmic griddle, cooking in a torrent of hard radiation.

The city was inhabited.

Faces were visible at windows. Elusive figures emerged at streetcorners, peered, withdrew. Scarp called to them; they shrank back into the hard-edged shadows.

'Well?' Arios demanded. 'They're human, aren't they?'

'What of it?' said Militor. 'Squatters, that's all. You saw how easy it was to push open that door. They've come in out of the desert to live in the ruins.'

'Maybe not. Descendants of the builders, I'd say. Perhaps the city never really was abandoned.' Arios looked at Scarp. 'Don't you agree?'

'They might be anything,' Scarp said. 'Squatters, descendants, even synthetics, even servants without masters, living on, waiting, living on, waiting—'

'Or projections cast by ancient machines,' Militor said. 'No human hand built this city.'

Arios snorted. They advanced quickly across the plaza and entered into the first of the grand avenues. The buildings flanking it were sealed. They proceeded to a major intersection, where they halted to inspect an open circular pit, fifteen feet in diameter, smooth-rimmed, descending into infinite darkness. Breckenridge had seen many such dark wells in his vision of the night before. He did not doubt now that he had left his sleeping body and had made an actual foray into the city last night.

Scarp flashed a light into the well. A copper-coloured metal ladder was visible along one face.

'Shall we go down?' Breckenridge asked.

'Later,' said Scarp.

The famous anthropologist had been drinking steadily all through the dinner party – wine, only wine, but plenty of it – and his eyes seemed glazed, his face flushed; nevertheless he continued to talk with superb clarity of perception and elegant precision of phrase, hardly pausing at all to construct his concepts. Perhaps he's merely quoting his own latest book from memory, Breckenridge thought, as he strained to follow the flow of ideas. '—a comparison between myth and what appears to have largely replaced it in modern societies, namely, politics. When the historian refers to the French Revolution it is always as a sequence of past happenings, a non-revertible series of events the remote consequences of which may still be felt at present. But to the French politician, as well as to his followers, the French Revolution is both a sequence belonging to the past – as to the historian – and an everlasting pattern which can be detected in the present French social structure and which provides a clue for its interpretation, a lead from which to infer the future developments. See, for instance, Michelet, who was a politically minded historian. He describes the French Revolution thus: "This day ... everything was possible ... future became present ... that is, no more time, a glimpse of eternity." ' The great man reached decisively for another glass of claret. His hand wavered; the glass toppled; a dark red torrent stained the tablecloth. Breckenridge experienced a sudden terrifying moment of complete disorientation, as though the walls and floor were

77

shifting places: he saw a parched desert plateau, four hooded figures, a blazing sky of strange constellations, a pulsating aurora sweeping the heavens with cold fire. A mighty walled city dominated the plain, and its frosty shadow, knifeblade-sharp, cut across Breckenridge's path. He shivered. The woman on Breckenridge's right laughed lightly and began to recite:

'I saw Eternity the other night
Like a great ring of pure and endless light.
   All calm, as it was bright;
And round beneath it, Time is hours, days, years,
   Driv'n by the spheres
Like a vast shadow mov'd; in which the world
   And all her train were hurl'd.'

'Excuse me,' Breckenridge said. 'I think I'm unwell.' He rushed from the dining room. In the hallway he turned towards the washroom and found himself staring into a steaming tropical marsh, all ferns and horsetails and giant insects. Dragonflies the size of pigeons whirred past him. The sleek rump of a brontosaurus rose like a bubbling aneurysm from the black surface of the swamp. Breckenridge recoiled and staggered away. On the other side of the hall lay the desert under the lash of a frightful noonday sun. He gripped the frame of a door and held himself upright, trembling, as his soul oscillated wildly across the hallucinatory aeons. 'I am Scarp,' said a quiet voice within him. 'You have come to the place where all times are one, where all errors can be unmade, where past and future are fluid and subject to redefinition.' Breckenridge felt powerful arms encircling and supporting him. 'Noel? Noel? Here, sit down.' Harry Munsey. Shiny pink skull, searching blue eyes. 'Jesus, Noel, you look like you're having some kind of bad trip. Merry sent me after you to find out—'

'It's okay,' Breckenridge said hoarsely. 'I'll be all right.'

'You want me to get her?'

'I'll be *all right*. Just let me steady myself a second.' He rose uncertainly. 'Okay. Let's go back inside.'

The anthropologist was still talking. A napkin covered the wine stain and he held a fresh glass aloft like a sacramental chalice. 'The key to everything, I think, lies in an idea that Franz Boas offered in 1898: "It would seem that mythological worlds have been built up only to be shattered again, and that new worlds were built from the fragments." '

Breckenridge said, 'The first men lived underground and there was no such thing as private property. One day there was an earthquake and the earth was rent apart. The light of day flooded the subterranean cavern where mankind dwelled. Clumsily, for the light dazzled their eyes, they came upward into the world of brightness and learned how to see. Seven days later they divided the fields among themselves and began to build the first walls as boundaries marking the limits of their land.'

By midday the city dwellers were losing their fear of the five intruders. Gradually, in twos and threes, they left their hiding places and gathered around the visitors until a substantial group had collected. They were dressed simply, in light robes, and they said nothing to the strangers, though they whispered frequently to one another. Among the group was the slender, dark-haired girl of Breckenridge's dream. 'Do you remember me?' he asked. She smiled and shrugged and answered softly in a liquid, incomprehensible language. Arios questioned her in six or seven tongues, but she shook her head to everything. Then she took Breckenridge by the hand and led him a few paces away, towards one of the street-wells. Pointing into it, she smiled. She pointed to Breckenridge, pointed to herself, to the surrounding buildings. She made a sweeping gesture taking in all the sky. She pointed again into the well. 'What are you trying to tell me?' he asked her. She answered in her own language. Breckenridge shook his head apologetically. She did a simple pantomime: eyes closed, head lolling against pressed-together hands. An image of sleep, certainly. She pointed to him. To herself. To the well. 'You want me to sleep with you?' he blurted. 'Down there?' He had to laugh at his own foolishness. It was ridiculous to assume the persistence of a cowardly, euphemistic metaphor like that across so many millennia. He gaped stupidly at her. She laughed – a silvery, tinkling laugh – and danced away from him, back towards her own people.

Their first night in the city they made camp in one of the great plazas. It was an octagonal space surrounded by low green buildings, sharp-angled, each faced on its plaza side with mirror-bright stone. About a hundred of the city-dwellers crouched in the shadows on the plaza's periphery, watching them. Scarp sprinkled fuel-pellets and kindled a fire; Militor distributed dinner; Horn played music as they ate; Arios, sitting apart, dictated a commentary into a recording device he carried, the size and texture of a large pearl. Afterwards they asked Breckenridge to tell a story, as usual, and he told them the tale of How Death Came to the World.

'Once upon a time,' he began, 'there were only a few people in the world and they lived in a green and fertile valley where winter never came and gardens bloomed all the year round. They spent their days laughing and swimming and lying in the sun, and in the evenings they feasted and sang and made love, and this went on without change, year in, year out, and no one ever fell ill or suffered from hunger, and no one ever died. Despite the serenity of this existence, one man in the village was unhappy. His name was Faust, and he was a restless, intelligent man with intense, burning eyes and a lean, un-smiling face. Faust felt that life must consist of something more than swimming and making love and plucking ripe fruit off vines. "There is something else to life," Faust insisted, "something unknown to us, something that eludes our grasp, something the lack of which keeps us from being truly happy. We are incomplete." The others listened to him and at first they were puzzled, for they had not known they were unhappy or incomplete; they had mistaken the ease and placidity of their existence for happiness. But after a while they started to believe that Faust might be right. They had not known how vacant their lives were until Faust had pointed it out. What can we do, they asked? How can we learn what the thing is that we lack? A wise old man suggested that they might ask the gods. So they elected Faust to visit the god Prometheus, who was said to be a friend to mankind, and ask him. Faust crossed hill and dale, mountain and river, and came at last to Prometheus on the storm-swept summit where he dwelled. He explained the situation and said, "Tell me, O Prometheus, why we feel so incomplete." The god replied, "It is because you do not have the use of fire. Without fire there can be no civilization; you are uncivilized, and your barbarism makes you unhappy. With fire you can cook your food and enjoy many interesting new flavours. With fire you can work metals, and create effective weapons and other tools." Faust considered this and said, "But where can we obtain fire? What is it? How is it used?"

' "I will bring fire to you," Prometheus answered.

'Prometheus then went to Zeus, the greatest of the gods, and said, "Zeus, the humans desire fire, and I seek your permission to bestow it upon them." But Zeus was hard of hearing and Prometheus lisped badly and in the language of the gods the words for fire and for death were very similar, and Zeus misunderstood and said, "How odd of them to desire such a thing, but I am a benevolent god, and deny my creatures nothing that they crave." So Zeus created a woman named Pandora and put death inside her and gave her to Prometheus, who took her back to the valley where mankind lived. "Here is Pandora," said Prometheus. "She will give you fire."

'As soon as Prometheus took his leave Faust came forward and embraced Pandora and lay with her. Her body was hot as flame, and as he held her in his arms death came forth from her and entered him, and he shivered and grew feverish, and cried out in ecstasy, "This is fire! I have mastered fire!" Within the hour death began to consume him, so that he grew weak and thin, and his skin became parched and yellowish, and he trembled like a leaf in a breeze. "Go!" he cried to the others. "Embrace her: She is the bringer of fire!" And he staggered off into the wilderness beyond the valley's edge, murmuring, "Thanks be to Prometheus for this gift." He lay down beneath a huge tree, and there he died, and it was the first time that death had visited a human being. And the tree died also.

'Then the other men of the village embraced Pandora, one after another, and death entered into them too, and they went from her to their own women and embraced them, so that soon all the men and women of the village were ablaze with death, and one by one their lives reached an end. Death remained in the village, passing into all who lived and into all who were born from their loins, and this is how death came to the world. Afterwards during a storm lightning struck the tree that had died when Faust had died, and set it ablaze, and a man whose name is forgotten thrust a dry branch into the blaze and lit it, and learned how to build a fire and how to keep the fire alive, and after that time men cooked their food and used fire to work metal into weapons, and so it was that civilization began.'

It was time to investigate one of the wells. Scarp, Arios, and Breckenridge would make the descent, with Militor and Horn remaining on the surface to cope with contingencies. They chose a well half a day's march from their campsite, deep into the city, a big one, broader and deeper than most they had seen. At its rim Scarp mounted a spherical fist-sized light that cast a dazzling blue-white beam into the opening. Then, lightly swinging himself out onto the metal ladder, he began to climb down, shrouded in a nimbus of molten brightness. Breckenridge peered after him. Scarp's head and shoulders remained visible for a long while, dwindling until he was only a point of darkness in motion deep within the cone of light, and then he could no longer be seen. 'Scarp?' Breckenridge called. After a moment came a muffled reply out of the depths. Scarp had reached bottom, somewhere beyond the range of the beam, and wanted them to join him.

Breckenridge followed. The descent seemed infinite. There was a stiffness in his left knee. He became a mere automaton, mechanically seizing the rungs; they were warm in his hands. His eyes, fixed on the pocked grey skin of the well's wall inches from his nose, grew glassy and unfocused. He passed through the zone of light as though sliding through the face of a mirror and moved downwards in darkness without a change of pace until his boot slammed unexpectedly into a solid floor where he had thought to encounter the next rung. The left boot; his knee, jamming, protested. Scarp lightly touched his shoulder. 'Step back here next to me,' he said. 'Take sliding steps and make sure you have a footing. For all we know, we're on some sort of ledge with a steep drop on all sides.'

They waited while Arios came down. His footfalls were like thunder in the well: boom, boom, boom, transmitted and amplified by the rungs. Then the men at the surface lowered the light, fixed to the end of a long cord, and at last they could look around.

They were in a kind of catacomb. The floor of the well was a platform of neatly dressed stone slabs which gave access to horizontal tunnels several times a man's height, stretching away to right and left, to fore and aft. The mouth of the well was a dim dot of light far above. Scarp, after inspecting the perimeter of the platform, flashed the beam into one of the tunnels, stared a moment, and cautiously entered. Breckenridge heard him cough. 'Dusty in here,' Scarp muttered. Then he said, 'You told us a story once about the King of the Dead Lands, Breckenridge. What was his name?'

'Thanatos.'

'Thanatos, yes. This must be his kingdom. Come and look.'

Arios and Breckenridge exchanged shrugs. Breckenridge stepped into the tunnel. The walls on both sides were lined from floor to ceiling with tiers of coffins, stacked eight or ten high and extending as far as the beam of light reached. The coffins were glass-faced and covered over with dense films of dust. Scarp drew his finger through the dust over one coffin and left deep tracks; clouds rose up, sending Breckenridge back, coughing and choking, to stumble into Arios. When the dust cleared they could see a figure within, seemingly asleep, the nude figure of a young man lying on his back. His expression was one of great serenity. Breckenridge shivered. Death's kingdom, yes, the place of Thanatos, the house of Pluto. He walked down the row, wiping coffin after coffin. An old man. A child. A young woman. An older woman. A whole population lay embalmed here. I died long ago, he thought, and I don't even sleep. I walk about beneath the earth. The silence was frightening here. 'The people of the city?' Scarp asked. 'The ancient inhabitants?'

'Very likely,' said Arios. His voice was as crisp as ever. He alone was not trembling. 'Slain in some inconceivable massacre? But what? But how?'

'They appear to have died natural deaths,' Breckenridge pointed out. 'Their bodies look whole and healthy. As though they were lying here asleep. Not dead, only sleeping.'

'A plague?' Scarp wondered. 'A sudden cloud of deadly gas? A taint of poison in their water supply?'

'If it had been sudden,' said Breckenridge, 'how would they have had time to build all these coffins? This whole tunnel – catacomb upon catacomb—' A network of passageways spanning the city's entire subterrain. Thousands of coffins. Millions. Breckenridge felt dazed by the presence of death on such a scale. The skeleton with the scythe, moving briskly about its work. Severed heads and hands and feet scattered like dandelions in the springtime meadow. The reign of Thanatos, King of Swords, Knight of Wands.

Thunder sounded behind them. Footfalls in the well.

Scarp scowled. 'I told them to wait up there. That fool Militor—'

Arios said, 'Militor should see this. Undoubtedly it's the resting place of the city dwellers. Undoubtedly these are human beings. Do you know what I imagine? A mass suicide. A unanimous decision to abandon the world of life. Years of preparation. The construction of tunnels, of machines for killing, a whole vast apparatus of immolation. And then the day appointed – long lines waiting to be processed – millions of men and women and children passing through the machines, gladly giving up their lives, going willingly to the coffins that await them—'

'And then,' Scarp said, 'there must have been only a few left and no one to process them. Living on, caretakers for the dead, perhaps, maintaining the machinery that preserves these millions of bodies—'

'Preserves them for what?' Arios asked.

'The day of resurrection,' said Breckenridge.

The footfalls in the well grew louder. Scarp glanced towards the tunnel's mouth. 'Militor?' he called. 'Horn?' He sounded angry. He walked towards the well. 'You were supposed to wait for us up—'

Breckenridge heard a grinding sound and whirled to see Arios tugging at the lid of a coffin – the one that held the serene young man. Instinctively he moved to halt the desecration, but he was too slow; the glass plate rose as Arios broke the seals, and, with a quick whooshing sound, a burst of greenish vapour rushed from the coffin. It hovered a moment in mid-air, speared by Arios' beam of light; then it congealed into a yellow precipitant and broke in a miniature rainstorm that stained the tunnel's stone floor. To Breckenridge's horror the young man's body jerked convulsively: muscles tightened into knots and almost instantly relaxed. 'He's alive!' Breckenridge cried.

'Was,' said Scarp.

Yes. The figure in the glass case was motionless. It changed colour and texture, turning black and withered. Scarp shoved Arios aside and slammed the lid closed, but that could do no good now. A dreadful new motion commenced within the coffin. In moments something shrivelled and twisted lay before them.

'Suspended animation,' said Arios. 'The city builders – they lie here, as human as we are, sleeping, not dead, sleeping. Sleeping! Militor! Militor, come quickly!'

Feingold said, 'Let me see if I have it straight. After the public offering our group will continue to hold 83 per cent of the Class B stock and 34 per cent of the voting common, which constitutes a controlling block. We'll let you have 100,000 five-year warrants and we'll agree to a conversion privilege on the 1992 $6\frac{1}{2}$ per cent debentures, plus we allow you the stipulated underwriting fee, providing your Argentinian friend takes up the agreed-upon allotment of debentures and follows through on his deal with us in Colorado. Okay?

Now, then, assuming the SEC has no objections, I'd like to outline the proposed interlocking directorates with Heitmark A.G. in Liechtenstein and Hellaphon S.A. in Athens, after which—'

The high, clear, rapid voice went on and on. Breckenridge toyed with his lunch, smiled frequently, nodded whenever he felt it was appropriate, and otherwise remained disconnected, listening only with the automatic-recorder part of his mind. They were sitting on the terrace of an open-air restaurant in Tiberias, at the edge of the Sea of Galilee, looking across to the bleak, brown Syrian hills on the far side. The December air was mild, the sun bright. Last week Breckenridge had visited Monaco, Zürich, and Milan. Yesterday Tel Aviv, tomorrow Haifa, next Tuesday Istanbul. Then on to Nairobi, Johannesburg, Peking, Singapore. Finally San Francisco and then home. Zap! Zap! A crazy round-the-world scramble in twenty days, cleaning up a lot of international business for the firm. It could all have been handled by telephone, or else some of these foreign tycoons could have come to New York, but Breckenridge had volunteered to do the junket. Why? Why? Sitting here ten thousand miles from home having lunch with a man whose office was down the street from his own. Crazy. Why all this running, Noel? Where do you think you'll get?

'Some more wine?' Feingold asked. 'What do you think of this Israeli stuff, anyway?'

'It goes well with the fish.' Breckenridge reached for Feingold's copy of the agreement. 'Here, let me initial all that.'

'Don't you want to check it over first?'

'Not necessary. I have faith in you, Sid.'

'Well, I wouldn't cheat you, that's true. But I could have made a mistake. I'm capable of making mistakes.'

'I don't think so,' Breckenridge said. He grinned. Feingold grinned. Behind the grin there was something chilly. Breckenridge looked away. You think I'm bending over backwards to treat you like a gentleman, he thought, because you know what people like me are really supposed to think about Jews, and I know you know, and you know I know you know, and –

and – well, screw it, Sid. Do I trust you? Maybe I do. Maybe I don't. But the basic fact is I just don't care. Stack the deck any way you like, Feingold. I just don't care. I wish I was on Mars. Or Pluto. Or the year Two Billion. Zap! Right across the whole continuum! Noel Breckenridge, freaking out! He heard himself say, 'Do you want to know my secret fantasy, Sid? I dream of waking up Jewish one day. It's so damned boring being a gentile, do you know that? I feel so bland, so straight, so sunny. I envy you all that feverish kinky complexity of soul. All that history. Ghettos, persecutions, escapes, schemes for survival and revenge, a sense of tribal unity born out of shared pain. It's so hard for a goy to develop some honest paranoia, you know? Let alone a little schiziness.' Feingold was still grinning. He filled Breckenridge's wine glass again. He showed no sign of having heard anything that might offend him. Maybe I didn't say anything, Breckenridge thought.

Feingold said, 'When you get back to New York, Noel, I'd like you out to our place for dinner. You and your wife. A weekend, maybe. Logs on the fire, thick steaks, plenty of good wine. You'll love our place.' Three Israeli jets roared low over Tiberias and vanished in the direction of Lebanon. 'Will you come? Can you fit it into your schedule?'

Some possible structural hypotheses:

LIFE AS MEANINGLESS CONDITION

Breckenridge on Wall Street.	The four seekers moving randomly.	The dead city.

LIFE RENDERED MEANINGFUL THROUGH ART

Breckenridge recollects ancient myths.	The four seekers elicit his presence and request the myths.	The dead city inhabited after all. The inhabitants listen to Breckenridge.

THE IMPACT OF ENTROPY

His tales are garbled dreams.	The seekers quarrel over theory.	The city dwellers speak an unknown language.

He is a double self.	The four seekers are unsure of the historical background.	Most of the city dwellers are asleep.

His audience was getting larger every night. They came from all parts of the city, silently arriving, drawn at sundown to the place where the visitors camped. Hundreds, now, squatting beyond the glow of the campfire. They listened intently, nodded, seemed to comprehend, murmured occasional comments to one another. How strange: they seemed to comprehend.

'The story of Samson and Odysseus,' Breckenridge announced. 'Samson is blind but mighty. His woman is known as Delilah. To them comes the wily chieftain Odysseus, making his way homeward from the land of Ithaca. He penetrates the maze in which Samson and Delilah live and hires himself to them as bond servant, giving his name as No Man. Delilah entices him to carry her off, and he abducts her. Samson is aware of the abduction but is unable to find them in the maze; he cries out in pain and rage, "No Man steals my wife! No Man steals my wife!' His servants are baffled by this and take no action. In fury Samson brings the maze crashing down on himself and dies, while Odysseus carries Delilah off to Sparta, where she is seduced by Paris, Prince of Troy. Odysseus thus loses her and by way of gaining revenge he seduces Helen, the Queen of Troy, and the Trojan War begins.'

And then he told the story of how mankind was created:

'In the beginning there was only a field of white sand. Lightning struck it, and where the lightning hit the sand it coagulated into a vessel of glass, and rainwater ran into the vessel and brought it to life, and from the vessel a she-wolf was born. Thunder entered her womb and fertilized her and she gave birth to twins, and they were not wolves but a human boy and a human girl. The wolf suckled the twins until they reached adulthood. Then they copulated and engendered children of their own. Because they were ashamed of their nakedness they killed the old wolf and made garments from her hide.'

And he told them the myth of the Wandering Jew, who scoffed at God and was condemned to drift through time until he himself was able to become God.

And he told them of the Golden Age and the Iron Age and the Age of Uranium.

And he told them how the waters and winds came into being, and the seasons, the months, day and night.

And he told them how art was born:
'Out of a hole in space pours a stream of pure life-force. Many men and women attempted to seize the flow, but they were burned to ashes by its intensity. At last, however, a man devised a way. He hollowed himself out until there was nothing at all inside his body and had himself dragged by a faithful dog to the place where the stream of energy descended from the heavens. Then the life-force entered him and filled him, and instead of destroying him it took possession of him and restored him to life. But the force overflowed within him, brimming over, and the only way he could deal with that was to fashion stories and sculptures and songs, for otherwise the force would engulf him and drown him. His name was Gilgamesh and he was the first of the artists of mankind.'

The city dwellers came by the thousand now. They listened and wept at Breckenridge's words.

Hypothesis of structural resolution:

He finds creative fulfilment.	The four seekers have bridged space and time to bring life out of death.	The sleeping city dwellers will be awakened.

Gradually the outlines of a master myth took place: the

creation, the creation of man, the origin of private property, the origin of death, the loss of innocence, the loss of faith, the end of the world, the coming of a redeemer to start the cycle anew. Soon the structure would be complete. When it was, Breckenridge thought, perhaps rains would fall on the desert, perhaps the world would be reborn.

Breckenridge slept. Sleeping, he experienced an inward glow of golden light. The girl he had encountered before came to him and took his hand and led him through the city. They walked for hours, it seemed, until they came to a well different from all the others, rectangular rather than circular and surrounded at street level by a low railing of bright metal mesh. 'Go down into this one,' she told him. 'When you reach the bottom, keep walking until you reach the room where the mechanisms of awakening are located.' He looked at her in amazement, realizing that her words had been comprehensible. 'Are you speaking my language,' he asked, 'or am I speaking yours?' She answered by smiling and pointing towards the well.

He stepped over the railing and began his descent. The well was deeper than the other one; the air in its depths was stale and dry. The golden glow lit his way for him to the bottom and thence along a low passageway with a rounded vault of a ceiling. After a long time he came to a large, brightly lit room filled with sleek grey machinery. It was much like the computer room at any large bank. Mounted on the walls were control panels, labelled in an unknown language but also clearly marked with squential symbols:

I II III IIII IIIII IIIIII

While he studied these he became aware of a sliding, hissing sound from the corridor beyond. He thought of sturdy metal cables passing one against the other; but then into the control room slowly came a creature something like a scorpion in form, considerably greater than a man in size. Its curved tubular thorax was dark and of a waxen texture; a dense mat of brown bristles, thick as straws, sprouted on its abdomen;

its many eyes were bright, alert, and malevolent. Breckenridge snatched up a steel bar that lay near his feet and tried to wield it like a lance as the monster approached. From its jaws, though, there looped a sudden lasso of newly spun silken thread that caught the end of the bar and jerked it from Breckenridge's grasp. Then a second loop, entangling his arms and shoulders. Struggle was useless. He was caught. The creature pulled him closer. Breckenridge saw fangs, powerful palpi, a scythe of a tail in which a dripping stinger had become erect. Breckenridge writhed in the monster's grip. He felt neither surprise nor fear; this seemed a necessary working out of some ancient fore-ordained pattern.

A cool silent voice within his skull said, 'Who are you?'

'Noel Breckenridge of New York City, born AD 1940.'

'Why do you intrude here?'

'I was summoned. If you want to know why, ask someone else.'

'Is it your purpose to awaken the sleepers?'

'Very possibly,' Breckenridge said.

'So the time has come?'

'Maybe it has,' said Breckenridge. All was still for a long moment. The monster made no hostile move. Breckenridge grew impatient. 'Well, what's the arrangement?' he said finally.

'The arrangement?'

'The terms under which I get my freedom. Am I supposed to tell you a lot of diverting stories? Will I have to serve you six months out of the year, forever more? Is there some precious object I'm obliged to bring you from the bottom of the sea? Maybe you have a riddle that I'm supposed to answer.'

The monster made no reply.

'Is that it?' Breckenridge demanded. 'A riddle?'

'Do you want it to be a riddle?'

'A riddle, yes.'

There was another endless pause. Breckenridge met the beady gaze steadily. At last the voice said, 'A riddle. A riddle. Very well. Tell me the answer to this. What goes on four legs in the morning, on two legs in the afternoon, on three legs in the evening?'

Breckenridge repeated it. He pondered. He frowned. He coughed. Then he laughed. 'A baby,' he said, 'crawls on all fours. A grown man walks upright. An old man requires the assistance of a cane. Therefore the answer to your riddle is—'

He left the sentence unfinished. The gleam went out of the monster's eyes; the silken loop binding Breckenridge dissolved; the creature began slowly and sadly to back away, withdrawing into the corridor from which it came. Its hissing, rustling sound persisted for a time, growing ever more faint.

Breckenridge turned and without hesitation pulled the switch marked I.

The aurora no longer appears in the night sky. A light rain has been falling frequently for some days, and the desert is turning green. The sleepers are awakening, millions of them, called forth from their coffins by the workings of automatic mechanisms. Breckenridge stands in the central plaza of the city, arms outspread, and the city dwellers, as they emerge from the subterranean sleeping places, make their way towards him. I am the resurrection and the life, he thinks. I am Orpheus the sweet singer. I am Homer the blind. I am Noel Breckenridge. He looks across the aeons to Harry Munsey. 'I was wrong,' he says. 'There's meaning everywhere, Harry. For Sam Smith as well as for Beethoven. For Noel Breckenridge as well as for Michelangelo. Dawn after dawn, simply being alive, being part of it all, part of the cosmic dance of life – that's the meaning, Harry. Look! Look!' The sun is high now – not a cruel sun but a mild. gentle one, its heat softened by a humid haze. This is the dream-time, when all mistakes are unmade, when all things become one. The city folk surround him. They come closer. Closer yet. They reach towards him. He experiences a delicious flash of white light. The world disappears.

'JFK Airport,' he told the taxi driver. The cab zoomed away. From the front seat came the voice of the radio with today's closing Dow Jones Industrials: 948.72, down 6.11. He reached the airport by half past five, and at seven he boarded a Pan Am flight for London. The next morning at nine, London time, he cabled his wife to say that he was well and planned to head south for the winter. Then he reported to the Air France counter for the nonstop flight to Morocco. Over the next week he cabled home from Rabat, Marrakech, and Timbuktu in Mali. The third cable said:

GUESS WHAT STOP I'M REALLY IN TIMBUKTU STOP HAVE RENTED
JEEP STOP I SET OUT INTO SAHARA TOMORROW STOP AM VERY
HAPPY STOP YES STOP VERY HAPPY STOP VERY VERY HAPPY
STOP STOP STOP

It was the last message he sent. The night it arrived in New York there was a spectacular celestial display, an aurora that brought thousands of people out into Central Park. There was rain in the southeastern Sahara four days later, the first recorded precipitation there in eight years and seven months. An earthquake was reported in southern Sicily, but it did little damage. Things were much quieter after that for everybody.

Ship-sister, star-sister

Sixteen light-years from earth today, in the fifth month of the voyage, and the silent throb of acceleration continues to drive the velocity higher. Three games of Go are in progress in the ship's lounge. The year-captain stands at the entrance to the lounge, casually watching the players: Roy and Sylvia, Leon and Chiang, Heinz and Elliot. Go has been a craze aboard ship for weeks. The players – some eighteen or twenty members of the expedition have caught the addiction by now – sit hour after hour, contemplating strategies, devising variations, grasping the smooth black or white stones between forefinger and second finger, putting the stones down against the wooden board with the proper smart sharp clacking sound. The year-captain himself does not play, though the game once interested him to the point of obsession, long ago; he finds his responsibilities so draining that an exercise in simulated territorial conquest does not attract him now. He comes here often to watch, however, remaining five or ten minutes, then going on about his duties.

The best of the players is Roy, the mathematician, a large, heavy man with a soft sleepy face. He sits with his eyes closed, awaiting in tranquillity his turn to play. 'I am purging myself of the need to win,' he told the year-captain yesterday when asked what occupies his mind while he waits. Purged or not, Roy wins more than half of his games, even though he gives most of his opponents a handicap of four or five stones.

He gives Sylvia a handicap of only two. She is a delicate woman, fine-boned and shy, a geneticist, and she plays well although slowly. She makes her move. At the sound of it Roy opens his eyes. He studies the board, points, and says, *'Atari,'* the conventional way of calling to his opponent's attention the fact that her move will enable him to capture several of her stones. Sylvia laughs lightly and retracts her move. After a moment she moves again. Roy nods and picks up a white stone, which he holds for nearly a minute before he places it.

The year-captain would like to speak with Sylvia about one of her experiments, but he sees she will be occupied with the game for another hour or more. The conversation can wait. No one hurries aboard this ship. They have plenty of time for everything: a lifetime, maybe, if no habitable planet can be found. The universe is theirs. He scans the board and tries to anticipate Sylvia's next move. Soft footsteps sound behind him. The year-captain turns. Noelle, the ship's communicator, is approaching the lounge. She is a slim sightless girl with long dark hair, and she customarily walks the corridors unaided: no sensors for her, not even a cane. Occasionally she stumbles, but usually her balance is excellent and her sense of the location of obstacles is superb. It is a kind of arrogance for the blind to shun assistance, perhaps. But also it is a kind of desperate poetry.

As she comes up to him she says, 'Good morning, year-captain.'

Noelle is infallible in making such identifications. She claims to be able to distinguish members of the expedition by the tiny characteristic sounds they make: their patterns of breathing, their coughs, the rustling of their clothing. Among the others there is some scepticism about this. Many aboard the ship believe that Noelle is reading their minds. She does not deny that she possesses the power of telepathy; but she insists that the only mind to which she has direct access is that of her twin sister Yvonne, far away on Earth.

He turns to her. His eyes meet hers: an automatic act, a habit. Hers, dark and clear, stare disconcertingly through his forehead. He says, 'I'll have a report for you to transmit in about two hours.'

'I'm ready whenever.' She smiles faintly. She listens a moment to the clacking of the Go stones. 'Three games being played?' she asks.

'Yes.'

'How strange that the game hasn't begun to lose its hold on them by this time.'

'Its grip is powerful,' the year-captain says.

'It must be. How good it is to be able to give yourself so completely to a game.'

'I wonder. Playing Go consumes a great deal of valuable time.'

'Time?' Noelle laughs. 'What is there to do with time, except to consume it?' After a moment she says, 'Is it a difficult game?'

'The rules are quite simple. The application of the rules is another matter entirely. It's a deeper and more subtle game than chess, I think.'

Her blank eyes wander across his face and suddenly lock into his. 'How long would it take for me to learn how to play?'

'You?'

'Why not? I also need amusement, year-captain.'

'The board has hundreds of intersections. Moves may be made at any of them. The patterns formed are complex and constantly changing. Someone who is unable to see—'

'My memory is excellent,' Noelle says. 'I can visualize the board and make the necessary corrections as play proceeds. You need only tell me where you put down your stones. And guide my hand, I suppose, when I make my moves.'

'I doubt that it'll work, Noelle.'

'Will you teach me anyway?'

The ship is sleek, tapered, graceful: a silver bullet streaking across the universe at a velocity that has at this point come to exceed a million kilometres per second. No. In fact the ship is no bullet at all, but rather something squat and awkward, as clumsy as any ordinary space-going vessel, with an elaborate spidery superstructure of extensor arms and antennas and observation booms and other externals. Yet because of its incredible speed the year-captain persists in thinking of it as sleek and tapered and graceful. It carries him without friction through the vast empty grey cloak of nospace at a velocity greater than that of light. He knows better, but he is unable to shake that streamlined image from his mind.

Already the expedition is sixteen light-years from Earth. That isn't an easy thing for him to grasp. He feels the force of it, but not the true meaning. He can tell himself, *Already we are sixteen kilometres from home*, and understand that readily enough. *Already we are sixteen hundred kilometres from home* – yes, he can understand that too. What about *Already we are sixteen million kilometres from home*? That much strains comprehension – a gulf, a gulf, a terrible empty dark gulf – but he thinks he is able to understand even so great a distance, after a fashion. Sixteen light-years, though? How can he explain that to himself? Brilliant stars flank the tube of nospace through which the ship now travels, and he knows that his grey-flecked beard will have turned entirely white before the light of those stars glitters in the night sky of Earth. Yet only a few months have elapsed since the departure of the expedition. How miraculous it is, he thinks, to have come so far so swiftly.

Even so, there is a greater miracle. He will ask Noelle to relay a message to Earth an hour after lunch, and he knows that he will have an acknowledgement from Control Central in Brazil before dinner. That seems an even greater miracle to him.

Her cabin is neat, austere, underfurnished: no paintings, no light-sculptures, nothing to please the visual sense, only a few small sleek bronze statuettes, a smooth oval slab of green stone, and some objects evidently chosen for their rich textures – a strip of nubby fabric stretched across a frame, a sea urchin's stony test, a collection of rough sandstone chunks. Everything is meticulously arranged. Does someone help her keep the place tidy? She moves serenely from point to point in the little room, never in danger of a collision; her confidence of motion is unnerving to the year-captain, who sits patiently waiting for her to settle down. She is pale, precisely groomed, her dark hair drawn tightly back from her forehead and held by an intricate ivory clasp. Her lips are full, her nose is rounded. She wears a soft flowing robe. Her body is attractive: he has seen her in the baths and knows of her high full breasts, her ample curving hips, her creamy perfect skin. Yet so far as he has heard she has had no shipboard liaisons. Is it because she is blind? Perhaps one tends not to think of a blind person as a potential sexual partner. Why should that be? Maybe because one hesitates to take advantage of a blind person in a sexual encounter, he suggests, and immediately catches himself up, startled, wondering why he should think of any sort of sexual relationship as *taking advantage*. Well, then, possibly compassion for her handicap gets in the way of erotic feeling; pity too easily becomes patronizing, and kills desire. He rejects that theory: glib, implausible. Could it be that people fear to approach her, suspecting that she is able to read their inmost thoughts? She has repeatedly denied any ability to enter minds other than her sister's. Besides, if you have nothing to hide, why be put off by her telepathy? No, it must be something else, and now he thinks he has isolated it: that Noelle is so self-contained, so serene, so much wrapped up in her blindness and her mind-power and her unfathomable communion with her distant sister, that no one dares to breach the crystalline barricades that guard her inner self. She is unapproached because she seems unapproachable; her strange perfection of soul sequesters her, keeping others at a distance the way extraordinary physical beauty can sometimes keep people at a distance. She does not arouse desire because she does not seem at all human. She gleams. She is a flawless machine, an integral part of the ship.

He unfolds the text of today's report to Earth. 'Not that there's anything new to tell them,' he says, 'but I suppose we have to file the daily communiqué all the same.'

'It would be cruel if we didn't. We mean so much to them.'

'I wonder.'

'Oh, yes. Yvonne says they take our messages from her as fast as they come in, and send them out on every channel. Word from us is terribly important to them.'

'As a diversion, nothing more. As the latest curiosity. Intrepid explorers venturing into the uncharted wilds of interstellar nospace.' His voice sounds harsh to him, his rhythms of speech coarse and blurting. His words surprise him. He had not known he felt this way about Earth. Still, he goes on. 'That's all we represent: novelty, vicarious adventure, a moment of amusement.'

'Do you mean that? It sounds so awfully cynical.'

He shrugs. 'Another six months and they'll be completely bored with us and our communiqués. Perhaps sooner than that. A year and they'll have forgotten us.'

She says, 'I don't see you as a cynical man. Yet you often say such' – she falters – 'such—'.

'Such blunt things? I'm a realist, I guess. Is that the same as a cynic?'

'Don't try to label yourself, year-captain.'

'I only try to look at things realistically.'

'You don't know what real is. You don't know what you are, year-captain.'

The conversation is suddenly out of control: much too charged, much too intimate. She has never spoken like this before. It is as if there is a malign electricity in the air, a prickly field that distorts their normal selves, making them unnaturally tense and aggressive. He feels panic. If he disturbs the delicate balance of Noelle's consciousness, will she still be able to make contact with far-off Yvonne?

He is unable to prevent himself from parrying: 'Do *you* know what I am, then?'

She tells him, 'You're a man in search of himself. That's why you volunteered to come all the way out here.'

'And why did you volunteer to come all the way out here, Noelle?' he asks helplessly.

She lets the lids slide slowly down over her unseeing eyes and offers no reply. He tries to salvage things a bit by saying more calmly into her tense silence, 'Never mind. I didn't intend to upset you. Shall we transmit the report?'

'Wait.'

'All right.'

She appears to be collecting herself. After a moment she says, less edgily, 'How do you think they see us at home? As creatures engaged in an epic voyage?'

'Right now, as superhuman creatures, epic voyage.'

'And later we'll become more ordinary in their eyes?'

'Later we'll become nothing to them. They'll forget us.'

'How sad.' Her tone tingles with a grace-note of irony. She may be laughing at him. 'And you, year-captain? Do you picture yourself as ordinary or as superhuman?'

'Something in between. Rather more than ordinary, but no demigod.'

'I regard myself as quite ordinary except in two respects,' she says sweetly.

'One is your telepathic communion with your sister and the other—' He hesitates, mysteriously uncomfortable at naming it. 'The other is your blindness.'

'Of course,' she says. Smiles. Radiantly. 'Shall we do the report now?'

'Have you made contact with Yvonne?'

'Yes. She's waiting.'

'Very well, then.' Glancing at his notes, he begins slowly to read: 'Shipday 117. Velocity ... Apparent location ...'

She naps after every transmission. They exhaust her. She was beginning to fade even before he reached the end of today's message; now, as he steps into the corridor, he knows she will be asleep before he closes the door. He leaves, frowning, troubled by the odd outburst of tension between them and by his mysterious attack of 'realism'. By what right does he say Earth will grow jaded with the voyagers? All during the years of preparation for this first interstellar journey the public excitement never flagged, indeed spurred the voyagers themselves on at times when their interminable training routines threatened *them* with boredom. Earth's messages, relayed by Yvonne to Noelle, vibrate with eager queries; the curiosity of the home-world has been overwhelming since the start. Tell us, tell us, tell us!

But there is so little to tell, really, except in that one trans-cendental area where there is so much. And how, really, can any of that be told?

How can *this*—

He pauses by the viewplate in the main transit corridor, a

rectangular window a dozen metres long that gives direct access to the external environment. The pearl-grey emptiness of nospace, dense and pervasive, presses tight against the skin of the ship. During the training period the members of the expedition had been warned to anticipate nothing in the way of outside inputs as they crossed the galaxy; they would be shuttling through a void of infinite length, a matter-free tube, and there would be no sights to entertain them, no backdrop of remote nebulas, no glittering stars, no stray meteors, not so much as a pair of colliding atoms yielding the tiniest momentary spark, only an eternal sameness, like a blank wall. They had been taught methods of coping with that: turn inward, demand no delights from the universe beyond the ship, make the ship itself your universe. And yet, and yet, how misguided those warnings had been! Nospace was not a wall but rather a window. It was impossible for those on earth to understand what revelations lay in that seeming emptiness. The year-captain, head throbbing from his encounter with Noelle, now revels in his keenest pleasure. A glance at the viewplate reveals that place where the immanent becomes the transcendent: the year-captain sees once again the infinite reverberating waves of energy that sweep through the greyness. What lies beyond the ship is neither a blank wall nor an empty tube; it is a stunning profusion of interlocking energy fields, linking everything; it is music that also is light, it is light that also is music, and those aboard the ship are sentient particles wholly enmeshed in that vast all-engulfing reverberation, that radiant song of gladness, that is the universe. The voyagers journey joyously towards the centre of all things, giving themselves gladly into the care of cosmic forces far surpassing human control and understanding. He presses his hands against the cool glass. He puts his face close to it. *What do I see, what do I feel, what am I experiencing?* It is instant revelation, every time. It is – almost, *almost!* – the sought-after oneness. Barriers remain, but yet he is aware of an altered sense of space and time, a knowledge of the awesome something that lurks in the vacancies between the spokes of the cosmos, something majestic and powerful; he knows that that something is part of himself, and he is part of it. When he stands at the viewplate he yearns to open the ship's great hatch and tumble into the eternal. But not yet, not yet. Barriers remain. The voyage has only begun. They grow closer every day to that which they seek, but the voyage has only begun.

How could we convey any of this to those who remain behind? How could we make them understand?

Not with words. Never with words.

Let them come out here and see for themselves—

He smiles. He trembles and does a little shivering wriggle of delight. He turns away from the viewplate, drained, ecstatic.

Noelle lies in uneasy dreams. She is aboard a ship, an archaic three-master struggling in an icy sea. The rigging sparkles with fierce icicles, which now and again snap free in the cruel gales and smash with little tinkling sounds against the deck. The deck wears a slippery shiny coating of thin hard ice, and footing is treacherous. Great eroded bergs heave wildly in the grey water, rising, slapping the waves, subsiding. If one of those bergs hits the hull, the ship will sink. So far they have been lucky about that, but now a more subtle menace is upon them. The sea is freezing over. It congeals, coagulates, becomes a viscous fluid surging sluggishly. Broad glossy plaques toss on the waves: new ice floes, colliding, grinding, churning; the floes are at war, destroying one another's edges, but some are making treaties, uniting to form a single implacable shield. When the sea freezes altogether the ship will be crushed. And now it is freezing. The ship can barely make headway. The sails belly out uselessly, straining at their lines. The wind makes a lyre out of the rigging as the ice-coated ropes twang and sing. The hull creaks like an old man; the grip of the ice is heavy. The timbers are yielding. The end is near. They will all perish. They will all perish. Noelle emerges from her cabin, goes above, seizes the railing, sways, prays, wonders when the wind's fist will punch through the stiff frozen canvas of the sails. Nothing can save them. But now! Yes, yes! A glow overhead! Yvonne, Yvonne! She comes. She hovers like a goddess in the black star-pocked sky. Soft golden light streams from her. She is smiling, and her smile thaws the sea. The ice relents. The air grows gentle. The ship is freed. It sails on, unhindered, towards the perfumed tropics.

In late afternoon Noelle drifts silently, wraithlike, into the control room where the year-captain is at work; she looks so weary and drawn that she is almost translucent; she seems unusually vulnerable, as though a harsh sound would shatter her. She has brought the year-captain Earth's answer to this morning's transmission. He takes from her the small, clear data-cube on which she has recorded her latest conversation with her sister. As Yvonne speaks in her mind, Noelle repeats the message aloud into a sensor disc, and it is captured on the cube. He wonders why she looks so wan. 'Is anything wrong?' he asks. She tells him that she has had some difficulty receiving the message; the signal from Earth was strangely fuzzy. She is perturbed by that.

'It was like static,' she says.

'Mental static?'

She is puzzled. Yvonne's tone is always pure, crystalline, wholly undistorted. Noelle has never had an experience like this before.

'Perhaps you were tired,' he suggests. 'Or maybe she was.'

He fits the cube into the playback slot, and Noelle's voice comes from the speakers. She sounds unfamiliar, strained and ill at ease; she fumbles words frequently and often asks Yvonne to repeat. The message, what he can make out of it, is the usual cheery stuff, predigested news from the home-world – politics, sports, the planetary weather, word of the arts and sciences, special greetings for three or four members of the expedition, expressions of general good wishes – everything light, shallow, amiable. The static disturbs him. What if the telepathic link should fail? What if they were to lose contact with Earth altogether? He asks himself why that should trouble him so. The ship is self-sufficient; it needs no guidance from Earth in order to function properly, nor do the voyagers really have to have daily information about events on the mother planet. Then why care if silence descends? Why not accept the fact that they are no longer earthbound in any way, that they have become virtually a new species as they leap, faster than light, outward into the stars? No. He cares. The link matters. He decides that it has to do with what they are experiencing in relation to the intense throbbing greyness outside, that interchange of energies, that growing sense of universal connection. They are making discoveries every day, not astronomical but – well, spiritual – and, the year-captain thinks, what a pity if none of this can ever be communicated to those who have remained behind. We must keep the link open.

'Maybe,' he says, 'we ought to let you and Yvonne rest for a few days.'

They look upon me as some sort of nun because I'm blind and special. I hate that, but there's nothing I can do to change it. I am what they think I am. I lie awake imagining men touching my body. The year-captain stands over me. I see his face clearly, the skin flushed and sweaty, the eyes gleaming. He strokes my breasts. He puts his lips to my lips. Suddenly, terribly, he embraces me and I scream. Why do I scream?

'You promised to teach me how to play,' she says, pouting a little. They are in the ship's lounge. Four games are under way: Elliot and Sylvia, Roy and Paco, David and Heinz, Mike and Bruce. Her pout fascinates him: such a little-girl gesture, so charming, so human. She seems to be in much better shape today, even though there was trouble again in the transmission, Yvonne complaining that the morning report was coming through indistinctly and noisily. Noelle has decided that the noise is some sort of local phenomenon, something like a sunspot effect, and will vanish once they are far enough from this sector of nospace. He is not as sure of this as she is, but she probably has a better understanding of such things than he. 'Teach me, year-captain,' she prods. 'I really do want to know how to play. Have faith in me.'

'All right,' he says. The game may prove valuable to her, a relaxing pastime, a timely distraction. 'This is the board. It has nineteen horizontal lines, nineteen vertical lines. The stones are played on the intersections of these lines, not on the squares that they form.' He takes her hand and traces, with the tips of her fingers, the pattern of intersecting lines. They have been printed with a thick ink, easily discernible against the flatness of the board. 'These nine dots are called stars,' he tells her. 'They serve as orientation points.' He touches her fingertips to the nine stars. 'We give the lines in this direction numbers, from one to nineteen, and we give the lines in the other direction letters, from A to T, leaving out I. Thus we can identify positions on the board. This is B10, this is D18, this is J4, do you follow?' He feels despair. How can she ever commit the board to memory? But she looks untroubled as she runs her hand along the edges of the board, murmuring, 'A, B, C, D . . .'

The other games have halted. Everyone in the lounge is watching them. He guides her hand towards the two trays of stones, the white and the black, and shows her the traditional way of picking up a stone between two fingers and clapping it down against the board. 'The stronger player uses the white stones,' he says. 'Black always moves first. The players take turns placing stones, one at a time, on any unoccupied intersection. Once a stone is placed it is never moved unless it is captured, when it is removed at once from the board.'

'And the purpose of the game?' she asks.

'To control the largest possible area with the smallest possible number of stones. You build walls. The score is reckoned by counting the number of vacant intersections within your walls, plus the number of prisoners you have taken.' Methodically he explains the technique of play to her: the placing of stones, the seizure of territory, the capture of opposing stones. He illustrates by setting up simulated situations on the board, calling out the location of each stone as he places it: 'Black holds P12, Q12, R12, S12, T12, and also P11, P10, P9, Q8, R8, S8, T8. White holds—' Somehow she visualizes the positions; she repeats the patterns after him, and asks questions that show she sees the board clearly in her mind. Within twenty minutes she understands the basic ploys. Several times, in describing manoeuvres to her, he gives her an incorrect coordinate – the board, after all, is not marked with numbers and letters, and he misgauges the points occasionally – but each time she corrects him, gently saying, 'N13? Don't you mean N12?'

At length she says, 'I think I follow everything now. Would you like to play a game?'

Consider your situation carefully. You are twenty years old, female, sightless. You have never married or even entered into a basic pairing. Your only real human contact is with your twin sister, who is like yourself blind and single. Her mind is fully open to yours. Yours is to hers. You and she are two halves of one soul, inexplicably embedded in separate bodies. With her, only with her, do you feel complete. Now you are asked to take part in a voyage to the stars, without her, a voyage that is sure to cut you off from her forever. You are told that if you leave Earth aboard the starship there is no chance that you will ever see your sister again. You are also told that your presence is important to the success of the voyage, for without your help it would take decades or even centuries for news of the starship to reach Earth, but if you are aboard it will be possible to maintain instantaneous communication across any distance. What should you do? Consider. Consider.

You consider. And you volunteer to go, of course. You are needed: how can you refuse? As for your sister, you will naturally lose the opportunity to touch her, to hold her close, to derive direct comfort from her presence. Otherwise you will lose nothing. Never 'see' her again? No. can 'see' her just as well, certainly, from a distance of a million light-years as you can from the next room. There can be no doubt of that.

The morning transmission. Noelle, sitting with her back to the year-captain, listens to what he reads her and sends it coursing over a gap of more than sixteen light-years. 'Wait,' she says. 'Yvonne is calling for a repeat. From *"metabolic"*.' He pauses, goes back, reads again: '*Metabolic balances remain normal, although, as earlier reported, some of the older members of the expedition have begun to show trace deficiencies of manganese and potassium. We are taking appropriate corrective steps, and—*' Noelle halts him with a brusque gesture. He waits, and she bends forward, forehead against the table, hands pressed tightly to her temples. 'Static again,' she says. 'It's worse today.'

'Are you getting through at all?'

'I'm getting through, yes. But I have to push, to push, to push. And still Yvonne asks for repeats. I don't know what's happening, year-captain.'

'The distance—'

'No!'

'Better than sixteen light-years.'

'No,' she says. 'We've already demonstrated that distance effects aren't a factor. If there's no falling-off of signal after a million kilometres, after one light-year, after ten light-years – no perceptible drop in clarity and accuracy whatever – then there shouldn't be any qualitative diminution suddenly at sixteen light-years. Don't you think I've thought about this?'

'Noelle—'

'Attenuation of signal is one thing, and interference is another. An attenuation curve is a gradual slope. Yvonne and I have had perfect contact from the day we left Earth until just a few days ago. And now – no, year-captain, it can't be attenuation. It has to be some sort of interference. A local effect.'

'Yes, like sunspots, I know. But—'

'Let's start again. Yvonne's calling for signal. Go on from *"manganese and potassium".*'

—'manganese and potassium. We are taking appropriate corrective steps—'

Playing Go seems to ease her tension. He has not played in years, and he is rusty at first, but within minutes the old associations return and he finds himself setting up chains of stones with skill. Although he expects her to play poorly, unable to remember the patterns on the board after the first few moves, she proves to have no difficulty keeping the entire array in her mind. Only in one respect has she overestimated herself: for all her precision of coordination, she is unable to place the stones exactly, tending rather to disturb the stones already on

107

the board as she makes her moves. After a little while she admits failure and thenceforth she calls out the plays she desires – M17, Q6, P6, R4, C11 – and he places the stones for her. In the beginning he plays unaggressively, assuming that as a novice she will be haphazard and weak, but soon he discovers that she is adroitly expanding and protecting her territory while pressing a sharp attack against his, and he begins to devise more cunning strategies. They play for two hours and he wins by sixteen points, a comfortable margin but nothing to boast about, considering that he is an experienced and adept player and that this is her first game.

The others are sceptical of her instant ability. 'Sure she plays well,' Heinz mutters. 'She's reading your mind, isn't she? She can see the board through your eyes and she knows what you're planning.'

'The only mind open to her is her sister's,' the year-captain says vehemently.

'How can you be sure she's telling the truth?'

The year-captain scowls. 'Play a game with her yourself. You'll see whether it's skill or mind-reading that's at work.'

Heinz, looking sullen, agrees. That evening he challenges Noelle; later he comes to the year-captain, abashed. 'She plays well. She almost beat me, and she did it fairly.'

The year-captain plays a second game with her. She sits almost motionless, eyes closed, lips compressed, offering the coordinates of her moves in a quiet bland monotone, like some sort of game-playing mechanism. She rarely takes long to decide on a move and she makes no blunders that must be retracted. Her capacity to devise game patterns has grown astonishingly; she nearly shuts him off from the centre, but he recovers the initiative and manages a narrow victory. Afterwards she loses once more to Heinz, but again she displays an increase of ability, and in the evening she defeats Chiang, a respected player. Now she becomes invincible. Undertaking two or three matches every day, she triumphs over Heinz, Sylvia, the year-captain, and Leon; Go has become something immense to her, something much more than a mere game, a simple test of strength; she focuses her energy on the board so intensely that her playing approaches the level of a religious discipline, a kind of meditation. On the fourth day she defeats Roy, the ship's champion, with such economy that everyone is dazzled. Roy can speak of nothing else. He demands a rematch and is defeated again.

Noelle wondered, as the ship was lifting from Earth, whether she really would be able to maintain contact with Yvonne across the vast span of interstellar space. She had nothing but faith to support her belief that the power that joined their minds was wholly unaffected by distance. They had often spoken to each other without difficulty from opposite sides of the planet, yes, but would it be so simple when they were half a galaxy apart? During the early hours of the voyage she and Yvonne kept up a virtually continuous linking, and the signal remained clear and sharp, with no perceptible falling off of reception, as the ship headed outward. Past the orbit of the moon, past the million-kilometre mark, past the orbit of Mars: clear and sharp, clear and sharp. They had passed the first test: clarity of signal was not a quantitative function of distance. But Noelle remained unsure of what would happen once the ship abandoned conventional power and shunted into nospace in order to attain faster-than-light velocity. She would then be in a space apart from Yvonne; in effect she would be in another universe; would she still be able to reach her sister's mind? Tension rose in her as the moment of the shunt approached, for she had no idea what life would be like for her in the absence of Yvonne. To face that dreadful silence, to find herself thrust into such terrible isolation – but it did not happen. They entered nospace and her awareness of Yvonne never flickered. *Here we are, wherever we are,* she said, and moments later came Yvonne's response, a cheery greeting from the old continuum. Clear and sharp, clear and sharp. Nor did the signal grow more tenuous in the weeks that followed. Clear and sharp, clear and sharp, until the static began.

The year-captain visualizes the contact between the two sisters as an arrow whistling from star to star, as fire speeding through a shining tube, as a river of pure force coursing down a celestial wave guide. He sees the joining of those two minds as a stream of pure light binding the moving ship to the far-off mother world. Sometimes he dreams of Yvonne and Noelle, Noelle and Yvonne, and the glowing bond that stretches between the sisters gives off so brilliant a radiance that he stirs and moans and presses his forehead into the pillow.

The interference grows worse. Neither Noelle nor Yvonne can explain what is happening; Noelle clings without conviction to her sunspot analogy. They still manage to make contact twice daily, but it is increasingly a strain on the sisters' resources, for every sentence must be repeated two or three times, and whole blocks of words now do not get through at all. Noelle has become thin and haggard. Go refreshes her, or at least diverts her from this failing of her powers. She has become a master of the game, awarding even Roy a two-stone handicap; although she occasionally loses, her play is always distinguished, extraordinarily original in its sweep and design. When she is not playing she tends to be remote and aloof. She is in all aspects a more elusive person than she was before the onset of this communications crisis.

Noelle dreams that her blindness has been taken from her. Sudden light surrounds her, and she opens her eyes, sits up, looks about in awe and wonder, saying to herself, This is a table, this is a chair, this is how my statuettes look, this is what my sea urchin is like. She is amazed by the beauty of everything in her room. She rises, goes forward, stumbling at first, groping, then magically gaining poise and balance, learning how to walk in this new way, judging the position of things not by echoes and air currents but rather by using her eyes. Information floods her. She moves about the ship, discovering the faces of her shipmates. You are Roy, you are Sylvia, you are Heinz, you are the year-captain. They look, surprisingly, very much as she had imagined them: Roy fleshy and red-faced, Sylvia fragile, the year-captain lean and fierce, Heinz like this,

Elliot like that, everyone matching expectations. Everyone beautiful. She goes to the window of which the others all talk, and looks out into the famous greyness. Yes, yes, it is as they say it is: a cosmos of wonders, a miracle of complex pulsating tones, level after level of incandescent reverberation sweeping outward towards the rim of the boundless universe. For an hour she stands before that dense burst of rippling energies, giving herself to it and taking it into herself, and then, and then, just as the ultimate moment of illumination is coming over her, she realizes that something is wrong. Yvonne is not with her. She reaches out and does not reach Yvonne. She has somehow traded her power for the gift of sight. Yvonne? Yvonne? All is still. Where is Yvonne? Yvonne is not with her. This is only a dream, Noelle tells herself, and I will soon awaken. But she cannot awaken. In terror she cries out. 'It's all right,' Yvonne whispers. 'I'm here, love, I'm here, I'm here, just as always.' Yes. Noelle feels the closeness. Trembling, she embraces her sister. Looks at her. I can see, Yvonne! I can see! Noelle realizes that in her first rapture she quite forgot to look at herself, though she rushed about looking at everything else. Mirrors have never been part of her world. She looks at Yvonne, which is like looking at herself, and Yvonne is beautiful, her hair dark and silken and lustrous, her face smooth and pale, her features fine of outline, her eyes – her blind eyes – alive and sparkling. Noelle tells Yvonne how beautiful she is, and Yvonne nods, and they laugh and hold one another close, and they begin to weep with pleasure and love and Noelle awakens, and the world is dark around her.

'I have the new communiqué to send,' the year-captain says wearily. 'Do you feel like trying again?'

'Of course I do.' She gives him a ferocious smile. 'Don't even hint at giving up, year-captain. There absolutely *has* to be some way around this interference.'

'Absolutely,' he says. He rustles his papers restlessly. 'Okay, Noelle. Let's go. Shipday 128. Velocity . . .'

'Give me another moment to get ready,' Noelle says.

He pauses. She closes her eyes and begins to enter the transmitting state. She is conscious, as ever, of Yvonne's presence. Even when no specific information is flowing between them, there is perpetual low-level contact, there is the sense that the other is near, that warm proprioceptive awareness such as one has of one's own arm or leg or lip. But between that impalpable subliminal contact and the actual transmission of specific content lie several key steps. Yvonne and Noelle are human biopsychic resonators constituting a long-range communications network; there is a tuning procedure for them as for any transmitters and receivers. Noelle opens herself to the radiant energy spectrum, vibratory, pulsating, that will carry her message to her earthbound sister. As the transmitting circuit in this interchange she must be the one to attain maximum energy flow. Quickly, intuitively, she activates her own energy centres, the one in the spine, the one in the solar plexus, the one at the top of the skull; energy pours from her and instantaneously spans the galaxy. But today there is an odd and troublesome splashback effect: monitoring the circuit, she is immediately aware that the signal has failed to reach Yvonne. Yvonne is there, Yvonne is tuned and expectant, yet something is jamming the channel and nothing gets through, not a single syllable. 'The interference is worse than ever,' she tells the year-captain. 'I feel as if I could put my hand out and *touch* Yvonne. But she's not reading me and nothing's coming back from her.' With a little shake of her shoulders Noelle alters the sending frequency; she feels a corresponding adjustment at Yvonne's end of the connection; but again they are thwarted, again there is total blockage. Her signal is going forth and is being soaked up by – what? How can such a thing happen?

Now she makes a determined effort to boost the output of the system. She addresses herself to the neural centre in her spine, exciting its energies, using them to drive the next centre to a more intense vibrational tone, harnessing that to push the highest centre of all to its greatest harmonic capacity. Up and down the energy bands she roves. Nothing. Nothing. She shivers; she huddles; she is physically emptied by the strain. 'I can't get through,' she murmurs. 'She's there, I can feel her there, I know she's working to read me. But I can't transmit any sort of intelligible coherent message.'

Almost seventeen light-years from Earth and the only communication channel is blocked. The year-captain is overwhelmed by frosty terrors. The ship, the self-sufficient autonomous ship, has become a mere gnat blowing in a hurricane. The voyagers hurtle blindly into the depths of an unknown universe, alone, alone, alone. He was so smug about not needing any link to earth, but now that the link is gone he shivers and cowers. Everything has been made new. There are no rules. Human beings have never been this far from home. He presses himself against the viewplate and the famous greyness just beyond, swirling and eddying, mocks him with its immensity. Leap into me, it calls, leap, leap, lose yourself in me, drown in me.

Behind him: the sound of soft footsteps. Noelle. She touches his hunched, knotted shoulders. 'It's all right,' she whispers. 'You're overreacting. Don't make such a tragedy out of it.' But it is. Her tragedy, more than anyone's, hers and Yvonne's. But also his, theirs, everybody's. Cut off. Lost in a foggy silence.

Down in the lounge people are singing. Boisterous voices, Elliot, Chiang, Leon.

'Travelin' Dan was a spacefarin' man
He jumped in the nospace tube.'

The year-captain whirls, seizes Noelle, pulls her against him. Feels her trembling. Comforts her, where a moment before she had been comforting him. 'Yes, yes, yes, yes,' he murmurs. With his arm around her shoulders he turns, so that both of them are facing the viewplate. As if she could see. Nospace dances and churns an inch from his nose. He feels a hot wind blowing through the ship, the khamsin, the sirocco, the simoom, the leveche, a sultry wind, a killing wind coming out of the grey strangeness, and he forces himself not to fear that wind. It is a wind of life, he tells himself, a wind of joy, a cool sweet wind, the mistral, the tramontana. Why should he think

113

there is anything to fear in the realm beyond the viewplate? How beautiful it is out there, how ecstatically beautiful! How sad that we can never tell anyone about it, now, except one another. A strange peace unexpectedly descends on him. Everything is going to be all right, he insists. No harm will come of what has happened. And perhaps some good. And perhaps some good. Benefits lurk in the darkest places.

She plays Go obsessively, beating everyone. She seems to live in the lounge twenty hours a day. Sometimes she takes on two opponents at once – an incredible feat, considering that she must hold the constantly changing intricacies of both boards in her memory – and defeats them both: two days after losing verbal-level contact with Yvonne, she simultaneously triumphs over Roy and Heinz before an audience of thirty. She looks animated and buoyant; the sorrow she must feel over the snapping of the link she takes care to conceal. She expresses it, the others suspect, only by her manic Go-playing. The year-captain is one of her most frequent adversaries, taking his turn at the board in the time he would have devoted to composing and dictating the communiqués for Earth. He had thought Go was over for him years ago, but he too is playing obsessively now, building walls and the unassailable fortresses known as eyes. There is reassurance in the rhythmic clacking march of the black and white stones. Noelle wins every game against him. She covers the board with eyes.

Who can explain the interference? No one believes that the problem is a function of anything so obvious as distance. Noelle has been quite convincing on that score: a signal that propagates perfectly for the first sixteen light-years of a journey ought not suddenly to deteriorate. There should at least have been prior sign of attenuation, and there was no attenuation, only noise interfering with and ultimately destroying the signal. Some force is intervening between the sisters. But what can it be? The idea that it is some physical effect analogous to sunspot static, that it is the product of radiation emitted by some giant star in whose vicinity they have lately been travelling, must in the end be rejected. There is no energy interface between realspace and nospace, no opportunity for any kind of electromagnetic intrusion. That much had been amply demonstrated long before any manned voyages were undertaken. The nospace tube is an impermeable wall. Nothing that has mass or charge can leap the barrier between the universe of accepted phenomena and the cocoon of nothingness that the ship's drive mechanism has woven about them, nor can a photon get across, nor even a slippery neutrino.

Many speculations excite the voyagers. The one force that *can* cross the barrier, Roy points out, is thought: intangible, unmeasurable, limitless. What if the sector of realspace corresponding to this region of the nospace tube is inhabited by beings of powerful telepathic capacity whose transmissions, flooding out over a sphere with a radius of many light-years, are able to cross the barrier just as readily as those of Yvonne? The alien mental emanations, Roy supposes, are smothering the signal from Earth.

Heinz extends this theory into a different possibility: that the interference is caused by denizens of nospace. There is a seeming paradox in this, since it has been shown mathematically that the nospace tube must be wholly matter-free except for the ship that travels through it; otherwise a body moving at speeds faster than light would generate destructive resonances as its mass exceeds infinity. But perhaps the equations are imperfectly understood. Heinz imagines giant incorporeal beings as big as asteroids, as big as planets, masses of pure energy or even pure mental force that drift freely through the tube. These beings may be sources of biopsychic transmissions that disrupt the Yvonne-Noelle circuit, or maybe they are actually *feeding* on the sisters' mental output, Heinz postulates. 'Angels,' he calls them. It is an implausible but striking concept that fascinates everyone for several days. Whether the 'angels' live within the tube as proposed by Heinz, or on some world just outside it as pictured by Roy, is unimportant at the moment; the consensus aboard ship is that the interference is the work of an alien intelligence, and that arouses wonder in all.

What to do? Leon, inclining towards Roy's hypothesis,

moves that they leave nospace immediately and seek the world or worlds where the 'angels' dwell. The year-captain objects, noting that the plan of the voyage obliges them to reach a distance of one hundred light-years from Earth before they begin their quest for habitable planets. Roy and Leon argue that the plan is merely a guide, arbitrarily conceived, and not received scriptural writ; they are free to depart from it if some pressing reason presents itself. Heinz, supporting the year-captain, remarks that there is no need actually to leave nospace regardless of the source of the alien transmissions; if the thoughts of these creatures can come in from beyond the tube, then Noelle's thoughts can surely go outward through the tube to them, and contact can be established without the need of deviating from the plan. After all, if the interference is the work of beings sharing the tube with them, and the voyagers seek them in vain outside the tube, it may be impossible to find them again once the ship returns to nospace. This approach seems reasonable, and the question is put to Noelle: Can you attempt to open a dialogue with these beings?

She laughs. 'I make no guarantees. I've never tried to talk to angels before. But I'll try, my friends. I'll try.'

BLACK (Year-Captain)	WHITE (Noelle)	
		Black remains on offensive through Move 89. White then breaks through weak north stones and encloses a major centre territory.
R16	Q4	Black is unable to reply adequately and
C4	E3	White runs a chain of stones along the
D17	D15	19th line. At Move 141 Black launches a
E16	K17	hopeless attack, easily crushed by White,
O17	E15	inside White's territory. Game ends at Move
H17	M17	196 after Black is faced with the
R6	Q6	cat-in-the-basket trap, by which it will
Q7	P6	lose a large group in the process of
R5	R4	capturing one stone.
D6	C11	Score: White 81, Black 62.
K3	H3	
N4	O4	
N3	O3	
R10	C8	
O15 . . .	M15 . . .	

She has never done anything like this before. It seems almost an act of infidelity, this opening of her mind to something or someone who is not Yvonne. But it must be done. She extends a tenuous tendril of thought that probes like a rivulet of quicksilver. Through the wall of the ship, into the surrounding greyness, upward, outward, towards, towards—

—angels?—

Angels. Oh. Brightness. Strength. Magnetism. Yes. Awareness now of a fierce roiling mass of concentrated energy close by. A mass in motion, laying a terrible stress on the fabric of the cosmos; the angel has angular momentum. It tumbles ponderously on its colossal axis. Who would have thought an angel could be so huge? Noelle is oppressed by the shifting weight of it as it makes its slow heavy axial swing. She moves closer. Oh. She is dazzled. *Too much light! Too much power!* She draws back, overwhelmed by the intensity of the other being's output. Such a mighty mind: she feels dwarfed. If she touches it with her mind she will be destroyed. She must step down the aperture, establish some kind of transformer to shield herself against the full blast of power that comes from it. It requires time and discipline. She works steadily, making adjustments, mastering new techniques, discovering capacities she had not known she possessed. And now. Yes. Try again. Slowly, slowly, slowly, with utmost care. Outward goes the tendril.

Yes.

Approaching the angel.

See? Here am I. Noelle. Noelle. Noelle. I come to you in love and fear. Touch me lightly. Just touch me—

Just a touch—

Touch—

Oh. Oh.

I see you. The light – eye of crystal – fountains of lava – oh, the light – your light – I see – I see—

Oh, like a god—

—and Semele wished to behold Zeus in all his brightness, and Zeus would have discouraged her; but Semele insisted and Zeus who loved her could not refuse her; so Zeus came upon her in full majesty and Semele was consumed by his glory, so

that only the ashes of her remained, but the son she had con-
ceived by Zeus, the boy Dionysus, was not destroyed, and Zeus
saved Dionysus and took him away sealed in his thigh, bringing
him forth afterwards and bestowing godhood upon him—

—oh God I am Semele—

She withdraws again. Rests, regroups her powers. The force of this being is frightening. But there are ways of insulating herself against destruction, of letting the overflow of energy dissipate itself. She will try once more. She knows she stands at the brink of wonders. Now. Now. The questing mind reaches forth.

I am Noelle. I come to you in love, angel.

Contact.

The universe is burning. Bursts of wild silver light streak across the metal dome of the sky. Words turn to ash. Walls smoulder and burst into flames. There is contact. A dancing solar flare—a stream of liquid fire – a flood tide of brilliant radiance, irresistible, unendurable, running into her, sweeping over her, penetrating her. Light everywhere.

—Semele.

The angel smiles and she quakes. *Open to me*, cries the vast tolling voice, and she opens and the force enters fully, sweeping through her

optic chiasma	thalamus
sylvian fissure	hypothalamus
medulla oblongata	limbic system
	reticular system

pons varolii
corpus callosum   cingulate sulcus
cuneus   orbital gyri
cingulate gyrus   caudate nucleus

—c e r e b r u m !—
claustrum   operculum
putamen   fornix
chloroid glomus medial lemniscus

dura mater
dural sinus
arachnoid granulation
subarachnoid space
pia mater

cerebellum
cerebellum
cerebellum

She has been in a coma for days, wandering in delirium. Troubled, fearful, the year-captain keeps a sombre vigil at her bedside. Sometimes she seems to rise towards consciousness; intelligible words, even whole sentences bubble dreamily from her lips. She talks of light, of a brilliant unbearable white glow, of arcs of energy, of intense solar eruptions. A star holds me, she mutters. She tells him that she has been conversing with a star. How poetic, the year-captain thinks: what a lovely metaphor. Conversing with a star. But where is she, what is happening to her? Her face is flushed; her eyes move about rapidly, darting like trapped fish beneath her closed lids. Mind to mind, she whispers, the star and I, mind to mind. She begins to hum – an edgy whining sound, climbing almost towards inaudibility, a high-frequency keening. It pains him to hear it: hard aural radiation. Then she is silent.

Her body goes rigid. A convulsion of some sort? No. She is awakening. He sees lightning bolts of perception flashing through her quivering musculature: the galvanized frog, twitching at the end of its leads. Her eyelids tremble. She makes a little moaning noise.

She looks up at him.

The year-captain says gently, 'Your eyes are open. I think you can see me now, Noelle. Your eyes are tracking me, aren't they?'

'I can see you, yes.' Her voice is hesitant, faltering, strange for a moment, a foreign voice, but then it becomes more like its usual self as she asks, 'How long was I away?'

'Eight ship-days. We were worried.'

'You look exactly as I thought you would look,' she says. 'Your face is hard. But not a dark face. Not a hostile face.'

'Do you want to talk about where you went, Noelle?'

She smiles. 'I talked with the ... angel.'

'Angel?'

'Not really an angel, year-captain. Not a physical being, either, not any kind of alien species. More like the energy creatures Heinz was discussing. But bigger. Bigger. I don't know what it was, year-captain.'

'You told me you were talking with a star.'

'—a star!'

'In your delirium. That's what you said.'

Her eyes blaze with excitement. 'A star! Yes! Yes, year-captain! I think I was, yes!'

'But what does that mean: talking to a star?'

She laughs. 'It means talking to a star, year-captain. A great ball of fiery gas, year-captain, and it has a mind, it has a consciousness. I think that's what it was. I'm sure now. I'm sure!'

'But how can a—'

The light goes abruptly from her eyes. She is travelling again; she is no longer with him. He waits beside her bed. An hour, two hours, half a day. What bizarre realm has she penetrated? Her breathing is a distant, impersonal drone. So far away from him now, so remote from any place he comprehends. At last her eyelids flicker. She looks up. Her face seems transfigured. To the year-captain she still appears to be partly in that other world beyond the ship. 'Yes,' she says. 'Not an angel, year-captain. A sun. A living intelligent sun.' Her eyes are radiant. 'A sun, a star, a sun,' she murmurs. 'I touched the consciousness of a sun. Do you believe that, year-captain? I found a network of stars that live, that think, that have minds, that have souls. That communicate. The whole universe is alive.'

'A star,' he says dully. 'The stars have minds.'

'Yes.'

'All of them? Our own sun too?'

'All of them. We came to the place in the galaxy where this star lives, and it was broadcasting on my wavelength, and its

120

output began overriding my link with Yvonne. That was the interference, year-captain. The big star broadcasting.'

This conversation has taken on for him the texture of a dream. He says quietly, 'Why didn't earth's sun override you and Yvonne when you were on earth?'

She shrugs. 'It isn't old enough. It takes – I don't know, billions of years – until they're mature, until they can transmit. Our sun isn't old enough, year-captain. None of the stars close to earth is old enough. But out here—'

'Are you in contact with it now?'

'Yes. With it and with many others. And with Yvonne.'

'Yvonne too?'

'She's back in the link with me. She's in the circuit.' Noelle pauses. 'I can bring others into the circuit. I could bring you in, year-captain.'

'Me?'

'You. Would you like to touch a star with your mind?'

'What will happen to me? Will it harm me?'

'Did it harm me, year-captain?'

'Will I still be me afterwards?'

'Am I still me, year-captain?'

'I'm afraid.'

'Open to me. Try. See what happens.'

'I'm afraid.'

'Touch a star, year-captain.'

He puts his hand on hers. 'Go ahead,' he says, and his soul becomes a solarium.

Afterwards, with the solar pulsations still reverberating in the mirror of his mind, with blue-white sparks leaping in his synapses, he says, 'What about the others?'

'I'll bring them in too.'

He feels a flicker of momentary resentment. He does not want to share the illumination. But in the instant that he conceives his resentment, he abolishes it. *Let them in.*

'Take my hand,' Noelle says.

They reach out together. One by one they touch the others. Roy. Sylvia. Heinz. Elliot. He feels Noelle surging in tandem with him, feels Yvonne, feels greater presences, luminous, eternal. All are joined. Ship-sister, star-sister: all become one. The year-captain realizes that the days of playing Go have ended. They are one person; they are beyond games.

'And now,' Noelle whispers, 'now we reach towards Earth. We put our strength into Yvonne, and Yvonne—'

Yvonne draws Earth's seven billion into the network.

The ship hurtles through the nospace tube. Soon the year-captain will initiate the searching for a habitable planet. If they discover one, they will settle there. If not, they will go on, and it will not matter at all, and the ship and its seven billion passengers will course onward forever, warmed by the light of the friendly stars.

A sea of faces

*Are not such floating fragments on the sea of the unconscious
called Freudian ships?*
—*Josephine Saxton*

Falling.

It's very much like dying, I suppose. That awareness of
infinite descent, that knowledge of the total absence of support.
It's all sky up here. Down below is neither land nor sea, only
colour without form, so distant that I can't even put a name to
the colour. The cosmos is torn open, and I plummet headlong,
arms and legs pinwheeling wildly, the grey stuff in my skull
centrifuging towards my ears. I'm dropping like Lucifer. *From
morn to noon he fell, from noon to dewy eve, A summer's day;
and with the setting sun Dropp'd from the zenith like a falling
star.* That's Milton. Even now my old liberal-arts education
stands me in good stead. *And when he falls, he falls like Lucifer, Never to hope again.* That's Shakespeare. It's all part of
the same thing. All of English literature was written by a single
man, whose sly persuasive voice ticks in my dizzy head as I
drop. God grant me a soft landing.

'She looks a little like you,' I told Irene. 'At least, it seemed
that way for one quick moment, when she turned towards the
window in my office and the sunlight caught the planes of her
face. Of course, it's the most superficial resemblance only, a
matter of bone structure, the placement of the eyes, the cut of
the hair. But your expressions, your inner selves externally
represented, are altogether dissimilar. You radiate unbounded
good health and vitality, Irene, and she slips so easily into the
classic schizoid fancies, the eyes alternately dreamy and darting, the forehead pale, flecked with sweat. She's very troubled.'

'What's her name?'

'Lowry. April Lowry.'

'A beautiful name. April. Young?'

'About twenty-three.'

'How sad, Richard. Schizoid, you said?'

'She retreats into nowhere without provocation. Lord knows what triggers it. When it happens she can go six or eight months without saying a word. The last attack was a year ago. These days she's feeling much better; she's willing to talk about herself a bit. She says it's as though there's a zone of weakness in the walls of her mind, an opening, a trap door, a funnel, something like that, and from time to time her soul is irresistibly drawn towards it and goes pouring through and disappears into God knows what, and there's nothing left of her but a shell. And eventually she comes back through the same passage. She's convinced that one of these times she won't come back.'

'Is there some way to help her?' Irene asked. 'What will you try? Drugs? Hypnosis? Shock? Sensory deprivation?'

'They've all been tried.'

'What then, Richard? What will you do?'

Suppose there is a way. Let's pretend there is a way. Is that an acceptable hypothesis? Let's pretend. Let's just pretend, and see what happens.

The vast ocean below me occupies the entirety of my field of vision. Its surface is convex, belly-up in the middle and curving vertiginously away from me at the periphery; the slope is so extreme that I wonder why the water doesn't all run run off towards the edges and drown the horizon. Not far beneath that shimmering swollen surface a gigantic pattern of crosshatchings and countertextures is visible, like an immense mural floating lightly submerged in the water. For a moment, as I plunge, the pattern resolves itself and becomes coherent: I see the face of Irene, a calm pale mask, the steady blue eyes focused lovingly on me. She fills the ocean. Her semblance covers an area greater than any continental mass. Firm chin, strong full lips, delicate tapering nose. She emanates a serene aura of inner peace that buoys me like an invisible net: I am falling easily now, pleasantly, arms outspread, face down, my entire body relaxed.

How beautiful she is! I continue to descend and the pattern shatters; the sea is abruptly full of metallic shards and splinters, flashing bright gold through the dark blue-green; then, when I am perhaps a thousand metres lower, the pattern suddenly reorganizes itself. A colossal face, again. I welcome Irene's return, but no, the face is the face of April, my silent sorrowful one. A haunted face, a face full of shadows: dark terrified eyes, flickering nostrils, sunken cheeks. A bit of one incisor is visible over the thin lower lip. O my poor sweet Taciturna. Needles of reflected sunlight glitter in her outspread waterborne hair. April's manifestation supplants serenity with turbulence; again I plummet out of control, again I am in the cosmic centrifuge, my breath is torn from me and a dread chill rushes past my tumbling body. Desperately I fight for poise and balance. I attain it, finally, and look down. The pattern has again broken; where April has been, I see only parallel bands of amber light, distorted by choppy refractions. Tiny white dots – islands, I suppose – now are evident in the glossy sea.

What a strange resemblance there is, at times, between April and Irene!

How confusing for me to confuse them. How dangerous for me.

—It's the riskiest kind of therapy you could have chosen, Dr Bjornstrand.
　—Risky for me, or risky for her?
　—Risky both for you and for your patient, I'd say.
　—So what else is new?
　—You asked me for an impartial evaluation, Dr Bjornstrand. If you don't care to accept my opinion—
　—I value your opinion highly, Erik.
　—But you're going to go through with the therapy as presently planned?
　—Of course I am.

This is the moment of splashdown.

I hit the water perfectly and go slicing through the sea's shining surface with surgical precision, knifing fifty metres deep, eighty, a hundred, cutting smoothly through the oceanic epithelium and the sturdy musculature beneath. Very well done, Dr Bjornstrand. High marks for form.

Perhaps this is deep enough.

I pivot, kick, turn upward, clutch at the brightness above me. I may have overextended myself, I realize. My lungs are on fire and the sky, so recently my home, seems terribly far away. But with vigorous strokes I pull myself up and come popping into the air like a stubborn cork.

I float idly a moment, catching my breath. Then I look around. The ferocious eye of the sun regards me from a late-morning height. The sea is warm and gentle, undulating seductively. There is an island only a few hundred metres away: an inviting beach of bright sand, a row of slender palms farther back. I swim towards it. As I near the shore, the bottomless dark depths give way to a sandy outlying sunken shelf, and the hue of the sea changes from deep blue to light green. Yet it is taking longer to reach land than I had expected. Perhaps my estimate of the distance was overly optimistic; for all my efforts, the island seems to be getting no closer. At moments it actually appears to be retreating from me. My arms grow heavy. My kick becomes sluggish. I am panting, wheezing, sputtering; something throbs behind my forehead. Suddenly, though, I see sun-streaked sand just below me. My feet touch bottom. I wade wearily ashore and fall to my knees on the margin of the beach.

—Can I call you April, Miss Lowry?

—Whatever.

—I don't think that that's a very threatening level of therapist-patient intimacy, do you?

—Not really.

—Do you always shrug every time you answer a question?

—I didn't know I did.

—You shrug. You also studiously avoid any show of facial expression. You try to be very unreadable, April.

—Maybe I feel safer that way.

—But who's the enemy?

—You'd know more about that than I would, doctor.

—Do you actually think so? I'm all the way over here. You're right there inside your own head. You'll know more than I ever will about you.

—You could always come inside my head if you wanted to.

—Wouldn't that frighten you?

—It would kill me.

—I wonder, April. You're much stronger than you think you are. You're also very beautiful, April. I know, it's beside the point. But you are.

It's just a small island. I can tell that by the way the shoreline curves rapidly away from me. I lie sprawled near the water's edge, face down, exhausted, fingers digging tensely into the warm moist sand. The sun is strong; I feel waves of heat going *thratata thratata* on my bare back. I wear only a ragged pair of faded blue jeans, very tight, cut off choppily at the knee. My belt is waterlogged and salt-cracked, as though I was adrift for days before making landfall. Perhaps I was. It's hard to maintain a reliable sense of time in this place.

I should get up. I should explore.

Yes. Getting up, now. A little dizzy, eh? Yes. But I walk steadily up the gentle slope of the beach. Fifty metres inland, the sand shades into sandy soil, loose, shallow; rounded white coral boulders poke through from below. Thirsty soil. Nevertheless, how lush everything is here. A wall of tangled vines and creepers. Long glossy tropical green leaves, smooth-edged, big-veined. The corrugated trunks of the palms. The soft sound of the surf, *fwissh, fwissh*, underlying all other textures. How blue the sea. How green the sky. *Fwissh.*

Is that the image of a face in the sky?

A woman's face, yes. Irene? April? The features are indistinct. But I definitely see it, yes, hovering a few hundred metres above the water as if projected from the sun-streaked sheet that is the skin of the ocean: a glow, a radiance, having the form of a delicate face – nostrils, lips, brows, cheeks, certainly a face, and not just one, either, for in the intensity of my stare I cause it to split and then to split again, so that a row of them hangs in the air, ten faces, a hundred, a thousand faces, faces all about me, a sea of faces. They seem quite grave. *Smile!* On command, the faces smile. Much better. The air itself is brighter for that smile. The faces merge, blur, sharpen, blur again, overlap in part, dance, shimmer, melt, flow. Illusions born of the heat. Daughters of the sun. Sweet mirages. I look past them, higher, into the clear reaches of the cloudless heavens.

Hawks!

Hawks here? Shouldn't I be seeing gulls? The birds whirl and swoop, dark figures against the blinding sky, wings outspread, feathers like fingers. I see their fierce hooked beaks. They snap great beetles from the steaming air and soar away, digesting. Then there are no birds, only the faces, still smiling. I turn my back on them and slowly move off through the underbrush to see what sort of place the sea has given me.

So long as I stay near the shore, I have no difficulty in walking; cutting through the densely vegetated interior might be a different matter. I sidle off to the left, following the nibbled line of beach. Before I have walked a hundred paces I have made a new discovery: the island is adrift.

Glancing seaward, I notice that on the horizon there lies a dark shore rimmed by black triangular mountains, one or two days' sail distant. Minutes ago I saw only open sea in that direction. Maybe the mountains have just this moment sprouted, but more likely the island, spinning slowly in the currents, has only now turned to reveal them. That must be the answer. I stand quite still for a long while and it seems to me that I behold those mountains now from one angle, now from a slightly different one. How else to explain such effects of parallax? The island freely drifts. It moves, and I move with it, upon the breast of the changeless unbounded sea.

The celebrated young American therapist Richard Bjornstrand commenced his experimental treatment of Miss April Lowry on the third of August, 1987. Within fifteen days the locus of disturbance had been identified, and Dr Bjornstrand had recommended consciousness-penetration treatment, a technique increasingly popular in the United States. Miss Lowry's physician was initially opposed to the suggestion, but further consultations demonstrated the potential value of such an approach, and on the nineteenth of September the entry procedures were initiated. We expect further reports from Dr Bjornstrand as the project develops.

Leonie said, 'But what if you fall in love with her?'

'What of it?' I asked. 'Therapists are always falling in love with their patients. Reich married one of his patients, and so did Fenichel, and dozens of the early analysts had affairs with their patients, and even Freud, who didn't, was known to observe—'

'Freud lived a long time ago,' Leonie said.

I have now walked entirely around the island. The circumambulation took me four hours, I estimate, since the sun was almost directly overhead when I began it and is now more than halfway towards the horizon. In these latitudes I suppose sunset comes quite early, perhaps by half past six, even in summer.

All during my walk this afternoon the island remained on a steady course, keping one side constantly towards the sea, the other towards that dark mountain-girt shore. Yet it has continued to drift, for there are minor oscillations in the position of the mountains relative to the island, and the shore itself appears gradually to grow closer. (Although that may be an illusion.) Faces appear and vanish and reappear in the lower reaches of the sky according to no predictable schedule of event or identity: April, Irene, April, Irene, Irene, April, April, Irene. Sometimes they smile at me. Sometimes they do not. I thought I saw one of the Irenes wink; I looked again and the face was April's.

The island, though quite small, has several distinct geographical zones. On the side where I first came ashore there is a row of close-set palms, crown to crown, beyond which the beach slopes towards the sea. I have arbitrarily labelled that side of the island as *east*. The western side is low and parched, and the vegetation is a tangle of scrub. On the north side is a high coral ridge, flat-faced and involute, descending steeply into the water. White wavelets batter tirelessly against the rounded spires and domes of that pocked coral wall. The island's southern shore has dunes, quite Saharesque, their yellowish-pink crests actually shifting ever so slightly as I watch. Inland, the island rises to a peak perhaps fifty metres above sea level, and evidently there are deep pockets of retained rainwater in the porous, decayed limestone of the undersurface, for the vegetation is profuse and vigorous. At several points I made brief forays to the interior, coming upon a swampy region of noisy sucking quicksand in one place, a cool dark glade interpenetrated with the tunnels and mounds of termites in another, a copse of wide-branching little fruit-bearing trees elsewhere.

Altogether the place is beautiful. I will have enough food and drink, and there are shelters. Nevertheless I long already for an end to the voyage. The bare sharp-tipped mountains of the mainland grow ever nearer; some day I will reach the shore, and my real work will begin.

The essence of this kind of therapy is risk. The therapist must be prepared to encounter forces well beyond his own strength, and to grapple with them in the knowledge that they might readily triumph over him. The patient, for her part, must accept the knowledge that the intrusion of the therapist into her consciousness may cause extensive alterations of the personality, not all of them for the better.

A bewildering day. The dawn was red-stained with purple veins – a swollen, grotesque, traumatic sky. Then came high winds; the palms rippled and swayed and great fronds were torn loose. A lull followed. I feared toppling trees and tidal waves, and pressed inland for half an hour, settling finally in a kind of natural amphitheatre of dead old coral, a weathered bowl thrust up from the sea millennia ago. Here I waited out the morning. Towards noon thick dark clouds obscured the heavens. I felt a sense of menace, of irresistible powers gathering their strength, such as I sometimes feel when I hear that tense little orchestral passage late in the Agnus Dei of the

Missa Solemnis, and instants later there descended on me hail, rain, sleet, high wind, furious heat, even snow – all weathers at once. I thought the earth would crack open and pour forth magma upon me. It was all over in five minutes, and every trace of the storm vanished. The clouds parted; the sun emerged, looking gentle and innocent; birds of many plumages wheeled in the air, warbling sweetly. The faces of Irene and April, infinitely reduplicated, blinked on and off against the backdrop of the sky. The mountainous shore hung fixed on the horizon, growing no nearer, getting no farther away, as though the day's turmoils had caused the frightened island to put down roots.

Rain during the night, warm and steamy. Clouds of gnats. An evil humming sound, greasily resonant, pervading everything. I slept, finally, and was awakened by a sound like a mighty thunderclap, and saw an enormous distorted sun rising slowly in the west.

We sat by the redwood table on Donald's patio: Irene, Donald, Erik, Paul, Anna, Leonie, me. Paul and Erik drank bourbon, and the rest of us sipped Shine, the new drink, essence of cannabis mixed with (I think) ginger beer and strawberry syrup. We were very high. 'There's no reason,' I said, 'why we shouldn't avail ourselves of the latest technological developments. Here's this unfortunate girl suffering from an undeterminable but crippling psychological malady, and the chance exists for me to enter her soul and—'

'Enter her *what*?' Donald asked.

'Her consciousness, her anima, her spirit, her mind, her whatever you want to call it.'

'Don't interrupt him,' Leonie said to Donald.

Irene said, 'Will you bring her to Erik for an impartial opinion first, at least?'

'What makes you think Erik is impartial?' Anna asked.

'He tries to be,' said Erik coolly. 'Yes, bring her to me, Dr Bjornstrand.'

'I know what you'll tell me.'

'Still. Even so.'

'Isn't this terribly dangerous?' Leonie asked. 'I mean, suppose your mind became stuck inside hers, Richard?'

'Stuck?'

'Isn't that possible? I don't actually know anything about the process, but—'

'I'll be entering her only in the most metaphorical sense,' I said. Irene laughed. Anna said, 'Do you actually believe that?' and gave Irene a sly look. Irene merely shook her head. 'I don't worry about Richard's fidelity,' she said, drawling her words.

Her face fills the sky today.

April. Irene. Whoever she is. She eclipses the sun, and lights the day with her own supernal radiance.

The course of the island has been reversed, and now it drifts out to sea. For three days I have watched the mountains of the mainland growing smaller. Evidently the currents have changed; or perhaps there are zones of resistance close to the shore, designed to keep at bay such wandering islands as mine. I must find a way to deal with this. I am convinced that I can do nothing for April unless I reach the mainland.

I have entered a calm place where the sea is a mirror and the sweltering air reflects the reflected images in an infinitely baffling regression. I see no face but my own, now, and I see it everywhere. A million versions of myself dance in the steamy haze. My jaws are stubbled and there is a bright red band of sunburn across my nose and upper cheeks. I grin and the multitudinous images grin at me. I reach towards them and they reach towards me. No land is in sight, no other islands – nothing, in fact, but this wall of reflections. I feel as though I am penned inside a box of polished metal. My shining image infests the burning atmosphere. I have a constant choking sensation; a terrible languor is coming over me; I pray for hurricanes, waterspouts, convulsions of the ocean bed, any sort of upheaval that will break the savage claustrophobic tension.

*

Is Irene my wife? My lover? My companion? My friend? My sister?

I am within April's consciousness and Irene is a figment.

It has begun to occur to me that this may be my therapy rather than April's.

I have set to work creating machinery to bring me back to the mainland. All this week I have painstakingly felled palm trees, using a series of blunt, soft hand axes chipped from slabs of dead coral. Hauling the trees to a promontory on the island's southern face, I lashed them loosely together with vines, setting them in the water so that they projected from both sides of the headland like the oars of a galley. By tugging at an unusually thick vine that runs down the spine of the whole construction, I am indeed able to make them operate like oars; and I have tied that master vine to an unusually massive palm that sprouts from the central ridge of the promontory. What I have built, in fact, is a kind of reciprocating engine; the currents, stirring the leafy crowns of my felled palms, impart a tension to the vines that link them, and the resistance of the huge central tree to the tug of the master vine causes the felled trees to sweep the water, driving the entire island shoreward. Through purposeful activity, said Goethe, we justify our existence in the eyes of God.

The 'oars' work well. I'm heading towards the mainland once again.

Heading towards the mainland very rapidly. Too rapidly, it seems. I think I may be caught in a powerful current.

The current definitely has seized my island and I'm being swept swiftly along, willy-nilly. I am approaching the island where Scylla waits. That surely is Scylla: that creature just ahead. There is no avoiding her; the force of the water is inexorable and my helpless oars dangle limply. The many-necked monster sits in plain sight on a barren rock, coiled into herself, waiting. Where shall I hide? Shall I scramble into the underbrush and huddle there until I am past her? Look, there: six heads, each with three rows of pointed teeth, and twelve snaky limbs. I suppose I could hide, but how cowardly, how useless. I will show myself to her. I stand exposed on the shore. I listen to her dread barking. How may I guard myself against Scylla's fangs? Irene smiles out of the low fleecy clouds. There's a way, she seems to be saying. I gather a cloud and fashion it into a simulacrum of myself. See: another Bjornstrand stands here, sunburned, half naked. I make a second replica, a third, complete to the stubble, complete to the blemishes. A dozen of them. Passive, empty, soulless. Will they deceive her? We'll see. The barking is ferocious now. She's close. My island whips through the channel. Strike, Scylla! Strike! The long necks rise and fall, rise and fall. I hear the screams of my other selves; I see their arms and legs thrashing as she seizes them and lifts them. Them she devours. Me she spares. I float safely past the hideous beast. April's face, reduplicated infinitely in the blue vault above me, is smiling. I have gained power by this encounter. I need have no further fears: I have become invulnerable. Do your worst, ocean! Bring me to Charybdis. I'm ready. Yes. Bring me to Charybdis.

The whole, D. H. Lawrence wrote, is a strange assembly of apparently incongruous parts, slipping past one another. I agree. But of course the incongruity is apparent rather than real, else there would be no whole.

I believe I have complete control over the island now. I can redesign it to serve my needs, and I have streamlined it, making it shipshaped, pointed at the bow, blunt at the stern. My conglomeration of felled palms has been replaced; now flexible projections of island-stuff flail the sea, propelling me steadily towards the mainland. Broad-leafed shade trees make the heat of day more bearable. At my command freshwater streams spring from the sand, cool, glistening.

Gradually I extend the sphere of my control beyond the

perimeter of the island. I have established a shark-free zone just off shore within an encircling reef. There I swim in perfect safety, and when hunger comes, I draw friendly fishes forth with my hands.

I fashion images out of clouds: April, Irene. I simulate the features of Dr Richard Bjornstrand in the heavens. I draw April and Irene together, and they blur, they become one woman.

Getting close to the coast now. Another day or two and I'll be there.

This is the mainland. I guide my island into a wide half-moon harbour, shadowed by the great naked mountains that rise like filed black teeth from the nearby interior. The island pushes out a sturdy woody cable that ties it to its berth; using the cable as a gangplank, I go ashore. The air is cooler here. The vegetation is sparse and cactusoidal: thick fleshy thorn-studded purplish barrels, mainly, taller than I. I strike one with a log and pale pink fluid gushes from it: I taste it and find it cool, sugary, vaguely intoxicating.

Cactus fluid sustains me during a five-day journey to the summit of the closest mountain. Bare feet slap against bare rock. Heat by day, lunar chill by night; the boulders twang at twilight as the warmth leaves them. At my back sprawls the sea, infinite, silent. The air is spangled with the frowning faces of women. I ascend by a slow spiral route, pausing frequently to rest, and push myself onward until at last I stand athwart the highest spine of the range. On the inland side the mountains drop away steeply into a tormented irregular valley, boulder-strewn and icy, slashed by glittering white lakes like so many narrow lesions. Beyond that is a zone of low breast-shaped hills, heavily forested, descending into a central lowlands out of which rises a pulsing fountain of light – jagged phosphorescent bursts of blue and gold and green and red that rocket into the air, attenuate, and are lost. I dare not approach that fountain; I will be consumed, I know, in its fierce intensity, for there the essence of April has its lair, the savage soul-core that must never be invaded by another.

I turn seaward and look to my left, down the coast. At first I see nothing extraordinary: a row of scalloped bays, some strips of sandy beach, a white line of surf, a wheeling flock of dark birds. But then I detect, far along the shore, a more remarkable feature. Two long slender promontories jut from the mainland like curved fingers, a thumb and a forefinger reaching towards one another, and in the wide gulf enclosed between them the sea churns in frenzy, as though it boils. At the vortex of the disturbance, though, all is calm. There! There is Charybdis! The maelstrom!

It would take me days to reach it overland. The sea route will be quicker. Hurrying down the slopes, I return to my island and sever the cable that binds it to shore. Perversely, it grows again. Some malign influence is negating my power. I sever; the cable reunites. I sever; it reunites. Again, again, again. Exasperated, I cause a fissure to pierce the island from edge to edge at the place where my cable is rooted; the entire segment surrounding that anchor breaks away and remains in the harbour, held fast, while the remainder of the island drifts towards the open sea.

Wait. The process of fission continues of its own momentum. The island is calving like a glacier, disintegrating, huge fragments breaking away. I leap desperately across yawning crevasses, holding always to the largest sector, struggling to rebuild my floating home, until I realize that nothing significant remains of the island, only an ever-diminishing raft of coral rock, halving and halving again. My island is no more than ten metres square now. Five. Less than five. Gone.

I always dreaded the ocean. That great inverted bowl of chilly water, resonating with booming salty sounds, infested with dark rubbery weeds, inhabited by toothy monsters – it preyed on my spirit, draining me, filling itself from me. Of course it was the northern sea I knew and hated, the dull dirty Atlantic, licking greasily at the Massachusetts coast. A black rocky shoreline, impenetrable mysteries of water, a line of morning debris cluttering the scanty sandy coves, a host of crabs and lesser scuttlers crawling everywhere. While swimming I imagined unfriendly sea beasts nosing around my dangling legs. I looked with distaste upon that invisible shimmering clutter of hairy-clawed planktonites, that fantasia of fibrous filaments and chittering antennae. And I dreaded most of all the slow lazy stirring of the Kraken, idly sliding its vast tentacles upward towards the boats of the surface. And here I am adrift on the sea's own breast. April's face in the sky wears a smile. The face of Irene flexes into a wink.

I am drawn towards the maelstrom. Swimming is unnecessary; the water carries me purposefully towards my goal. Yet I swim, all the same, stroke after stroke, yielding nothing to the force of the sea. The first promontory is coming into view. I swim all the more energetically. I will not allow the whirlpool to capture me; I must give myself willingly to it.

Now I swing round and round in the outer gyres of Charybdis. This is the place through which the spirit is drained: I can see April's pallid face like an empty plastic mask, hovering, drawn downward, disappearing chin-first through the whirlpool's vortex, reappearing, going down once more, an infinite cycle of drownings and disappearances and returns and resurrections. I must follow her.

No use pretending to swim here. One can only keep one's arms and legs pressed close together and yield, as one is sluiced down through level after level of the maelstrom until one reaches the heart of the eddy, and then – *swoosh!* – the ultimate descent. Now I plummet. The tumble takes forever. *From morn to noon he fell, from noon to dewy eve.* I rocket downward through the hollow heart of the whirlpool, gripped in a monstrous suction, until abruptly I am delivered to a dark region of cold quiet water: far below the surface of the sea. My lungs ache; my rib cage, distended over a bloated lump of hot depleted air, shoots angry protests into my armpits. I glide along the smooth vertical face of a submerged mountain. My feet find lodging on a ledge; I grope my way along it and come at length to the mouth of a cave, set at a sharp angle against the steep wall of stone. I topple into it.

Within, I find an air-filled pocket of a room, dank, slippery, lit by some inexplicable inner glow. April is there, huddled against the back of the cave. She is naked, shivering, sullen, her hair pasted in damp strands to the pale column of her neck. Seeing me, she rises but does not come forward. Her breasts are small, her hips narrow, her thighs slender: a child's body.

I reach a hand towards her. 'Come. Let's swim out of here together, April.'

'No. It's impossible. I'll drown.'

'I'll be with you.'

'Even so,' she says. 'I'll drown, I know it.'

'What are you going to do, then? Just stay in here?'

'For the time being.'

'Until when?'

'Until it's safe to come out,' she says.

'When will that be?'

'I'll know.'

'I'll wait with you. All right?'

I don't hurry her. At last she says, 'Let's go now.'

This time I am the one who hesitates, to my own surprise. It is as if there has been an interchange of strength in this cave and I have been weakened. I draw back, but she takes my hand and leads me firmly to the mouth of the cave. I see the water swirling outside, held at bay because it has no way of expelling the bubble of air that fills our pocket in the mountain wall. April begins to glide down the slick passageway that takes us from the cave. She is excited, radiant, eyes bright, breasts heaving. 'Come,' she says. 'Now! *Now!*'

We spill out of the cave together.

The water hammers me. I gasp, choke, tumble. The pressure is appalling. My eardrums scream shrill complaints. Columns of water force themselves into my nostrils. I feel the whirlpool dancing madly far above me. In terror I turn and try to scramble back into the cave, but it will not have me, and rebounding impotently against a shield of air, I let myself be engulfed by the water. I am beginning to drown, I think. My eyes deliver no images. Dimly I am aware of April tugging at me, grasping me, pulling me upward. What will she do, swim through the whirlpool from below? All is darkness. I perceive only the touch of her hand. I struggle to focus my eyes, and finally I see her through a purple chaos. How much like Irene she looks! Which is she, April or Irene? It scarcely matters. Drowning is my occupation now. It will all be over soon. Let me go, I tell her, let me go, let me do my drowning and be done with it. Save yourself. Save yourself. Save yourself. But she pays no heed and continues to tug.

We erupt into the sunlight.

Bobbing at the surface, we bask in glorious warmth. 'Look,' she cries. 'There's an island! Swim, Richard, swim! We'll be there in ten minutes. We can rest there.'

Irene's face fills the sky.

'Swim!' April urges.

I try. I am without strength. A few strokes and I lapse into stupor. April, apparently unaware, is far ahead of me, cutting energetically through the water, streaking towards the island. April, I call. April. April, help me. I think of the beach, the warm moist sand, the row of palms, the intricate texture of the white coral boulders. Yes. Time to go home. Irene is waiting for me. April! April!

She scrambles ashore. Her slim bare form glistens in the hot sunlight.

April?

The sea has me. I drift away, foolish flotsam, borne again towards the maelstrom.

Down. Down. No way to fight it. April is gone. I see only Irene, shimmering in the waves. Down.

This cool dark cave.

Where am I? I don't know.

Who am I? Dr Richard Bjornstrand? April Lowry? Both of those? Neither of those? I think I'm Bjornstrand. Was. Here, Dickie Dickie Dickie.

How do I get out of here? I don't know.

I'll wait. Sooner or later I'll be strong enough to swim out. Sooner. Later. We'll see.

Irene?

April?

Here, Dickie Dickie Dickie. Here.

Where?

Here.

The dybbuk of Mazel Tov IV

My grandson David will have his bar mitzvah next spring. No one in our family has undergone that rite in at least three hundred years – certainly not since we Levins settled in Old Israel, the Israel on Earth, soon after the European holocaust. My friend Eliahu asked me not long ago how I feel about David's bar mitzvah, whether the idea of it angers me, whether I see it as a disturbing element. No, I replied: the boy is a Jew, after all; let him have a bar mitzvah if he wants one. These are times of transition and upheaval, as all times are. David is not bound by the attitudes of his ancestors.

'Since when is a Jew not bound by the attitudes of his ancestors?' Eliahu asked.

'You know what I mean,' I said.

Indeed he did. We are bound but yet free. If anything governs us out of the past it is the tribal bond itself, not the philosophies of our departed kinsmen. We accept what we choose to accept; nevertheless we remain Jews. I come from a family that has liked to say – especially to gentiles – that we are Jews but not Jewish, that is, we acknowledge and cherish our ancient heritage but we do not care to entangle ourselves in outmoded rituals and folkways. This is what my forefathers declared, as far back as those secular-minded Levins who three centuries ago fought to win and guard the freedom of the land of Israel. (Old Israel, I mean.) I would say the same here, if there were any gentiles on this world to whom such things had to be explained. But of course in this New Israel in the stars we have only ourselves, no gentiles within a dozen light-years, unless you count our neighbours the Kunivaru as gentiles. (Can creatures that are not human rightly be called gentiles? I'm not sure the term applies. Besides, the Kunivaru now insist that they are Jews. My mind spins. It's an issue of Talmudic complexity, and God knows I'm no Talmudist. Hillel, Akiva, Rashi, help me!) Anyway, come the fifth day of Sivan my son's son will have his bar mitzvah, and I'll play the proud grandpa as pious old Jews have done for six thousand years.

All things are connected. That my grandson would have a bar mitzvah is merely the latest link in a chain of events that goes back to – when? To the day the Kunivaru decided to embrace Judaism? To the day the dybbuk entered Seul the Kunivar? To the day we refugees from Earth discovered the fertile planet that we sometimes call New Israel and sometimes call Mazel Tov IV? To the day of the Final Pogrom on Earth? Reb Yossele the Hasid might say that David's bar mitzvah was determined on the day the Lord God fashioned Adam out of dust. But I think that would be overdoing things.

The day the dybbuk took possession of the body of Seul the Kunivar was probably where it really started. Until then things were relatively uncomplicated here. The Hasidim had their settlement, we Israelis had ours, and the natives, the Kunivaru, had the rest of the planet; and generally we all kept out of one another's way. After the dybbuk everything changed. It happened more than forty years ago, in the first generation after the Landing, on the ninth day of Tishri in the year 6302. I was working in the fields, for Tishri is a harvest month. The day was hot, and I worked swiftly, singing and humming. As I moved down the long rows of crackle-pods, tagging those that were ready to be gathered, a Kunivar appeared at the crest of the hill that overlooks our kibbutz. It seemed to be in some distress, for it came staggering and lurching down the hillside with extraordinary clumsiness, tripping over its own four legs as if it barely knew how to manage them. When it was about a hundred metres from me it cried out, 'Shimon! Help me, Shimon! In God's name help me!'

There were several strange things about this outcry, and I perceived them gradually, the most trivial first. It seemed odd that a Kunivar would address me by my given name, for they are a formal people. It seemed more odd that a Kunivar would speak to me in quite decent Hebrew, for at that time none of them had learned our language. It seemed most odd of all – but

I was slow to discern it — that a Kunivar would have the very voice, dark and resonant, of my dear dead friend Joseph Avneri.

The Kunivar stumbled into the cultivated part of the field and halted, trembling terribly. Its fine green fur was pasted into hummocks by perspiration and its great golden eyes rolled and crossed in a ghastly way. It stood flat-footed, splaying its legs out under the four corners of its chunky body like the legs of a table, and clasped its long powerful arms around its chest. I recognized the Kunivar as Seul, a subchief of the local village, with whom we of the kibbutz had had occasional dealings.

'What help can I give you?' I asked. 'What has happened to you, Seul?'

'Shimon — Shimon—' A frightful moan came from the Kunivar. 'Oh, God, Shimon, it goes beyond all belief! How can I bear this? How can I even comprehend it?'

No doubt of it. The Kunivar was speaking in the voice of Joseph Avneri.

'Seul?' I said hesitantly.

'My name is Joseph Avneri.'

'Joseph Avneri died a year ago last Elul. I didn't realize you were such a clever mimic, Seul.'

'Mimic? You speak to me of mimicry, Shimon? It's no mimicry. I am your Joseph, dead but still aware, thrown for my sins into this monstrous alien body. Are you Jew enough to know what a dybbuk is, Shimon?'

'A wandering ghost, yes, who takes possession of the body of a living being.'

'I have become a dybbuk.'

'There are no dybbuks. Dybbuks are phantoms out of mediaeval folklore,' I said.

'You hear the voice of one.'

'This is impossible,' I said.

'I agree, Shimon, I agree.' He sounded calmer now. 'It's entirely impossible. I don't believe in dybbuks either, any more than I believe in Zeus, the Minotaur, werewolves, gorgons, or golems. But how else do you explain me?'

'You are Seul the Kunivar, playing a clever trick.'

'Do you really think so? Listen to me, Shimon: I knew you when we were boys in Tiberias. I rescued you when we were fishing in the lake and our boat overturned. I was with you the day you met Leah whom you married. I was godfather to your son Yigal. I studied with you at the university in Jerusalem. I fled with you in the fiery days of the Final Pogrom. I stood watch with you aboard the Ark in the years of our flight from earth. Do you remember, Shimon? Do you remember Jerusalem? The Old City, the Mount of Olives, the Tomb of Absalom, the Western Wall? Am I a Kunivar, Shimon, to know of the Western Wall?'

'There is no survival of consciousness after death,' I said stubbornly.

'A year ago I would have agreed with you. But who am I if I am not the spirit of Joseph Avneri? How can you account for me any other way? Dear God, do you think I *want* to believe this, Shimon? You know what a scoffer I was. But it's real.'

'Perhaps I'm having a very vivid hallucination.'

'Call the others, then. If ten people have the same hallucination, is it still a hallucination? Be reasonable, Shimon! Here I stand before you, telling you things that only I could know, and you deny that I am—'

'Be reasonable?' I said. 'Where does reason enter into this? Do you expect me to believe in ghosts, Joseph, in wandering demons, in dybbuks? Am I some superstition-ridden peasant out of the Polish woods? Is this the Middle Ages?'

'You called me Joseph,' he said quietly.

'I can hardly call you Seul when you speak in that voice.'

'Then you believe in me!'

'No.'

'Look, Shimon, did you ever know a bigger sceptic than Joseph Avneri? I had no use for the Torah, I said Moses was fictional, I ploughed the fields on Yom Kippur, I laughed in God's nonexistent face. What is life, I said? And I answered: a mere accident, a transient biological phenomenon. Yet here I am. I remember the moment of my death. For a full year I've

144

wandered this world, bodiless, perceiving things, unable to communicate. And today I find myself cast into this creature's body, and I know myself for a dybbuk. If *I* believe, Shimon, how can you dare disbelieve? In the name of our friendship, have faith in what I tell you!'

'You have actually become a dybbuk?'

'I have become a dybbuk,' he said.

I shrugged. 'Very well, Joseph. You're a dybbuk. It's madness, but I believe.' I stared in astonishment at the Kunivar. Did I believe? Did I believe that I believed? How could I not believe? There was no other way for the voice of Joseph Avneri to be coming from the throat of a Kunivar. Sweat streamed down my body. I was face to face with the impossible, and all my philosophy was shattered. Anything was possible now. God might appear as a burning bush. The sun might stand still. No, I told myself. Believe only one irrational thing at a time, Shimon. Evidently there are dybbuks; well, then, there are dybbuks. But everything else pertaining to the Invisible World remains unreal until it manifests itself.

I said, 'Why do you think this has happened to you?'

'It could only be as a punishment.'

'For what, Joseph?'

'My experiments. You knew I was doing research into the Kunivaru metabolism, didn't you?'

'Yes, certainly. But—'

'Did you know I performed surgical experiments on live Kunivaru in our hospital? That I used patients, without informing them or anyone else, in studies of a forbidden kind? It was vivisection, Shimon.'

'*What?*'

'There were things I needed to know, and there was only one way I could discover them. The hunger for knowledge led me into sin. I told myself that these creatures were ill, that they would shortly die anyway, and that it might benefit everyone if I opened them while they still lived, you see? Besides, they weren't human beings, Shimon, they were only animals – very intelligent animals, true, but still only—'

'No, Joseph. I can believe in dybbuks more readily than I can believe this. You, doing such a thing? My calm rational friend, my scientist, my wise one?' I shuddered and stepped a few paces back from him. 'Auschwitz!' I cried. 'Buchenwald! Dachau! Do those names mean anything to you? "They weren't human beings," the Nazi surgeon said. "They were only Jews, and our need for scientific knowledge is such that—" That was only three hundred years ago, Joseph. And you, a Jew, a Jew of all people, to—'

'I know, Shimon, I know. Spare me the lecture. I sinned terribly, and for my sins I've been given this grotesque body, this gross, hideous, heavy body, these four legs which I can hardly coordinate, this crooked spine, this foul hot furry pelt. I still don't believe in a God, Shimon, but I think I believe in some sort of compensating force that balances accounts in this universe, and the account has been balanced for me, oh, yes, Shimon! I've had six hours of terror and loathing today such as I never dreamed could be experienced. To enter this body, to fry in this heat, to wander these hills trapped in such a mass of flesh, to feel myself being bombarded with the sensory perceptions of a being so alien – it's been hell, I tell you that without exaggeration. I would have died of shock in the first ten minutes if I didn't already happen to be dead. Only now, seeing you, talking to you, do I begin to get control of myself. Help me, Shimon.'

'What do you want me to do?'

'Get me out of here. This is torment. I'm a dead man; I'm entitled to rest the way the other dead ones rest. Free me, Shimon.'

'How?'

'How? How? Do I know? Am I an expert on dybbuks? Must I direct my own exorcism? If you knew what an effort it is simply to hold this body upright, to make its tongue form Hebrew words, to say things in a way you'll understand—' Suddenly the Kunivar sagged to his knees, a slow, complex folding process that reminded me of the manner in which the camels of Old Earth lowered themselves to the ground. The alien creature began to sputter and moan and wave his arms about; foam appeared on his wide rubbery lips. 'God in Heaven, Shimon,' Joseph cried, 'set me free!'

I called for my son Yigal and he came running swiftly from the far side of the fields, a lean healthy boy, only eleven years old but already long-legged, strong-bodied. Without going into details I indicated the suffering Kunivar and told Yigal to get help from the kibbutz. A few minutes later he came back leading seven or eight men – Abrasha, Itzhak, Uri, Nahum, and some others. It took the full strength of all of us to lift the Kunivar into the hopper of a harvesting machine and transport him to our hospital. Two of the doctors – Moshe Shiloah and someone else – began to examine the stricken alien, and I sent Yigal to the Kunivaru village to tell the chief that Seul had collapsed in our fields.

The doctors quickly diagnosed the problem as a case of heat prostration. They were discussing the sort of injection the Kunivar should receive when Joseph Avneri, breaking a silence that had lasted since Seul had fallen, announced his presence within the Kunivar's body. Uri and Nahum had remained in the hospital room with me; not wanting this craziness to become general knowledge in the kibbutz, I took them outside and told them to forget whatever ravings they had heard. When I returned, the doctors were busy with their preparations and Joseph was patiently explaining to them that he was a dybbuk who had involuntarily taken possession of the Kunivar. 'The heat has driven the poor creature insane,' Moshe Shiloah murmured, and rammed a huge needle into one of Seul's thighs.

'Make them listen to me,' Joseph said.

'You know that voice,' I told the doctors. 'Something very unusual has happened here.'

But they were no more willing to believe in dybbuks than they were in rivers that flow uphill. Joseph continued to protest, and the doctors continued methodically to fill Seul's body with sedatives and restoratives and other potions. Even when Joseph began to speak of last year's kibbutz gossip – who had been sleeping with whom behind whose back, who had illicitly been peddling goods from the community storehouse to the Kuni-

147

varu – they paid no attention. It was as though they had so much difficulty believing that a Kunivar could speak Hebrew that they were unable to make sense out of what he was saying, and took Joseph's words to be Seul's delirium. Suddenly Joseph raised his voice for the first time, calling out in a loud, angry tone, 'You, Moshe Shiloah! Aboard the Ark I found you in bed with the wife of Teviah Kohn, remember? Would a Kunivar have known such a thing?'

Moshe Shiloah gasped, reddened, and dropped his hypodermic. The other doctor was nearly as astonished.

'What is this?' Moshe Shiloah asked. 'How can this be?'

'Deny me now!' Joseph roared. 'Can you deny me?'

The doctors faced the same problems of acceptance that I had had, that Joseph himself had grappled with. We were all of us rational men in this kibbutz, and the supernatural had no place in our lives. But there was no arguing the phenomenon away. There was the voice of Joseph Avneri emerging from the throat of Seul the Kunivar, and the voice was saying things that only Joseph would have said, and Joseph had been dead more than a year. Call it a dybbuk, call it hallucination, call it anything: Joseph's presence could not be ignored.

Locking the door, Moshe Shiloah said to me, 'We must deal with this somehow.'

Tensely we discussed the situation. It was, we agreed, a delicate and difficult matter. Joseph, raging and tortured, demanded to be exorcised and allowed to sleep the sleep of the dead; unless we placated him he would make us all suffer. In his pain, in his fury, he might say anything, he might reveal everything he knew about our private lives; a dead man is beyond all of society's rules of common decency. We could not expose ourselves to that. But what could we do about him? Chain him in an outbuilding and hide him in solitary confinement? Hardly. Unhappy Joseph deserved better of us than that; and there was Seul to consider, poor supplanted Seul, the dybbuk's unwilling host. We could not keep a Kunivar in the kibbutz, imprisoned or free, even if his body did house the spirit of one of our own people, nor could we let the shell of Seul go back to the Kunivaru village with Joseph as a furious passenger trapped inside. What to do? Separate soul from body, somehow: restore Seul to wholeness and send Joseph to the limbo of the dead. But how? There was nothing in the standard pharmacopoeia about dybbuks. What to do? What to do?

I sent for Shmarya Asch and Yakov Ben-Zion, who headed the kibbutz council that month, and for Shlomo Feig, our rabbi, a shrewd and sturdy man, very unorthodox in his orthodoxy, almost as secular as the rest of us. They questioned Joseph Avneri extensively, and he told them the whole tale, his scandalous secret experiments, his post-mortem year as a wandering spirit, his sudden painful incarnation within Seul. At length Shmarya Asch turned to Moshe Shiloah and snapped, 'There must be some therapy for such a case.'

'I know of none.'

'This is schizophrenia,' said Shmarya Asch in his firm, dogmatic way. 'There are cures for schizophrenia. There are drugs, there are electric shock treatments, there are – you know these things better than I, Moshe.'

'This is not schizophrenia,' Moshe Shiloah retorted. 'This is a case of demonic possession. I have no training in treating such maladies.'

'Demonic possession?' Shmarya bellowed. 'Have you lost your mind?'

'Peace, peace, all of you,' Shlomo Feig said, as everyone began to shout at once. The rabbi's voice cut sharply through the tumult and silenced us all. He was a man of great strength, physical as well as moral, to whom the entire kibbutz inevitably turned for guidance although there was virtually no one among us who observed the major rites of Judaism. He said, 'I find this as hard to comprehend as any of you. But the evidence triumphs over my scepticism. How can we deny that Joseph Avneri has returned as a dybbuk? Moshe, you know no way of causing this intruder to leave the Kunivar's body?'

'None,' said Moshe Shiloah.

'Maybe the Kunivaru themselves know a way,' Yakov Ben-Zion suggested.

'Exactly,' said the rabbi. 'My next point. These Kunivaru

are a primitive folk. They live closer to the world of magic and witchcraft, of demons and spirits, than we do whose minds are schooled in the habits of reason. Perhaps such cases of possession occur often among them. Perhaps they have techniques for driving out unwanted spirits. Let us turn to them, and let them cure their own.'

Before long Yigal arrived, bringing with him six Kunivaru, including Gyaymar, the village chief. They wholly filled the little hospital room, bustling around in it like a delegation of huge furry centaurs; I was oppressed by the acrid smell of so many of them in one small space, and although they had always been friendly to us, never raising an objection when we appeared as refugees to settle on their planet, I felt fear of them now as I had never felt before. Clustering about Seul, they asked questions of him in their own supple language, and when Joseph Avneri replied in Hebrew they whispered things to each other unintelligible to us. Then, unexpectedly, the voice of Seul broke through, speaking in halting spastic monosyllables that revealed the terrible shock his nervous system must have received; then the alien faded and Joseph Avneri spoke once more with the Kunivar's lips, begging forgiveness, asking for release.

Turning to Gyaymar, Shlomo Feig said, 'Have such things happened on this world before?'

'Oh, yes, yes,' the chief replied. 'Many times. When one of us dies having a guilty soul, repose is denied, and the spirit may undergo strange migrations before forgiveness comes. What was the nature of this man's sin?'

'It would be difficult to explain to one who is not Jewish,' said the rabbi hastily, glancing away. 'The important question is whether you have a means of undoing what has befallen the unfortunate Seul, whose sufferings we all lament.'

'We have a means, yes,' said Gyaymar the chief.

The six Kunivaru hoisted Seul to their shoulders and carried him from the kibbutz; we were told that we might accompany them if we cared to do so. I went along, and Moshe Shiloah, and Shmarya Asch, and Yakov Ben-Zion, and the rabbi, and perhaps some others. The Kunivaru took their comrade not to their village but to a meadow several kilometres to the east, down in the direction of the place where the Hasidim lived. Not long after the Landing the Kunivaru had let us know that the meadow was sacred to them, and none of us had ever entered it.

It was a lovely place, green and moist, a gently sloping basin crisscrossed by a dozen cool little streams. Depositing Seul beside one of the streams, the Kunivaru went off into the woods bordering the meadow to gather firewood and herbs. We remained close by Seul. 'This will do no good,' Joseph Avneri muttered more than once. 'A waste of time, a foolish expense of energy.' Three of the Kunivaru started to build a bonfire. Two sat nearby, shredding the herbs, making heaps of leaves, stems, roots. Gradually more of their kind appeared until the meadow was filled with them; it seemed that the whole village, some four hundred Kunivaru, was turning out to watch or to participate in the rite. Many of them carried musical instruments, trumpets and drums, rattles and clappers, lyres, lutes, small harps, percussive boards, wooden flutes, everything intricate and fanciful of design; we had not suspected such cultural complexity. The priests – I assume they were priests, Kunivaru of stature and dignity – wore ornate ceremonial helmets and heavy golden mantles of sea-beast fur. The ordinary townsfolk carried ribbons and streamers, bits of bright fabric, polished mirrors of stone, and other ornamental devices. When he saw how elaborate a function it was going to be, Moshe Shiloah, an amateur anthropologist at heart, ran back to the kibbutz to fetch camera and recorder. He returned, breathless, just as the rite commenced.

And a glorious rite it was: incense, a grandly blazing bonfire, the pungent fragrance of freshly picked herbs, some heavy-footed quasi-orgiastic dancing, and a choir punching out harsh, sharp-edged arrhythmic melodies. Gyaymar and the high priest of the village performed an elegant antiphonal chant, uttering long curling intertwining melismas and sprinkling Seul with a sweet-smelling pink fluid out of a baroquely carved wooden censer. Never have I beheld such stirring pageantry. But Joseph's gloomy prediction was correct; it was all entirely useless. Two hours of intensive exorcism had no effect. When the ceremony ended – the ultimate punctuation marks were five terrible shouts from the high priest – the dybbuk remained firmly in possession of Seul. 'You have not conquered me,' Joseph declared in a bleak tone.

Gyaymar said, 'It seems we have no power to command an earthborn soul.'

'What will we do now?' demanded Yakov Ben-Zion of no one in particular. 'Our science and their witchcraft both fail.'

Joseph Avneri pointed towards the east, towards the village of the Hasidim, and murmured something indistinct.

'No!' cried Rabbi Shlomo Feig, who stood closest to the dybbuk at that moment.

'What did he say?' I asked.

'It was nothing,' the rabbi said. 'It was foolishness. The long ceremony has left him fatigued, and his mind wanders. Pay no attention.'

I moved nearer to my old friend. 'Tell me, Joseph.'

'I said,' the dybbuk replied slowly, 'that perhaps we should send for the Baal Shem.'

'Foolishness!' said Shlomo Feig, and spat.

'Why this anger?' Shmarya Asch wanted to know. 'You, Rabbi Shlomo, you were one of the first to advocate employing Kunivaru sorcerers in this business. You gladly bring in alien witch doctors, rabbi, and grow angry when someone suggests that your fellow Jew be given a chance to drive out the demon? Be consistent, Shlomo!'

Rabbi Shlomo's strong face grew mottled with rage. It was strange to see this calm, even-tempered man becoming so excited. 'I will have nothing to do with Hasidim!' he exclaimed.

'I think this is a matter of professional rivalries,' Moshe Shiloah commented.

The rabbi said, 'To give recognition to all that is most superstitious in Judaism, to all that is most irrational and grotesque and outmoded and mediaeval? No! No!'

'But dybbuks *are* irrational and grotesque and outmoded and mediaeval,' said Joseph Avneri. 'Who better to exorcise one than a rabbi whose soul is still rooted in ancient beliefs?'

'I forbid this!' Shlomo Feig sputtered. 'If the Baal Shem is summoned I will . . . I will—'

'Rabbi,' Joseph said, shouting now, 'this is a matter of my tortured soul against your offended spiritual pride. Give way! Give way! Get me the Baal Shem!'

'I refuse!'

'Look!' called Yakov Ben-Zion. The dispute had suddenly become academic. Uninvited, our Hasidic cousins were arriving at the sacred meadow, a long procession of them, eerie prehistoric-looking figures clad in their traditional long black robes, wide-brimmed hats, heavy beards, dangling side-locks; and at the head of the group marched their tzaddik, their holy man, their prophet, their leader, Reb Shmuel the Baal Shem.

It was certainly never our idea to bring Hasidim with us when we fled out of the smouldering ruins of the Land of Israel. Our intention was to leave Earth and all its sorrows far behind, to start anew on another world where we could at last build an enduring Jewish homeland, free for once of our eternal gentile enemies and free, also, of the religious fanatics among our own kind whose presence had long been a drain on our vitality. We needed no mystics, no ecstatics, no weepers, no moaners, no leapers, no chanters; we needed only workers, farmers, machinists, engineers, builders. But how could we refuse them a place on the Ark? It was their good fortune to come upon us just as we were making the final preparations for our flight. The nightmare that had darkened our sleep for three centuries had been made real: the Homeland lay in flames, our armies had been shattered out of ambush, Philistines wielding long knives strode through our devastated cities. Our ship was ready to leap to the stars. We were not cowards but simply realists, for it was folly to think we could do battle any longer, and if some fragment of our ancient nation were to survive, it could only survive far from that bitter world Earth. So we were going to go; and here were suppliants asking us for succour, Reb Shmuel and his thirty followers. How could we turn them away, knowing they would certainly perish? They were human beings, they were Jews. For all our misgivings, we let them come on board.

And then we wandered across the heavens year after year, and then we came to a star that had no name, only a number, and then we found its fourth planet to be sweet and fertile, a happier world than Earth, and we thanked the God in whom we did not believe for the good luck that He had granted us, and we cried out to each other in congratulation, Mazel tov! Mazel tov! Good luck, good luck, good luck! And someone looked in an old book and saw that *Mazel* once had had an astrological connotation, that in the days of the Bible it had meant not only 'luck' but a lucky star, and so we named our lucky star Mazel Tov, and we made our landfall on Mazel Tov IV, which was to be the New Israel. Here we found no enemies, no Egyptians, no Assyrians, no Romans, no Cossacks, no Nazis, no Arabs, only the Kunivaru, kindly people of a simple nature, who solemnly studied our pantomimed explanations and replied to us in gestures, saying, Be welcome, there is more land here than we will ever need. And we built our kibbutz.

But we had no desire to live close to those people of the past, the Hasidim, and they had scant love for us, for they saw us as pagans, godless Jews who were worse than gentiles, and they went off to build a muddy little village of their own. Sometimes on clear nights we heard their lusty singing, but otherwise there was scarcely any contact between us and them.

I could understand Rabbi Shlomo's hostility to the idea of intervention by the Baal Shem. These Hasidim represented the mystic side of Judaism, the dark uncontrollable Dionysiac side, the skeleton in the tribal closet; Shlomo Feig might be amused or charmed by a rite of exorcism performed by furry centaurs, but when Jews took part in the same sort of supernaturalism it was distressing to him. Then, too, there was the ugly fact that the sane, sensible Rabbi Shlomo had virtually no followers at all among the sane, sensible secularized Jews of our kibbutz, whereas Reb Shmuel's Hasidim looked upon him with awe, regarding him as a miracle worker, a seer, a saint. Still, Rabbi Shlomo's understandable jealousies and prejudices aside, Joseph Avneri was right: dybbuks were vapours out of the realm of the fantastic, and the fantastic was the Baal Shem's kingdom.

He was an improbably tall, angular figure, almost skeletal, with gaunt cheekbones, a soft, thickly curling beard, and gentle dreamy eyes. I suppose he was about fifty years old, though I would have believed it if they said he was thirty or seventy or ninety. His sense of the dramatic was unfailing; now – it was late afternoon – he took up a position with the setting sun at his back, so that his long shadow engulfed us all, and spread forth his arms, and said, 'We have heard reports of a dybbuk among you.'

'There is no dybbuk!' Rabbi Shlomo retorted fiercely.

The Baal Shem smiled. 'But there is a Kunivar who speaks with an Israeli voice?'

'There has been an odd transformation, yes,' Rabbi Shlomo conceded. 'But in this age, on this planet, no one can take dybbuks seriously.'

'That is, *you* cannot take dybbuks seriously,' said the Baal Shem.

'I do!' cried Joseph Avneri in exasperation. 'I! I! I am the dybbuk! I, Joseph Avneri, dead a year ago last Elul, doomed for my sins to inhabit this Kunivar carcass. A Jew, Reb Shmuel, a dead Jew, a pitiful sinful miserable Yid. Who'll let me out? Who'll set me free?'

'There is no dybbuk?' the Baal Shem said amiably.

'This Kunivar has gone insane,' said Shlomo Feig.

We coughed and shifted our feet. If anyone had gone insane it was our rabbi, denying in this fashion the phenomenon that he himself had acknowledged as genuine, however reluctantly, only a few hours before. Envy, wounded pride, and stubbornness had unbalanced his judgement. Joseph Avneri, enraged, began to bellow the Aleph Beth Gimel, the Shma Yisroel, anything that might prove his dybbukhood. The Baal Shem waited patiently, arms outspread, saying nothing. Rabbi Shlomo, confronting him, his powerful stocky figure dwarfed by the long-legged Hasid, maintained energetically that there had to be some rational explanation for the metamorphosis of Seul the Kunivar.

When Shlomo Feig at length fell silent, the Baal Shem said, 'There is a dybbuk in this Kunivar. Do you think, Rabbi

Shlomo, that dybbuks ceased their wanderings when the shtetls of Poland were destroyed? Nothing is lost in the sight of God, Rabbi. Jews go to the stars; the Torah and the Talmud and the Zohar have gone also to the stars; dybbuks too may be found in these strange worlds. Rabbi, may I bring peace to this troubled spirit and to this weary Kunivar?'

'Do whatever you want,' Shlomo Feig muttered in disgust, and strode away scowling.

Reb Shmuel at once commenced the exorcism. He called first for a minyan. Eight of his Hasidim stepped forward. I exchanged a glance with Shmarya Asch, and we shrugged and came forward too, but the Baal Shem, smiling, waved us away and beckoned two more of his followers into the circle. They began to sing; to my everlasting shame I have no idea what the singing was about, for the words were Yiddish of a Galitzianer sort, nearly as alien to me as the Kunivaru tongue. They sang for ten or fifteen minutes; the Hasidim grew more animated, clapping their hands, dancing about their Baal Shem; suddenly Reb Shmuel lowered his arms to his sides, silencing them, and quietly began to recite Hebrew phrases, which after a moment I recognized as those of the Ninety-first Psalm: the Lord is my refuge and my fortress, in him will I trust. The psalm rolled melodiously to its comforting conclusion, its promise of deliverance and salvation. For a long moment all was still. Then in a terrifying voice, not loud but immensely commanding, the Baal Shem ordered the spirit of Joseph Avneri to quit the body of Seul the Kunivar. 'Out! Out! In God's name out, and off to your eternal rest!' One of the Hasidim handed Reb Shmuel a shofar. The Baal Shem put the ram's horn to his lips and blew a single titanic blast.

Joseph Avneri whimpered. The Kunivar that housed him took three awkward, toppling steps. 'Oy, mama, mama,' Joseph cried. The Kunivar's head snapped back; his arms shot straight out at his sides; he tumbled clumsily to his four knees. An aeon went by. Then Seul rose – smoothly, this time, with natural Kunivaru grace – and went to the Baal Shem, and knelt, and touched the tzaddik's black robe. So we knew the thing was done.

Instants later the tension broke. Two of the Kunivaru priests rushed towards the Baal Shem, and then Gyaymar, and then some of the musicians, and then it seemed the whole tribe was pressing close upon him, trying to touch the holy man. The Hasidim, looking worried, murmured their concern, but the Baal Shem, towering over the surging mob, calmly blessed the Kunivaru, stroking the dense fur of their backs. After some minutes of this the Kunivaru set up a rhythmic chant, and it was a while before I realized what they were saying. Moshe Shiloah and Yakov Ben-Zion caught the sense of it about the same time I did, and we began to laugh, and then our laughter died away.

'What do their words mean?' the Baal Shem called out.

'They are saying,' I told him, 'that they are convinced of the power of your god. They wish to become Jews.'

For the first time Reb Shmuel's poise and serenity shattered. His eyes flashed ferociously and he pushed at the crowding Kunivaru, opening an avenue between them. Coming up to me, he snapped. 'Such a thing is an absurdity!'

'Nevertheless, look at them. They worship you, Reb Shmuel.'

'I refuse their worship.'

'You worked a miracle. Can you blame them for adoring you and hungering after your faith?'

'Let them adore,' said the Baal Shem. 'But how can they become Jews? It would be a mockery.'

I shook my head. 'What was it you told Rabbi Shlomo? Nothing is lost in the sight of God. There have always been converts to Judaism; we never invite them, but we never turn them away if they're sincere, eh, Reb Shmuel? Even here in the stars, there is continuity of tradition, and tradition says we harden not our hearts to those who seek the truth of God. These are a good people: let them be received into Israel.'

'No,' the Baal Shem said. 'A Jew must first of all be human.'

'Show me that in the Torah.'

'The Torah! You joke with me. A Jew must first of all be human. Were cats allowed to become Jews? Were horses?'

'These people are neither cats nor horses, Reb Shmuel. They are as human as we are.'

'No! No!'

'If there can be a dybbuk on Mazel Tov IV,' I said, 'then there can also be Jews with six limbs and green fur.'

'No. No. No. *No!*'

The Baal Shem had had enough of this debate. Shoving aside the clutching hands of the Kunivaru in a most unsaintly way, he gathered his followers and stalked off, a tower of offended dignity, bidding us no farewells.

But how can true faith be denied? The Hasidim offered no encouragement, so the Kunivaru came to us; they learned Hebrew and we loaned them books, and Rabbi Shlomo gave them religious instruction, and in their own time and in their own way they entered into Judaism. All this was years ago, in the first generation after the Landing. Most of those who lived in those days are dead now – Rabbi Shlomo, Reb Shmuel the Baal Shem, Moshe Shiloah, Shmarya Asch. I was a young man then. I know a good deal more now, and if I am no closer to God than I ever was, perhaps He has grown closer to me. I eat meat and butter at the same meal, and I plough my land on the Sabbath, but those are old habits that have little to do with belief or the absence of belief.

We are much closer to the Kunivaru, too, than we were in those early days; they no longer seem like alien beings to us, but merely neighbours whose bodies have a different form. The younger ones of our kibbutz are especially drawn to them. The year before last Rabbi Lhaoyir the Kunivar suggested to some of our boys that they come for lessons to the Talmud Torah, the religious school, that he runs in the Kunivaru village; since the death of Shlomo Feig there has been no one in the kibbutz to give such instruction. When Reb Yossele, the son and successor of Reb Shmuel the Baal Shem, heard this, he raised strong objections. If your boys will take instruction, he said, at least send them to us, and not to green monsters. My son Yigal threw him out of the kibbutz. We would rather let our boys learn the Torah from green monsters, Yigal told Reb Yossele, than have them raised to be Hasidim.

And so my son's son has had his lessons at the Talmud Torah

of Rabbi Lhaoyir the Kunivar, and next spring he will have his bar mitzvah. Once I would have been appalled by such goings-on, but now I say only, How strange, how unexpected, how interesting! Truly the Lord, if He exists, must have a keen sense of humour. I like a god who can smile and wink, who doesn't take himself too seriously. The Kunivaru are Jews! Yes! They are preparing David for his bar mitzvah! Yes! Today is Yom Kippur, and I hear the sound of the shofar coming from their village! Yes! Yes. So be it. So be it, yes, and all praise be to Him.

Getting across

1

On the first day of summer my month-wife, Silena Ruiz, filched our district's master programme from the Ganfield Hold computer centre and disappeared with it. A guard at the Hold has confessed that she won admittance by seducing him, then gave him a drug. Some say she is in Conning Town now, others have heard rumours that she has been seen in Morton Court, still others maintain her destination was the Mill. I suppose it does not matter where she has gone. What matters is that we are without our programme. We have lived without it for eleven days, and things are starting to break down. The heat is abominable, but we must switch every thermostat to manual override before we can use our cooling system; I think we will boil in our skins before the job is done. A malfunction of the scanners that control our refuse compactor has stilled the garbage collectors, which will not go forth unless they have a place to dump what they collect. Since no one knows the proper command to give the compactor, rubbish accumulates, forming pestilential hills on every street, and dense swarms of flies or worse hover over the sprawling mounds. Beginning on the fourth day our police also began to go immobile – who can say why? – and by now all of them stand halted in their tracks. Some are already starting to rust, since the maintenance schedules are out of phase. Word has gone out that we are without protection, and outlanders cross into the district with impunity, molesting our women, stealing our children, raiding our stocks of foodstuffs. In Ganfield Hold platoons of weary sweating technicians toil constantly to replace the missing programme, but it might be months, even years, before they are able to devise a new one.

In theory, duplicate programmes are stored in several places within the community against just such a calamity. In fact, we have none. The one kept in the district captain's office turned out to be some twenty years obsolete; the one in the care of the soulfather's house had been devoured by rats; the programme held in the vaults of the tax collectors appeared to be intact, but when it was placed in the input slot it mysteriously failed to activate the computers. So we are helpless: an entire district, hundreds of thousands of human beings, cut loose to drift on the tides of chance. Silena, Silena, Silena! To disable all of Ganfield, to make our already burdensome lives more difficult, to expose me to the hatred of my neighbours – why, Silena? Why?

People glare at me on the streets. They hold me responsible, in a way, for all this. They point and mutter; in another few days they will be spitting and cursing, and if no relief comes soon they may be throwing stones. Look, I want to shout, she was only my month-wife and she acted entirely on her own. I assure you I had no idea she would do such a thing. And yet they blame me. At the wealthy houses of Morton Court they will dine tonight on babes stolen in Ganfield this day, and I am held accountable.

What will I do? Where can I turn?

I may have to flee. The thought of crossing district lines chills me. Is it the peril of death I fear, or only the loss of all that is familiar? Probably both: I have no hunger for dying and no wish to leave Ganfield. Yet I will go, no matter how difficult it will be to find sanctuary if I get safely across the line. If they continue to hold me tainted by Silena's crime I will have no choice. I think I would rather die at the hands of strangers than perish at those of my own people.

2

This sweltering night I find myself atop Ganfield Tower, seeking cool breezes and the shelter of darkness. Half the district has had the idea of escaping the heat by coming up here to-night, it seems; to get away from the angry eyes and tightened lips I have climbed to the fifth parapet, where only the bold and the foolish ordinarily go. I am neither, yet here I am.

As I move slowly around the tower's rim, warily clinging to

the old and eroded guardrail, I have a view of our entire district. Ganfield is like a shallow basin in form, gently sloping upward from the central spike that is the tower to a rise on the district perimeter. They say that a broad lake once occupied the site where Ganfield now stands; it was drained and covered over centuries ago, when the need for new living space became extreme. Yesterday I heard that great pumps are used to keep the ancient lake from breaking through into our cellars, and that before very long the pumps will fail or shut themselves down for maintenance, and we will be flooded. Perhaps so. Ganfield once devoured the lake; will the lake now have Ganfield? Will we tumble into the dark waters and be swallowed, with no one to mourn us?

I look out over Ganfield. These tall brick boxes are our dwellings, twenty storeys high but dwarfed from my vantage point far above. This sliver of land, black in the smoky moonlight, is our pitiful scrap of community park. These low flat-topped buildings are our shops, a helter-skelter cluster. This is our industrial zone, such that it is. That squat shadow-cloaked bulk just north of the tower is Ganfield Hold, where our crippled computers slip one by one into idleness. I have spent nearly my whole life within this one narrow swing of the compasses that is Ganfield. When I was a boy and affairs were not nearly so harsh between one district and its neighbour, my father took me on holiday to Morton Court, and another time to the Mill. When I was a young man I was sent on business across three districts to Parley Close. I remember those journeys as clearly and vividly as though I had dreamed them. But everything is quite different now and it is twenty years since I last left Ganfield. I am not one of your privileged commuters, gaily making transit from zone to zone. All the world is one great city, so it is said, with the deserts settled and the rivers bridged and all the open places filled, a universal city that has abolished the old boundaries, and yet it is twenty years since I passed from one district to the next. I wonder: are we one city, then, or merely thousands of contentious fragmented tiny states?

Look here, along the perimeter. There are no more boundaries, but what is this? This is our boundary, Ganfield Crescent, that wide curving boulevard surrounding the district. Are you a man of some other zone? Then cross the Crescent at risk of life. Do you see our police machines, blunt-snouted, glossy, formidably powerful, strewn like boulders in the broad avenue? They will interrogate you, and if your answers are uneasy, they may destroy you. Of course they can do no one any harm tonight.

Look outward now, at our horde of brawling neighbours. I see beyond the Crescent to the east the gaunt spires of Conning Town, and on the west, descending stepwise into the jumbled valley, the shabby dark-walled buildings of the Mill, with happy Morton Court on the far side, and somewhere in the smoky distance other places, Folkstone and Budleigh and Hawk Nest and Parley Close and Kingston and Old Grove and all the rest, the districts, the myriad districts, part of the chain that stretches from sea to sea, from shore to shore, spanning our continent paunch by haunch, the districts, the chips of gaudy glass making up the global mosaic, the infinitely numerous communities that are the segments of the all-encompassing world-city. Tonight at the capital they are planning next month's rainfall patterns for districts that the planners have never seen. District food allocations – inadequate, always inadequate – are being devised by men to whom our appetites are purely abstract entities. Do they believe in our existence, at the capital? Do they really think there is such a place as Ganfield? What if we sent them a delegation of notable citizens to ask for help in replacing our lost programme? Would they care? Would they even listen? For that matter, is there a capital at all? How can I who has never seen nearby Old Grove accept, on faith alone, the existence of a far-off governing centre, aloof, inaccessible, shrouded in myth? Maybe it is only a construct of some cunning subterranean machine that is our real ruler. That would not surprise me. Nothing surprises me. There is no capital. There are no central planners. Beyond the horizon everything is mist.

3

In the office, at least, no one dares show hostility to me. There are no scowls, no glares, no snide references to the missing programme. I am, after all, chief deputy to the District Commissioner of Nutrition, and since the commissioner is usually absent, I am in effect in charge of the department. If Silena's crime does not destroy my career, it might prove to have been unwise for my subordinates to treat me with disdain. In any case we are so busy that there is no time for such gambits. We are responsible for keeping the community properly fed; our tasks have been greatly complicated by the loss of the programme, for there is no reliable way now of processing our allocation sheets, and we must requisition and distribute food by guesswork and memory. How many bales of plankton cubes do we consume each week? How many kilos of proteoid mix? How much bread for the shops of Lower Ganfield? What fads of diet are likely to sweep the district this month? If demand and supply fall into imbalance as a result of our miscalculations, there could be widespread acts of violence, forays into neighbouring districts, even renewed outbreaks of cannibalism within Ganfield itself. So we must draw up our estimates with the greatest precision. What a terrible spiritual isolation we feel, deciding such things with no computers to guide us!

4

On the fourteenth day of the crisis the district captain summons me. His message comes in late afternoon, when we all are dizzy with fatigue, choked by humidity. For several hours I have been tangled in complex dealings with a high official of the Marine Nutrients Board; this is an arm of the central city government, and I must therefore show the greatest tact, lest Ganfield's plankton quotas be arbitrarily lowered by a bureaucrat's sudden pique. Telephone contact is uncertain – the Marine Nutrients Board has its headquarters in Melrose New Port, half a continent away on the southeastern coast – and the line sputters and blurs with distortions that our computers, if the master programme were in operation, would normally erase. As we reach a crisis in the negotiation my subdeputy gives me a note: DISTRICT CAPTAIN WANTS TO SEE YOU. 'Not now,' I say in silent lip-talk. The haggling proceeds. A few minutes later comes another note: IT'S URGENT. I shake my head, brush the note from my desk. The subdeputy retreats to the outer office, where I see him engaged in frantic discussion with a man in the grey and green uniform of the district captain's staff. The messenger points vehemently at me. Just then the phone line goes dead. I slam the instrument down and call to the messenger, 'What is it?'

'The captain, sir. To his office at once, please.'

'Impossible.'

He displays a warrant bearing the captain's seal. 'He requires your immediate presence.'

'Tell him I have delicate business to complete,' I reply. 'Another fifteen minutes, maybe.'

He shakes his head. 'I am not empowered to allow a delay.'

'Is this an arrest, then?'

'A summons.'

'But with the force of an arrest?'

'With the force of an arrest, yes,' he tells me.

I shrug and yield. All burdens drop from me. Let the subdeputy deal with the Marine Nutrients Board; let the clerk in the outer office do it, or no one at all; let the whole district starve. I no longer care. I am summoned. My responsibilities are discharged. I give over my desk to the subdeputy and summarize for him, in perhaps a hundred words, my intricate hours of negotiation. All that is someone else's problem now.

The messenger leads me from the building into the hot, dank street. The sky is dark and heavy with rain, and evidently it has been raining some while, for the sewers are backing up and angry swirls of muddy water run shin-deep through the gutters. The drainage system, too, is controlled from Ganfield Hold, and must now be failing. We hurry across the narrow plaza fronting my office, skirt a gush of sewage-laden outflow, push into a close-packed crowd of irritable workers heading for home. The messenger's uniform creates an invisible sphere of untouchability for us; the throngs part readily and close again behind us. Wordlessly I am conducted to the stone-faced building of the district captain, and quickly to his office. It is no unfamiliar place to me, but coming here as a prisoner is quite different from attending a meeting of the district council. My shoulders are slumped, my eyes look towards the threadbare carpeting.

The district captain appears. He is a man of sixty, silver-haired, upright, his eyes frank and direct, his features reflecting little of the strain his position must impose. He has governed our district ten years. He greets me by name, but without warmth, and says, 'You've heard nothing from your woman?'

'I would have reported it if I had.'

'Perhaps. Perhaps. Have you any idea where she is?'

'I know only the common rumours,' I say. 'Conning Town, Morton Court, the Mill.'

'She is in none of those places.'

'Are you sure?'

'I have consulted the captains of those districts,' he says. 'They deny any knowledge of her. Of course, one has no reason to trust their word, but on the other hand, why would they bother to deceive me?' His eyes fasten on mine. 'What part did you play in the stealing of the programme?'

'None, sir.'

'She never spoke to you of treasonable things?'

'Never.'

'There is strong feeling in Ganfield that a conspiracy existed.'

'If so, I knew nothing of it.'

He judges me with a piercing look. After a long pause he says heavily, 'She has destroyed us, you know. We can function at the present level of order for another six weeks, possibly, without the programme – if there is no plague, if we are not flooded, if we are not overrun with bandits from outside. After that the accumulated effects of many minor breakdowns will paralyse us. We will fall into chaos. We will strangle on our own wastes, starve, suffocate, revert to savagery, live like beasts until the end – who knows? Without the master programme we are lost. Why did she do this to us?'

'I have no theories,' I say. 'She kept her own counsel. Her independence of soul is what attracted me to her.'

166

'Very well. Let her independence of soul be what attracts you to her now. Find her and bring back the programme.'

'Find her? Where?'

'That is for you to discover.'

'I know nothing of the world outside Ganfield!'

'You will learn,' the captain says coolly. 'There are those here who would indict you for treason. I see no value in this. How does it help us to punish you? But we can *use* you. You are a clever and resourceful man; you can make your way through the hostile districts, and you can gather information, and you could well succeed in tracking her. If anyone has influence over her, you do: if you find her, you perhaps can induce her to surrender the programme. No one else could hope to accomplish that. Go. We offer you immunity from prosecution in return for your cooperation.'

The world spins wildly about me. My skin burns with shock. 'Will I have safe conduct through the neighbouring districts?' I ask.

'To whatever extent we can arrange. That will not be much, I fear.'

'You'll give me an escort, then? Two or three men?'

'We feel you will travel more effectively alone. A party of several men takes on the character of an invading force; you would be met with suspicion and worse.'

'Diplomatic credentials, at least?'

'A letter of identification, calling on all captains to honour your mission and treat you with courtesy.'

I know how much value such a letter will have in Hawk Nest or Folkstone.

'This frightens me,' I say.

He nods, not unkindly. 'I understand that. Yet someone must seek her, and who else is there but you? We grant you a day to make your preparations. You will depart on the morning after next, and God hasten your return.'

5

Preparations. How can I prepare myself? What maps should I collect, when my destination is unknown? Returning to the office is unthinkable; I go straight home, and for hours I wander from one room to the other as if I face execution at dawn. At last I gather myself and fix a small meal, but most of it remains on my plate. No friends call; I call no one. Since Silena's disappearance my friends have fallen away from me. I sleep poorly. During the night there are hoarse shouts and shrill alarms in the street; I learn from the morning newscast that five men of Conning Town, here to loot, had been seized by one of the new vigilante groups that have replaced the police machines, and were summarily put to death. I find no cheer in that, thinking that I might be in Conning Town in a day or so.

What clues to Silena's route? I ask to speak with the guard from whom she wangled entry into Ganfield Hold. He has been a prisoner ever since; the captain is too busy to decide his fate, and he languishes meanwhile. He is a small thick-bodied man with stubbly red hair and a sweaty forehead; his eyes are bright with anger and his nostrils quiver. 'What is there to say?' he demands. 'I was on duty at the Hold. She came in. I had never seen her before, though I knew she must be high caste. Her cloak was open. She seemed naked beneath it. She was in a state of excitement.'

'What did she tell you?'

'That she desired me. Those were her first words.' Yes. I could see Silena doing that, though I had difficulty in imagining her long slender form enfolded in this squat little man's embrace. 'She said she knew of me and was eager for me to have her.'

'And then?'

'I sealed the gate. We went to an inner room where there is a cot. It was a quiet time of day; I thought no harm would come. She dropped her cloak. Her body—'

'Never mind her body.' I could see it all too well in the eye of my mind, the sleek thighs, the taut belly, the small high breasts, the cascade of chocolate hair falling to her shoulders. 'What did you talk about? Did she say anything of a political kind? Some slogan, some words against the government?'

'Nothing. We lay together naked a while, only fondling one another. Then she said she had a drug with her, one which

168

would enance the sensations of love tenfold. It was a dark powder. I drank it in water; she drank it also, or seemed to. Instantly I was asleep. When I awoke the Hold was in uproar and I was a prisoner.' He glowers at me. 'I should have suspected a trick from the start. Such women do not hunger for men like me. How did I ever injure you? Why did you choose me to be the victim of your scheme?'

'Her scheme,' I say. 'Not mine. I had no part in it. Her motive is a mystery to me. If I could discover where she has gone, I would seek her and wring answers from her. Any help you could give me might earn you a pardon and your freedom.'

'I know nothing,' he says sullenly. 'She came in, she snared me, she drugged me, she stole the programme.'

'Think. Not a word? Possibly she mentioned the name of some other district.'

'Nothing.'

A pawn is all he is, innocent, useless. As I leave he cries out to me to intercede for him, but what can I do? 'Your woman ruined me!' he roars.

'She may have ruined us all,' I reply.

At my request a district prosecutor accompanies me to Silena's apartment, which has been under official seal since her disappearance. Its contents have been thoroughly examined, but maybe there is some clue I alone would notice. Entering, I feel a sharp pang of loss, for the sight of Silena's possessions reminds me of happier times. These things are painfully familiar to me: her neat array of books, her clothing, her furnishings, her bed. I knew her only eleven weeks, she was my month-wife only for two; I had not realized she had come to mean so much to me so quickly. We look around, the prosecutor and I. The books testify to the agility of her restless mind: little light fiction, mainly works of serious history, analyses of social problems, forecasts of conditions to come. Holman, *The Era of the World City*. Sawtelle, *Megalopolis Triumphant*. Doxiadis, *The New World of Urban Man*. Heggebend, *Fifty Billion Lives*. Marks, *Calcutta Is Everywhere*. Chasin, *The New Community*. I take a few of the books down, fondling them as though they were Silena. Many times when I had spent an evening here she reached for one of those books, Sawtelle or Heggebend or Marks or Chasin, to read me a passage that amplified some point she was making. Idly I turn pages. Dozens of paragraphs are underscored with fine, precise lines, and lengthy marginal comments are abundant. 'We've analysed all of that for possible significance,' the prosecutor remarks. 'The only thing we've concluded is that she thinks the world is too crowded for comfort.' A ratcheting laugh. 'As who doesn't?' He points to a stack of green-bound pamphlets at the end of a lower shelf. 'These, on the other hand, may be useful in your search. Do you know anything about them?'

The stack consists of nine copies of something called *Walden Three*: a Utopian fantasy, apparently, set in an idyllic land of streams and forests. The booklets are unfamiliar to me; Silena must have obtained them recently. Why nine copies? Was she acting as a distributor? They bear the imprint of a publishing house in Kingston. Ganfield and Kingston severed trade relations long ago; material published there is uncommon here. 'I've never seen them,' I say. 'Where do you think she got them?'

'There are three main routes for subversive literature originating in Kingston. One is—'

'Is this pamphlet subversive, then?'

'Oh, very much so. It argues for complete reversal of the social trends of the last hundred years. As I was saying: there are three main routes for subversive literature originating in Kingston. We have traced one chain of distribution running by way of Wisleigh and Cedar Mall, another through Old Grove, Hawk Nest, and Conning Town, and the third via Parley Close and the Mill. It is plausible that your woman is in Kingston now, having travelled along one of these underground distribution routes, sheltered by her fellow subversives all the way. But we have no way of confirming this.' He smiles emptily. 'She could be in any of the other communities along the three routes. Or in none of them.'

'I should think of Kingston, though, as my ultimate goal, until I learn anything to the contrary. Is that right?'

'What else can you do?'

What else, indeed? I must search at random through an unknown number of hostile districts, having no clue other than the vague one implicit in the place of origin of these nine booklets, while time ticks on and Ganfield slips deeper day by day into confusion.

The prosecutor's office supplies me with useful things: maps, letters of introduction, a commuter's passport that should enable me to cross at least some district lines unmolested, and an assortment of local currencies as well as banknotes issued by the central bank and therefore valid in most districts. Against my wishes I am given also a weapon – a small heat-pistol – and in addition a capsule that I can swallow in the event that a quick and easy death becomes desirable. As the final stage in my preparation I spend an hour conferring with a secret agent, now retired, whose career of espionage took him safely into hundreds of communities as far away as Threadmuir and Reed Meadow. What advice does he give someone about to try to get across? 'Maintain your poise,' he says. 'Be confident and self-assured, as though you belong in whatever place you find yourself. Never slink. Look all men in the eye. However, say no more than is necessary. Be watchful at all times. Don't relax your guard.' Such precepts I could have evolved without his aid. He has nothing in the nature of specific hints for survival. Each district, he says, presents unique problems, constantly changing; nothing can be anticipated, everything must be met as it arises. How comforting!

At nightfall I go to the soulfather's house, in the shadow of Ganfield Tower. To leave without a blessing seems unwise. But there is something stagy and unspontaneous about my visit, and my faith flees as I enter. In the dim antechamber I light the nine candles, I pluck the five blades of grass from the ceremonial vase, I do the other proper ritual things, but my spirit remains chilled and hollow, and I am unable to pray. The soulfather himself, having been told of my mission, grants me audience – gaunt old man with impenetrable eyes set in deep bony rims – and favours me with a gentle feather-light embrace. 'Go in safety,' he murmurs. 'God watches over you.' I wish I felt sure of that. Going home, I take the most roundabout possible route, as if trying to drink in as much of Ganfield as I can on my last night. The diminishing past flows through me like a river running dry. My birthplace, my school, the streets where I played, the dormitory where I spent my adolescence, the home of my first month-wife. Farewell. Farewell. Tomorrow I go across. I return to my apartment alone; once more my sleep is fitful; an hour after dawn I find myself, astonished by it, waiting in line among the commuters at the mouth of the transit tube, bound for Conning Town. And so my crossing begins.

6

Aboard the tube no one speaks. Faces are tense, bodies are held rigid in the plastic seats. Occasionally someone on the other side of the aisle glances at me as though wondering who this newcomer to the commuter group may be, but his eyes quickly slide away as I take notice. I know none of these commuters, though they must have dwelled in Ganfield as long as I; their lives have never intersected mine before. Engineers, merchants, diplomats, whatever – their careers are tied to districts other than their own. It is one of the anomalies of our ever more fragmented and stratified society that some regular contact still survives between community and community; a certain number of people must journey each day to outlying districts, where they work encapsulated, isolated, among unfriendly strangers.

We plunge eastward at unimaginable speed. Surely we are past the boundaries of Ganfield by now and under alien territory. A glowing sign on the wall of the car announces our route: CONNING TOWN–HAWK NEST–OLD GROVE–KINGSTON–FOLKSTONE–PARLEY CLOSE–BUDLEIGH–CEDAR MALL–THE MILL–MORTON COURT–GANFIELD, a wide loop through our most immediate neighbours. I try to visualize the separate links in this chain of districts, each a community of three or four hundred thousand loyal and patriotic citizens, each with its own special tone, its flavour, its distinctive quality, its apparatus of government, its customs and rituals. But I can imagine them merely as a cluster of Ganfields, every place very much like the one I have just left. I know this is not so. The world-city is no homogenous collection of uniformities, a global bundle of indistinguishable suburbs. No, there is incredible diversity, a host of unique urban cores bound by common need into a fragile unity. No master plan brought them into being; each evolved at a separate point in time, to serve the necessities of a particular purpose. This community sprawls gracefully along a curving river, that one boldly mounts the slopes of stark hills; here the prevailing architecture reflects an easy, gentle climate, there it wars with unfriendly nature; form follows topography and local function, creating individuality. The world is a richness: why then do I see only ten thousand Ganfields?

Of course it is not so simple. We are caught in the tension between forces which encourage distinctiveness and forces compelling all communities towards identicality. Centrifugal forces broke down the huge ancient cities, the Londons and Tokyos and New Yorks, into neighbourhood communities that seized quasi-autonomous powers. Those giant cities were too unwieldy to survive; density of population, making long-distance transport unfeasible and communication difficult, shattered the urban fabric, destroyed the authority of the central government, and left the closely knit small-scale subcity as the only viable unit. Two dynamic and contradictory processes now asserted themselves. Pride and the quest for local advantage led each community towards specialization: this one a centre primarily of industrial production, this one devoted to advanced education, this to finance, this to the processing of raw materials, this to wholesale marketing of commodities, this to retail distribution, and so on, the shape and texture of each district defined by its chosen function. And yet the new decentralization required a high degree of redundancy, duplication of governmental structures, of utilities, of community services; for its own safety each district felt the need to transform itself into a microcosm of the former full city. Ideally we should have hovered in perfect balance between specialization and redundancy, all communities striving to fulfil the needs of all other communities with the least possible overlap and waste of resources; in fact, our human frailty has brought into being

173

these irreversible trends of rivalry and irrational fear, dividing district from district, so that against our own self-interest we sever year after year our bonds of interdependence and stubbornly seek self-sufficiency at the district level. Since this is impossible, our lives grow constantly more impoverished. In the end all districts will be the same and we will have created a world of pathetic limping Ganfields, devoid of grace, lacking in variety.

So. The tube-train halts. This is Conning Town. I am across the first district line. I make my exit in a file of solemn-faced commuters. Imitating them, I approach a colossal cyclopean scanning machine and present my passport. It is unmarked by visas; theirs are gaudy with scores of them. I tremble, but the machine accepts me and slams down a stamp that fluoresces a brilliant shimmering crimson against the pale lavender page:

* DISTRICT OF CONNING TOWN *
* ENTRY VISA *
* 24-HOUR VALIDITY *

Dated to the hour, minute, second. Welcome, stranger, but get out of town before sunrise!

Up the purring ramp, into the street. Bright morning sunlight pries apart the slim sooty close-ranked towers of Conning Town. The air is cool and sweet, strange to me after so many sweltering days in programmeless demechanized Ganfield. Does our foul air drift across the border and offend them? Sullen eyes study me; those about me know me for an outsider. Their clothing is alien in style, pinched in at the shoulders, flaring at the waist. I find myself adopting an inane smile in response to their dour glares.

For an hour I walk aimlessly through the downtown section until my first fears melt and a comic cockiness takes possession of me: I pretend to myself that I am a native, and enjoy the flimsy imposture. This place is not much unlike Ganfield, yet nothing is quite the same. The sidewalks are wider; the street lamps have slender arching necks instead of angular ones; the fire hydrants are green and gold, not blue and orange. The police machines have flatter domes than ours, ringed with ten or twelve spy-eyes where ours have six or eight. Different, different, all different.

Three times I am halted by police machines. I produce my passport, display my visa, am allowed to continue. So far getting across has been easier than I imagined. No one molests me here. I suppose I look harmless. Why did I think my foreignness alone would lead these people to attack me? Ganfield is not at war with its neighbours, after all.

Drifting eastward in search of a bookstore, I pass through a shabby residential neighbourhood and through a zone of dismal factories before I reach an area of small shops. Then in late afternoon I discover three bookstores on the same block, but they are antiseptic places, not the sort that might carry subversive propaganda like *Walden Three*. The first two are wholly automated, blank-walled charge-plate-and-scanner operations. The third has a human clerk, a man of about thirty with drooping yellow moustachios and alert blue eyes. He recognizes the style of my clothing and says, 'Ganfield, eh? Lot of trouble over there.'

'You've heard?'

'Just stories. Computer breakdown, isn't it?'

I nod. 'Something like that.'

'No police, no garbage removal, no weather control, hardly anything working – that's what they say.' He seems neither surprised nor disturbed to have an outlander in his shop. His manner is amiable and relaxed. Is he fishing for data about our vulnerability, though? I must be careful not to tell him anything that might be used against us. But evidently they already know everything here. He says, 'It's a little like dropping back into the Stone Age for you people, I guess. It must be a real traumatic thing.'

'We're coping,' I say, stiffly casual.

'How did it happen, anyway?'

I give him a wary shrug. 'I'm not sure about that.' Still revealing nothing. But then something in his tone of a moment before catches me belatedly and neutralizes some of the reflexive automatic suspicion with which I have met his questions. I glance around. No one else is in the shop. I let something conspiratorial creep into my voice and say, 'It might not even be so traumatic, actually, once we get used to it. I mean, there once was a time when we didn't rely so heavily on machines to do our thinking for us, and we survived, and even managed pretty well. I was reading a little book last week that seemed to be saying we might profit by trying to return to the old way of life. Book published in Kingston.'

'*Walden Three.*' Not a question but a statement.

'That's it.' My eyes query his. 'You've read it?'

'Seen it.'

'A lot of sense in that book, I think.'

He smiles warmly. 'I think so too. You get much Kingston stuff over in Ganfield?'

'Very little, actually.'

'Not much here, either.'

'But there's some.'

'Some, yes,' he says.

Have I stumbled upon a member of Silena's underground movement? I say eagerly, 'You know, maybe you could help me meet some people who—'

'No.'

'No?'

'No.' His eyes are still friendly but his face is tense. 'There's nothing like that around here,' he says, his voice suddenly flat and remote. 'You'd have to go over into Hawk Nest.'

'I'm told that that's a nasty place.'

'Nevertheless. Hawk Nest is where you want to go. Nate and Holly Borden's shop, just off Box Street.' Abruptly his manner shifts to one of exaggerated bland clerkishness. 'Anything else I can do for you, sir? If you're interested in supernovels we've got a couple of good new double-amplified cassettes, just in. Perhaps I can show you—'

'Thank you, no.' I smile, shake my head, leave the store. A police machine waits outside. Its dome rotates, eye after eye scans me intently; finally its resonant voice says, 'Your passport, please.' This routine is familiar by now. I produce the document. Through the bookshop window I see the clerk bleakly watching. The police machine says, 'What is your place of residence in Conning Town?'

'I have none. I'm here on a twenty-four-hour visa.'

'Where will you spend the night?'

'In a hotel, I suppose.'

'Please show your room confirmation.'

'I haven't made arrangements yet,' I tell it.

I long moment of silence: the machine is conferring with its central, no doubt, keying into the master programme of Conning Town for instructions. At length it says, 'You are advised to obtain a legitimate reservation and display it to a monitor at the earliest opportunity within the next four hours. Failure to do so will result in cancellation of your visa and immediate expulsion from Conning Town.' Some ominous clicks come from the depths of the machine. 'You are now under formal surveillance,' it announces.

Brimming with questions, I return hastily to the bookshop. The clerk is displeased to see me. Anyone who attracts monitors to his shop – 'monitors' is what they call police machines here, it seems – is unwelcome. 'Can you tell me how to reach the nearest decent hotel?' I ask.

'You won't find one.'

'No decent hotels?'

'No hotels. None where you could get a room, anyway. We have only two or three transient houses, and accommodations are allocated months in advance to regular commuters.'

'Does the monitor know that?'

'Of course.'

'Where are strangers supposed to stay, then?'

The clerk shrugs. 'There's no structural programme here for strangers as such. The regular commuters have regular arrangements. Unauthorized intruders don't belong here at all. You fall somewhere in between, I imagine. There's no legal way for you to spend the night in Conning Town.'

'But my visa—'

'Even so.'

'I'd better go on into Hawk Nest, I suppose.'

'It's late. You've missed the last tube. You've got no choice but to stay, unless you want to try a border crossing on foot in the dark. I wouldn't recommend that.'

'Stay? But where?'

'Sleep in the street. If you're lucky the monitors will leave you alone.'

'Some quiet back alley, I suppose.'

'No,' he says. 'You sleep in an out-of-the-way place and you'll surely get sliced up by night-bandits. Go to one of the designated sleeping streets. In the middle of a big crowd you might just go unnoticed, even though you're under surveillance.' As he speaks he moves about the shop, closing it down for the night. He looks restless and uncomfortable. I take out my map of Conning Town and he shows me where to go. The map is some years out of date, apparently; he corrects it with irritable swipes of his pencil. We leave the shop together. I invite him to come with me to some restaurant as my guest, but he looks at me as if I carry plague. 'Goodbye,' he says. 'Good luck.'

7

Alone, apart from the handful of other diners, I take my evening meal at a squalid, dimly lit automated cafeteria at the edge of downtown. Silent machines offer me thin acrid soup, pale spongy bread, and a leaden stew containing lumpy ingredients of undeterminable origin, for which I pay with yellow plastic counters of Conning Town currency. Emerging undelighted, I observe a reddish glow in the western sky: it may be a lovely sunset or, for all I know, may be a sign that Ganfield is burning. I look about for monitors. My four-hour grace period has nearly expired. I must disappear shortly into a throng. It seems too early for sleep, but I am only a few blocks from the place where the bookshop clerk suggested I should pass the night, and I go to it. Just as well: when I reach it – a wide plaza bordered by grey buildings of ornate façade – I find it already filling up with street-sleepers. There must be eight hundred of them, men, women, family groups, settling down in little squares of cobbled territory that are obviously claimed night after night under some system of squatters' rights. Others constantly arrive, flowing inward from the plaza's three entrances, finding their places, laying out foam cushions or mounds of clothing as their mattresses. It is a friendly crowd: these people are linked by bonds of neighbourliness, a common poverty. They laugh, embrace, play games of chance, exchange whispered confidences, bicker, transact business, and join together in the rites of the local religion, performing a routine that involves six people clasping hands and chanting. Privacy seems obsolete here. They undress freely before one another and there are instances of open coupling. The gaiety of the scene – a mediaeval carnival is what it suggests to me, a Brueghelesque romp – is marred only by my awareness that this horde of revellers is homeless under the inhospitable skies, vulnerable to rain, sleet, damp fog, snow, and the other unkindnesses of winter and summer in these latitudes. In Ganfield we have just a scattering of streetsleepers, those who have lost their residential licences and are temporarily forced into the open, but here it seems to be an established institution, as though Conning Town declared a moratorium some years ago on new residential construction without at the same time checking the increase of population.

Stepping over and around and between people, I reach the centre of the plaza and select an unoccupied bit of pavement. But in a moment a little ruddy-faced woman arrives, excited and animated, and with a Conning Town accent so thick I can barely understand her she tells me she holds claim here. Her eyes are bright with menace; her hands are not far from becoming claws; several nearby squatters sit up and regard me threateningly. I apologize for my error and withdraw, stumbling over a child and narrowly missing overturning a bubbling cooking pot. Onward. Not here. Not here. A hand emerges from a pile of blankets and strokes my leg as I look around in perplexity. Not here. A man with a painted face rises out of a miniature green tent and speaks to me in a language I do not understand. Not here. I move on again and again, thinking that I will be jostled out of the plaza entirely, excluded, disqualified even to sleep in this district's streets, but finally I find a cramped corner where the occupants indicate I am welcome. 'Yes?' I say. They grin and gesture. Gratefully I seize the spot.

Darkness has come. The plaza continues to fill; at least a thousand people have arrived after me, cramming into every vacancy, and the flow does not abate. I hear booming laughter, idle chatter, earnest romantic persuasion, the brittle sound of domestic quarrelling. Someone passes a jug of wine around, even to me: bitter stuff, fermented clam juice its probable base, but I appreciate the gesture. The night is warm, almost sticky. The scent of unfamiliar food drifts on the air – something sharp, spicy, a heavy pungent smell. Curry? Is this then truly Calcutta? I close my eyes and huddle into myself. The hard cobblestones are cold beneath me. I have no mattress and I feel unable to remove my clothes before so many strangers. It will be hard for me to sleep in this madhouse, I think. But gradually the hubbub diminishes and – exhausted, drained – I slide into a deep troubled sleep.

Ugly dreams. The asphyxiating pressure of a surging mob. Rivers leaping their channels. Towers toppling. Fountains of mud bursting from a thousand lofty windows. Bands of steel encircling my thighs; my legs, useless, withering away. A torrent of lice sweeping over me. A frosty hand touching me. Touching me. Touching me. Pulling me up from sleep.

Harsh white light drenches me. I blink, cringe, cover my eyes. Shortly I perceive that a monitor stands over me. About me the sleepers are awake, backing away, murmuring, pointing.

'Your street-sleeping permit, please.'

Caught. I mumble excuses, plead ignorance of the law, beg forgiveness. But a police machine is neither malevolent nor merciful; it merely follows its programme. It demands my passport and scans my visa. Then it reminds me I have been under surveillance. Having failed to obtain a hotel room as ordered, having neglected to report to a monitor within the prescribed interval, I am subject to expulsion.

'Very well,' I say. 'Conduct me to the border of Hawk Nest.'

'You will return at once to Ganfield.'

'I have business in Hawk Nest.'

'Illegal entrants are returned to their district of origin.'

'What does it matter to you where I go, so long as I get out of Conning Town?'

'Illegal entrants are returned to their district of origin,' the machine tells me inexorably.

I dare not go back with so little accomplished. Still arguing with the monitor, I am led from the plaza through dark cavernous streets towards the mouth of a transit tube. On the station level a second monitor is given charge of me. 'In three hours,' the monitor that apprehended me informs me, 'the Ganfield-bound train will arrive.'

The first monitor rolls away.

Too late I realize that the machine has neglected to return my passport.

8

Monitor number two shows little interest in me. Patrolling the tube station, it swings in a wide arc around me, keeping a scanner perfunctorily trained on me but making no attempt to interfere with what I do. If I try to flee, of course, it will destroy me. Fretfully I study my maps. Hawk Nest lies to the northeast of Conning Town; if this is the tube station that I think it is, the border is not far. Five minutes' walk, perhaps. Passportless, there is no place I can go except Ganfield: my commuter status is revoked. But legalities count for little in Hawk Nest.

How to escape?

I concoct a plan. Its simplicity seems absurd, yet absurdity is often useful when dealing with machines. The monitor is instructed to put me aboard the train for Ganfield, yes. But not necessarily to keep me there.

I wait out the weary hours to dawn. I hear the crash of compressed air far up the tunnel. Snub-nosed, silken-smooth, the train slides into the station. The monitor orders me aboard. I walk into the car, cross it quickly, and exit by the open door on the far side of the platform. Even if the monitor has observed this manoeuvre, it can hardly fire across a crowded train. As I leave the car I break into a trot, darting past startled travellers, and sprint upstairs into the misty morning. At street level running is unwise. I drop back to a rapid walking pace and melt into the throngs of early workers. The street is Crystal Boulevard. Good. I have memorized a route: Crystal Boulevard to Flagstone Square, thence via Mechanic Street to the border.

Presumably all monitors, linked to whatever central nervous system the machines of the district of Conning Town utilize, have instantaneously been apprised of my disappearance. But that is not the same as knowing where to find me. I head northward on Crystal Boulevard – its name shows a dark sense of irony, or else the severe transformations time can work – and, borne by the flow of pedestrian traffic, enter Flagstone Square, a grimy, lopsided plaza out of which, on the left, snakes curving Mechanic Street. I go unintercepted on this thoroughfare of small shops. The place to anticipate trouble is at the border.

I am there in a few minutes. It is a wide dusty street, silent and empty, lined on the Conning Town side by a row of blocky brick warehouses, on the Hawk Nest side by a string of low ragged buildings, some in ruins, the best of them defiantly slatternly. There is no barrier. To fence a district border is unlawful except in time of war, and I have heard of no war between Conning Town and Hawk Nest.

Dare I cross? Police machines of two species patrol the street: flat-domed ones of Conning Town and black, hexagonheaded ones of Hawk Nest. Surely one or the other will gun me down in the no man's land between districts. But I have no choice. I must keep going forward.

I run out into the street at a moment when two police machines, passing one another on opposite orbits, have left an unpatrolled space perhaps a block long. Midway in my crossing the Conning Town monitor spies me and blares a command. The words are unintelligible to me and I keep running, zigzagging in the hope of avoiding the bolt that very likely will follow. But the machine does not shoot; I must already be on the Hawk Nest side of the line, and Conning Town no longer cares what becomes of me.

The Hawk Nest machine has noticed me. It rolls towards me as I stumble, breathless and gasping, onto the kerb. 'Halt!' it cries. 'Present your documents!' At that moment a red-bearded man, fierce-eyed, wide-shouldered, steps out of a decaying building close by me. A scheme assembles itself in my mind. Do the customs of sponsorship and sanctuary hold good in this harsh district?

'Brother!' I cry. 'What luck!' I embrace him, and before he can fling me off I murmur, 'I am from Ganfield. I seek sanctuary here. Help me!'

The machine has reached me. It goes into an interrogatory stance and I say, 'This is my brother who offers me the privilege of sanctuary. Ask him! Ask him!'

'Is this true?' the machine inquires.

Redbeard, unsmiling, spits and mutters, 'My brother, yes. A political refugee. I'll stand sponsor to him. I vouch for him. Let him be.'

The machine clicks, hums, assimilates. To me it says, 'You will register as a sponsored refugee within twelve hours or leave Hawk Nest.' Without another word it rolls away.

I offer my sudden saviour warm thanks. He scowls, shakes his head, spits once again. 'We owe each other nothing,' he says brusquely, and goes striding down the street.

9

In Hawk Nest nature has followed art. The name, I have heard, once had purely neutral connotations: some real-estate developer's high-flown metaphor, nothing more. Yet it determined the district's character, for gradually Hawk Nest became the home of predators that it is today, where all men are strangers, where every man is his brother's enemy.

Other districts have their slums. Hawk Nest *is* a slum. I am told they live here by looting, cheating, extorting, and manipulating. An odd economic base for an entire community, but maybe it works for them. The atmosphere is menacing. The only police machines seem to be those that patrol the border. I sense emanations of violence just beyond the corner of my eye: rapes and garrotings in shadowy byways, flashing knives and muffled groans, covert cannibal feasts. Perhaps my imagination works too hard. Certainly I have gone unthreatened so far; those I meet on the streets pay no heed to me, indeed will not even return my glance. Still, I keep my heat-pistol close by my hand as I walk through these shabby, deteriorating outskirts. Sinister faces peer at me through cracked, dirt-veiled windows. If I am attacked, will I have to fire in order to defend myself? God spare me from having to answer that.

10

Why is there a bookshop in this town of murder and rubble and decay? Here is Box Street, and here, in an oily pocket of spare-parts depots and fly-specked quick-lunch counters, is Nate and Holly Borden's place. Five times as deep as it is broad, dusty, dimly lit, shelves overflowing with old books and pamphlets: an improbable outpost of the nineteenth century, somehow displaced in time. There is no one in it but a large, impassive woman seated at the counter, fleshy, puffy-faced, motionless. Her eyes, oddly intense, glitter like glass discs set in a mound of dough. She regards me without curiosity.

I say, 'I'm looking for Holly Borden.'

'You've found her,' she replies, deep in the baritone range.

'I've come across from Ganfield by way of Conning Town.'

No response from her to this.

I continue, 'I'm travelling without a passport. They confiscated it in Conning Town and I ran the border.'

She nods. And waits. No show of interest.

'I wonder if you could sell me a copy of *Walden Three*,' I say.

Now she stirs a little. 'Why do you want one?'

'I'm curious about it. It's not available in Ganfield.'

'How do you know I have one?'

'Is anything illegal in Hawk Nest?'

She seems annoyed that I have answered a question with a question. 'How do you know *I* have a copy of that book?'

'A bookshop clerk in Conning Town said you might.'

A pause. 'All right. Suppose I do. Did you come all the way from Ganfield just to buy a book?' Suddenly she leans forward and smiles – a warm, keen, penetrating smile that wholly transforms her face: now she is keyed up, alert, responsive, shrewd, commanding. 'What's your game?' she asks.

'My game?'

'What are you playing? What are you up to here?'

It is the moment for total honesty. 'I'm looking for a woman named Silena Ruiz, from Ganfield. Have you heard of her?'

'Yes. She's not in Hawk Nest.'

'I think she's in Kingston. I'd like to find her.'

'Why? To arrest her?'

'Just to talk to her. I have plenty to discuss with her. She was my month-wife when she left Ganfield.'

'The month must be nearly up,' Holly Borden says.

'Even so,' I reply. 'Can you help me reach her?'

'Why should I trust you?'

'Why not?'

She ponders that briefly. She studies my face. I feel the heat of her scrutiny. At length she says, 'I expect to be making a journey to Kingston soon. I suppose I could take you with me.'

11

She opens a trap door; I descend into a room beneath the bookshop. After a good many hours a thin, grey-haired man brings me a tray of food. 'Call me Nate,' he says. Overhead I hear indistinct conversations, laughter, the thumping of boots on the wooden floor. In Ganfield famine may be setting in by now. Rats will be dancing around Ganfield Hold. How long will they keep me here? Am I a prisoner? Two days. Three. Nate will answer no questions. I have books, a cot, a sink, a drinking glass. On the third day the trap door opens. Holly Borden peers down. 'We're ready to leave,' she says.

The expedition consists just of the two of us. She is going to Kingston to buy books, and travels on a commercial passport that allows for one helper. Nate drives us to the tube-mouth in mid-afternoon. It no longer seems unusual to me to be passing from district to district; they are not such alien and hostile places, merely different from the place I know. I see myself bound on an odyssey that carries me across hundreds of districts, even thousands, the whole patchwork frenzy of our world. Why return to Ganfield? Why not go on, ever eastward, to the great ocean and beyond, to the unimaginable strangenesses on the far side?

Here we are in Kingston. An old district, one of the oldest. We are the only ones who journey hither today from Hawk Nest. There is only a perfunctory inspection of passports. The police machines of Kingston are tall, long-armed, with fluted bodies ornamented in stripes of red and green: quite a gay effect. I am becoming an expert in local variations of police-machine design. Kingston itself is a district of low pastel buildings arranged in spokelike boulevards radiating from the famed university that is its chief enterprise. No one from Ganfield has been admitted to the university in my memory.

Holly is expecting friends to meet her, but they have not come. We wait fifteen minutes. 'Never mind,' she says. 'We'll walk.' I carry the luggage. The air is soft and mild; the sun, sloping towards Folkstone and Budleigh, is still high. I feel oddly serene. It is as if I have perceived a divine purpose, an overriding plan, in the structure of our society, in our sprawling city of many cities, our network of steel and concrete clinging like an armour of scales to the skin of our planet. But what is that purpose? What is that plan? The essence of it eludes me; I am aware only that it must exist. A cheery delusion.

Fifty paces from the station we are abruptly surrounded by a dozen or more buoyant young men who emerge from an intersecting street. They are naked but for green loincloths; their hair and beards are untrimmed and unkempt; they have a fierce and barbaric look. Several carry long unsheathed knives strapped to their waists. They circle wildly around us, laughing, jabbing at us with their fingertips. 'This is a holy district!' they cry. 'We need no blasphemous strangers here! Why must you intrude on us?'

'What do they want?' I whisper. 'Are we in danger?'

'They are a band of priests,' Holly replies. 'Do as they say and we will come to no harm.'

They press close. Leaping, dancing, they shower us with sprays of perspiration. 'Where are you from?' they demand. 'Ganfield,' I say. 'Hawk Nest,' says Holly. They seem playful yet dangerous. Surging about me, they empty my pockets in a series of quick jostling forays: I lose my heat-pistol, my maps, my useless letters of introduction, my various currencies, everything, even my suicide capsule. These things they pass among themselves, exclaiming over them; then the heat-pistol and some of the currency are returned to me. 'Ganfield,' they murmur. 'Hawk Nest!' There is distaste in their voices. 'Filthy places,' they say. 'Places scorned by God,' they say. They seize our hands and haul us about, making us spin. Heavy-bodied Holly is surprisingly graceful, breaking into a serene lumbering dance that makes them applaud in wonder.

One, the tallest of the group, catches our wrists and says, 'What is your business in Kingston?'

'I come to purchase books,' Holly declares.

'I come to find my month-wife Silena,' say I.

'Silena! Silena! Silena!' Her name becomes a jubilant incantation on their lips. 'His month-wife! Silena! His month-wife! Silena! Silena! Silena!'

The tall one thrusts his face against mine and says, 'We offer you a choice. Come and make prayer with us, or die on the spot.'

'We choose to pray,' I tell him.

They tug at our arms, urging us impatiently onward. Down street after street until at last we arrive at holy ground: a garden plot, insignificant in area, planted with unfamiliar bushes and flowers, tended with evident care. They push us inside.

'Kneel,' they say.

'Kiss the sacred earth.'

'Adore the things that grow in it, strangers.'

'Give thanks to God for the breath you have just drawn.'

'And for the breath you are about to draw.'

'Sing!'

'Weep!'

'Laugh!'

'Touch the soil!'
'Worship!'

12

Silena's room is cool and quiet, in the upper storey of a
residence overlooking the university grounds. She wears a soft
green robe of coarse texture, no jewellery, no face-paint. Her
demeanour is calm and self-assured. I had forgotten the deli-
cacy of her features, the cool malicious sparkle of her dark
eyes.

'The master programme?' she says, smiling. 'I destroyed it!'

The depth of my love for her unmans me. Standing before
her, I feel my knees turning to water. In my eyes she is bathed
in a glittering aura of sensuality. I struggle to control myself.
'You destroyed nothing,' I say. 'Your voice betrays the lie.'

'You think I still have the programme?'

'I know you do.'

'Well, yes,' she admits coolly. 'I do.'

My fingers tremble. My throat parches. An adolescent foolishness seeks to engulf me.

'Why did you steal it?' I ask.

'Out of love of mischief.'

'I see the lie in your smile. What was the true reason?'

'Does it matter?'

'The district is paralysed, Silena. Thousands of people suffer.
We are at the mercy of raiders from adjoining districts. Many
have already died of the heat, the stink of garbage, the failure
of the hospital equipment. Why did you take the programme?'

'Perhaps I had political reasons.'

'Which were?'

'To demonstrate to the people of Ganfield how utterly
dependent on these machines they have allowed themselves to
become.'

'We knew that already,' I say. 'If you meant only to
dramatize our weaknesses, you were pressing the obvious.
What was the point of crippling us? What could you gain
from it?'

'Amusement?'

'Something more than that. You're not that shallow, Silena.'

'Something more than that, then. By crippling Ganfield I help to change things. That's the purpose of any political act. To display the need for change, so that change may come about.'

'Simply displaying the need is not enough.'

'It's a place to begin.'

'Do you think stealing our programme was a rational way to bring change, Silena?'

'Are you happy?' she retorts. 'Is this the kind of world you want?'

'It's the world we have to live in, whether we like it or not. And we need that programme in order to go on coping. Without it we are plunged into chaos.'

'Fine. Let chaos come. Let everything fall apart, so we can rebuild it.'

'Easy enough to say, Silena. What about the innocent victims of your revolutionary zeal, though?'

She shrugs. 'There are always innocent victims in any revolution.' In a sinuous movement she rises and approaches me. The closeness of her body is dazzling and maddening. With exaggerated voluptuousness she croons, 'Stay here. Forget Ganfield. Life is good here. These people are building something worth having.'

'Let me have the programme,' I say.

'They must have replaced it by now.'

'Replacing it is impossible. The programme is vital to Ganfield, Silena. Let me have it.'

She emits an icy laugh.

'I beg you, Silena.'

'How boring you are!'

'I love you.'

'You love nothing but the status quo. The shape of things as they are gives you great joy. You have the soul of a bureaucrat.'

'If you have always had such contempt for me, why did you become my month-wife?'

She laughs again. 'For sport, perhaps.'

Her words are like knives. Suddenly, to my own astonishment, I am brandishing the heat-pistol. 'Give me the programme or I'll kill you!' I cry.

She is amused. 'Go. Shoot. Can you get the programme from a dead Silena?'

'Give it to me.'

'How silly you look holding that gun!'

'I don't have to kill you,' I tell her. 'I can merely wound you. This pistol is capable of inflicting light burns that scar the skin. Shall I give you blemishes, Silena?'

'Whatever you wish. I'm at your mercy.'

I aim the pistol at her thigh. Silena's face remains expressionless. My arm stiffens and begins to quiver. I struggle with the rebellious muscles, but I succeed in steadying my aim only for a moment before the tremors return. An exultant gleam enters her eyes. A flush of excitement spreads over her face. 'Shoot,' she says defiantly. 'Why don't you shoot me?'

She knows me too well. We stand in a frozen tableau for an endless moment outside time – a minute, an hour, a second? – and then my arm sags to my side. I put the pistol away. It never would have been possible for me to fire it. A powerful feeling assails me of having passed through some subtle climax: it will all be downhill from here for me, and we both know it. Sweat drenches me. I feel defeated, broken.

Silena's features reveal intense scorn. She has attained some exalted level of consciousness in these past few moments where all acts become gratuitous, where love and hate and revolution and betrayal and loyalty are indistinguishable from one another. She smiles the smile of someone who has scored the winning point in a game the rules of which will never be explained to me.

'You little bureaucrat,' she says calmly. 'Here!'

From a closet she brings forth a small parcel which she tosses disdainfully to me. It contains a drum of computer film. 'The programme?' I ask. 'This must be some joke. You wouldn't actually give it to me, Silena.'

'You hold the master programme of Ganfield in your hand.'

'Really, now?'

'Really really,' she says. 'The authentic item. Go on. Go. Get out. Save your stinking Ganfield.'

'Silena—'

'Go.'

13

The rest is tedious but simple. I locate Holly Borden, who has purchased a load of books. I help her with them, and we return via tube to Hawk Nest. There I take refuge beneath the bookshop once more while a call is routed through Old Grove, Parley Close, the Mill, and possibly some other districts to the district captain of Ganfield. It takes two days to complete the circuit, since district rivalries make a roundabout relay necessary. Ultimately I am connected and convey my happy news: I have the programme, though I have lost my passport and am forbidden to cross Conning Town. Through diplomatic channels a new passport is conveyed to me a few days later, and I take the tube home the long way, via Budleigh, Cedar Mall, and Morton Court. Ganfield is hideous, all filth and disarray, close to the point of irreversible collapse; its citizens have lapsed into a deadly stasis and wait their doom placidly. But I have returned with the programme.

The captain praises my heroism. I will be rewarded, he says. I will have promotion to the highest ranks of the civil service, with hope of ascent to the district council.

But I take pale pleasure from his words. Silena's contempt still governs my thoughts. *Bureaucrat. Bureaucrat.*

14

Still, Ganfield is saved. The police machines have begun to move again.

Arthur C. Clarke
The View from Serendip 95p

Speculations on Space, Science and the Sea, together with fragments o f an Equatorial Autobiography.

'The film *2001* turned him into a cult figure . . . His enthusiasm is so immense he finds it impossible to be dull . . . his "continuing love affair" with Sri Lanka, his deep sea diving, his work on the film are as absorbing as anything he ever wrote'
COLIN WILSON, EVENING NEWS

'Gives voice to the romantic side of scientific enquiry'
NEW YORK TIMES

Bob Shaw
Who Goes Here? 75p

'One of the most impressive writers of the genre' SUNDAY TIMES

In the 24th century, men join the Space Legion to forget – a memory-erasing machine makes sure they do just that. The machine erases all traces of guilt, but for recruit Warren Peace it has wiped out everything. He must have a very nasty past indeed . . . Into battle with the Legion, and Warren faces vicious predators in fearsome conflict without the slightest idea why he's been stupid enough to sign on in the first place!

'Very funny . . . incidents run amok' THE TIMES